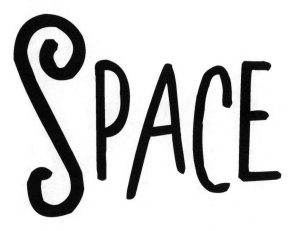

SPACE

Recollections of a
Girl on Edge

MARGARET
VINCENT

SPACE
RECOLLECTIONS OF A GIRL ON EDGE

iUniverse books may be ordered through booksellers or by contacting:

iUniverse
1663 Liberty Drive
Bloomington, IN 47403
www.iuniverse.com
1-800-Authors (1-800-288-4677)

ISBN: 978-1-5320-6632-0 (sc)
ISBN: 978-1-5320-6631-3 (e)

Library of Congress Control Number: 2019900957

Print information available on the last page.

iUniverse rev. date: 03/25/2019

Preface

Now, though mankind at our present level of awareness interprets time as consecutive, uni-directional and irreversible, to many mystics and some physicists time is an artifice created by our limited ability to perceive it as it actually is, an eternal present.

It has also been noted that retrograde healing may sometimes take place particularly where there have not been observers of the event of concern---that is, that it has not been observed by any form of consciousness.....

Chapter One

My mother liked to search the heavens.

This activity would come in spurts but could go on for days. She would leave me downstairs with my sisters in the evenings when my father worked the night shift at the 7-11, so she could go up on the roof of our apartment building to see the stars. There she would stand, scanning the sky for hours. She had been told by a doctor that she had super sharp vision, 20/5, instead of 20/20 like most people. This meant she could see at twenty feet what most normal-visioned people could only see at five feet. Naturally this predisposed her to see a lot of what others didn't, quite easily, and inspired her to keep looking. My mother had probably seen more shooting stars by the time she was twelve than most people do in two lifetimes, if you believe in people having more than one lifetime, which she did.

She took me up on the roof to help her search the heavens once. She became very bossy up there and 'assigned' me to one side of the roof, in a corner where I could keep an eye on two sides of the sky, with her on the other, to look out for meteors ---she needed me up there because she announced, "there was a meteor shower and they'd be coming through fast and furious."

So there I stood that night for at least an hour and there's nothing, nothing but stars winking at me and I couldn't even see those too well because of all the lights around. After about 40 minutes I started whining to go downstairs but my mother got mad and told me to be quiet, that they'd start up soon. Before she even finished the word 'soon', she started screaming and I jerked around to see a huge blue streak streaming across the sky then my mother losing her balance, toppling forward to almost fly over the three foot wall there to keep people like us from falling off. I ran over to her but by then she had stabilized herself.

"That was a close one--- maybe you need to give this up for a while," I yelled.

""It wasn't THAT!" she screamed. "Didn't you see it?"

"Yuh. A really big meteor."

"Not THAT!" my mother yelled like I was an idiot. "Raynelle!" she shouted and grabbed my head in both hands like I wasn't listening to her. "There were lights--- IN AN OVAL SHAPE, like a ship! Behind the meteor! But they just stayed a few seconds then disappeared…just faded away!"

"Oh," I told her. "Sorry I didn't see that, just the meteor." Deep in my heart I was sure she was seeing things, just the way people do when they really, really want to see something, eventually they'll see it. We went downstairs after that, those real narrow crooked stairs with cob webs around them and a step might completely give out if you weren't very light on your feet. My mother was still muttering about it definitely being some sort of space vehicle and how she wished they had come down for us because that's what she'd been waiting for all these years. It took her three days to calm down after that.

She claimed to have gotten very, very close to a space ship once. It was parked in a field in her home town of Lonely, Missouri. She said the thing was shaped liked a cigar with all kinds of lights on each side and that she just happened to be driving by there that night with a boyfriend--- when there it was. She felt that the beings in there knew her and wanted to communicate with her, so she convinced the boyfriend to get out of their car and start toward it. The boy became afraid and froze in his tracks after a few yards, but mother didn't, just kept on trudging towards it. At the last moment though, it just took off and swept up into the night sky. Gone. Just a blur, faster than anything you could ever imagine. They both just stood there and watched it go, then the boy started back to the car, talking about how it was the beer he'd had that night that made him see that.

But not my mother. She was positive not only that it had been there but that it had wanted to contact her. This is one of the stories she had told me several times when I was little. After a while though she stopped talking about all this because my father was so sure there was no such thing as space beings that he would get into a frenzy every time she mentioned the word space and just not talk to her for a few days to punish her. This is why she never even mentioned those lights from our building, that she was completely convinced were a space ship, to my father. He had already said he had always thought she was a little loony deep down and seeing the ship when she was a teenager just proved it. So after a while you wouldn't hear my mother mention anything about this whole subject at all and my little sisters never even learned about any of it it. I think with everything else going on in her life, after a while mother probably forgot about it too.

Chapter Two

You could tell things had started looking up around our apartment after Ravena, my middle sister's seventh birthday.

She hadn't left any of her gum around the floor and also my youngest sister Wanda had stayed in her own bed for five nights running. Not only that, my father had called from down town and told us he had a new job with maybe three times as much money and we'd be moving to another apartment before long, one uptown with a doorman. Well needless to say we were all pretty psyched. Especially my mother ---she was looking pretty again there for a while, not putting on all that makeup which she used to say she needed. "I have a fair skin, that's all, you don't see it so much anymore, a natural blond." I knew she was right about the skin. I got it too along with that wiry red hair from my father that stuck out in all directions like I had my finger in a socket.

That afternoon an envelope appeared mysteriously under the door from the waste land of the hall outside; it was always so dark out there it made my flesh creep. You could never be sure you might not trip on something and who knows what it might be? So I always ran from the stairs to our apartment door. At least there were some lights along the stairs, bad as they were. Anyway Wanda was first to catch sight of it---a fat envelope just under the door. She got down onto her hands and knees and skittered like a crab over to it, afraid someone else might get it first, but my eagle-eyed mother, jumped to snatch it away from her as if she just knew there was something magical in there, and there was. Mother grabbed that envelope and dashed into her bedroom with it but we're all hustling in right behind her, suspecting something new, wondering what's up. You could just feel the strange powerful energy out of that envelope. So she sits in the bed for a second after closing the door behind her like she's making a wish but we get it open a crack, with each of our heads just peering through that crack one right over another like the three stories of our building. She holds it up to the window light where even we could see there's something thick and greenish in most of it with the very tail-end rectangle part clear in the light, then she tears it open like it'll sear her hand if she holds it still a second longer and all the green stuff flies out and lands all over the floor. Money. We all run in screaming to grab some but not before she's down on her hands and knees with that blonde hair dangling in front of her face like a yellow curtain and she's scooping it up as fast as she can then stuffing it into her bra where she knows none of us will venture. Then Wanda started a screaming "How much is it mom! How much! And then, "Can't I get that dragon down at Custard's?" She's squealing about this used grey dragon she's had her eye on at Custard's thrift store ever since she first laid eyes on the thing one year ago. I'm sure it didn't come out of the factory grey, there's years of manhandling and wear on that poor thing. But Wanda is young and has the most heart of all of us---I think she feels sorry for it because one of its blue button eyes is gone.

"Hush!" My mother expounds, "we don't have money for nonsense like that."

Then she looks sternly at all of us and hands the money to me. I expected this. Mother, in spite of many talents, never did quite learn to read at any but a half-baked level and can't count her way out of a paper bag, especially when it comes to so much money. So she pulls it solemnly out of her oversized bra and hands it to me, slowly, one by one, like she's counting it. "COUNT it, Dear," she orders, not usually one for endearments but I guess this situation clearly demanded special attention. I was the only one who got A's in math and the oldest; it had to happen. "I want it back," she tells me while I'm counting, like somehow I might have imagined otherwise.

But I was used to this, just maybe on a smaller scale. "Don't distract me," I mumble sternly, "or I'll have to do the whole thing over again. We'll be here all night." At that they all shut their mouths and stare at my hands until I finished the counting, then pile the bills together neatly like I'm dealing a deck of cards and commence to count again.

"Alright, alright," my mother fumes. "She's gotta count it again. Come on, Raynelle."

"How much?" my little sisters both squeak and my mother touches my hand earnestly as I finish the final count.

"Well?" Mother says finally.

"Four hundred," I announced proudly. "Four HUNDRED dollars."

"Where'd we get it?" pipes up Wanda, still a little upset from having it yanked out of her hand.

"Daddy of course!" pipes up Ravena.

"Of course," says Mother taking the money back solemnly, folding it, and sticking it back in the bra.

"Things are going to change around here," Mother announced later that night after sweeping the kitchen floor, something I couldn't remember seeing her do for some time. "I heard from Daddy today and he said there will be more money, every few days or so."

"But where is he?" whined Ravena, frowning, saying what was on everybody else's mind.

"He's staying with a friend right now. Just getting adjusted to his new job, it's uptown, he'll be back soon. There's a lot of responsibility you know, there has to be, making so much money." She grimaced as she leaned down to push the dirt pile towards the cover of an old Glamour magazine, as if she was holding the weight of all his responsibility on her shoulders.

We all went to bed happy that night. At least I did, just thrilled by the possibility that we would be moving out of that awful building. I could envision the doorman at the next building: svelte and handsome, with sleek shiny black hair, multi-lingual of course so that he could talk to all his wealthy tenants, including my father who had come up from Costa Rica.

<hr />

Days passed and everyday after school everybody was studying that front door just waiting for either Daddy or another envelope to work its way under there---but nothing appeared. No one would say a word about it. The air seemed a little thicker in the apartment with the nervousness of it all. Where my mother had been looking jolly and pretty, bare-faced for her, there were now those deep frown lines again and a grimace around her mouth like a pair of parentheses. As far as I could tell, she still had the money which had to be a good thing, especially if there wasn't any more coming for a while--- but the refrigerator was beginning to look clearer and cleaner like things do when they become empty.

So it was a big surprise to me when after a few more nights, in waltzed Mother with a friend from downstairs carrying a big cardboard box. Course we all gathered around it and it was near as quiet as an empty church in there while she slowly peeled open the big box. She wouldn't tell us what was in it though; it was like she was putting on a show, first going to the kitchen to get her carving knife, then she handed it carefully to her friend Raul from downstairs, like she's handing him some diamond studded magic wand; then he hovers over the box for a minute and stares at each one of us. "Bet you can't guess what's in here!" he finally shouted then hunched over and pounced on the box, fast as a hawk grabbing up a mouse. And he's done. But then he opens the flaps slowly to prolong the suspense. Meanwhile being the smallest, Wanda was closer than anyone else, screams "Television!" and threw herself on top of the box. My mother, with many tisks and grumblings, grabbed Wanda and put behind her ample legs.

"Yes," Mother announced at last. "A new digital flat screen TV. Do you know how long I've waited for one of these?" Fact is none of us knew that, nor that she even had ever wanted one at all. Mother wasn't one to share her innermost desires with us or maybe with anyone, I don't know. Anyway there we all were with this big dumb TV and I'm thinking this thing had to cost more than four hundred dollars. And I'm right, because the next thing I hear is her announcing that we'll all have to be very careful and save money because she's on the hook for a hundred dollars each month to pay for the thing. Well needless to say I was a little bummed out by this---it looked like not only were we not getting any more money, but we had a new problem. And I didn't even want another TV. There was a hard cold feeling right in the pit of my stomach as I started to suspect that my father may not really have had a new job and maybe the financial affairs of our family would be handled by my mother without even the occasional common sense of my father, at least for a while. I knew instead of having that refrigerator full of baloney and cool aide and lots of different cereals in the cupboard, we were probably in for hard times with the major meal of the day our free lunch at school.

To be honest, sometimes this all seems pretty confusing to me; but all I say is true because for the most part anyway I am a stickler for the truth. That's what one of my teachers said when I finally turned in the kid who had been copying off my papers for five months. I wouldn't have turned the kid in if he hadn't beaten up a little boy on the playground that day. I'd figured if the teacher's not smart enough to see what's going on in her own classroom, oh well. Sometimes I think she wanted him to cheat because it was clear that was the only way he was going to pass the grade. All in all I don't think grown ups know that much, they want you to think they do but really I think most of them are like kids in big bodies who really aren't sure exactly what's going on.

Chapter Three

Well, I can tell you things did begin to change after that and, not for the best. There was no word from my father and no more money magically slid under our door. My mother began to wear more make-up again and pretty soon I think she was just putting new layers over the old ones without even washing it off at night. She looked tired and was always complaining about how we were going to make the payments on her new TV. But she did enjoy that thing. Every time I saw her she was perched in front of it sucking on a Pepsi, from the second I got home from school to when I went to bed at night. I could still hear the drone of late night TV whenever I woke up, sometimes in the wee hours of the morning. She slept on the old sofa most of the time and would be there snoring in the morning while I did my best to help my sisters get ready for school.

Truth is, I wouldn't have done it because I knew it wasn't right, but I felt sorry for my mother. The fact is I even felt a little guilty because deep in my heart I felt … well, all in all, *better* than she was. I know she had some hard times being raised in a hard scrabble mud-poor family in Arkansas and had to quit school in the eighth grade. She said it was because she had to work on their two acre farm but I think she just put off learning to read year after year until the school kicked her out or maybe she just couldn't stand it anymore. I mean it must be pretty worrisome to be thirteen and developed and all and still got to fumble your way through a sentence any second grader could read. She said she had dyslexia or something and that was the problem. I don't know.

I never met her parents--- my grandparents; her mother died at an early age of some sickness she blamed on her husband, don't know what exactly, and mother never saw him after he left the home when she was twelve. Mother never described exactly why but she hated the man and never did want to see him again, for how he treated her. I began to have an idea what that was, but I'm not going into that. So I tried to be good to my mother, maybe from pity. Here I am only twelve almost and not only can I read and write, but I'm a good reader, I mean really good. If I like a book, I can get through it in one day---that includes staying up all night reading it with my tiny lamp pulled under the covers so as not to wake up my sisters who would immediately start up a wailing that would have the entire apartment building up pounding at our door. Fact is, not only am I a good reader I'm good in just about everything at school and you should see the look on my mother's face when I hand her my report cards. She definitely can spot those big A's, though she may not be able to read the comments and always has me read them to her, and they are good---for the most part. Now and then if there's something like "she has a cocky attitude,'" or "she'd do even better if she studied," well, I don't read that part. I don't think that's cheating, Mother never said I have to report every single word.

As for my father, well, he didn't have it much better than she did, from what I can tell. When I asked him what it was like growing up, he just smiles and rolls his eyes around like one of those google-eyed doll babies Wanda loves and goes back to his computer games. I'll admit sometimes when I was little I felt jealous of those games, seemed like he got so wrapped up in it all. When I got older of course, I realized it was just a machine and even used to like those moments when he was home glued to it, seemed like he knew I was there and cared. Sometimes he let me play too but in general it was enough to just sit near him.

I do know my father met mother while she was holding down a waitress job at Kingley's Barbecue Pit. He winked and told me the moment she leaned over the counter he fell in love; it took me a while to figure out what he meant by that. They moved in together and got married and from what I can gather I was born eight and three quarters months later---I was a week premature they said.

A few days after getting the TV, there was a knock on the door. My mother answered it, taking her time unlocking the three deadbolts my father installed there. Standing in front of her in his uniform was our upstairs neighbor Ralph who worked as a janitor at the local city jail. He just wanted to tell us he said, that he saw my father there dressed in an orange suit last night. "At first I thought no, no it ain't him, can't be Horace, he has a good job down town," he was mumbling all the while twisting his cap in his hands like he's throttling a chicken; then he shouted, "I was cleaning there you know, my job, and there he was, told me to tell you he was there. Couldn't make his call because he said yer phone was uh... disconnected." Ralph looked around the room like he's searching for proof of this. Well us girls are just standing there behind mother like three people lined up in a firing squad but it's mother who collapses right there in front of us into a pile of quivering white flesh. We stand stock still for some seconds, like this can't be happening, then we all including Ralph, grab my poor mother and drag her as carefully as we can to the lumpy old sofa while she's steady muttering about water. We got her some and she gathered her senses. "This can't be!" she whispers, he just told me a couple days back, on he's got a good job now." That was on our downstairs neighbor Ida's phone which we used since ours was disconnected.

It turns out the good job was selling pot, that's right marijuana. So we all headed down to the city jail the next day and watched mother cry in the little cubicle while Daddy sat in his day-glo orange suit looking at his lap then smiling at each one of us through the Plexiglas window and saying nothing, like it's just another day. Finally he says, "I thought--- I really thought this would be IT, the money…it was so much, like just there for the getting. But they caught me. I didn't feel like I was doing anything wrong, all I had was a pound or so, not so much… don't they have anything better to do? I wasn't doing really wrong,nothing, still at my job at the convenience store, coming out of there locking up at three in the morning and this cop. He's just standing on the corner watching me, then he comes up and puts the cuffs on me. Just slaps them on. That's the truth--- they violated my rights, as usual." The faster he talked the thicker his accent got, until he's speaking Spanish and mother who still doesn't know the language in spite of father trying to teach her for ten years, interrupts him.

"Horace! What will we DO! I bought a thin screen! We were DEPENDING on you!" she shrieks.

"What? Try to be sympathetic Earlene. Maybe they'll let me go…I have a clean record except that one DUI but that was a few years back. Three years I think." He stared at the wall behind us, looking thoughtful, and rubbed his nose.

"I don't care!" my mother yelled. "You'll be here for years, I know how these things work. We'll have no one, NOTHING!" Then she started sobbing.

"No, it couldn't be," he said calmly. "I was really just using it, I've developed a bit of a habit," he said as a guard walked by, then muttered some cuss word and coughed into his fist. "But I know some guys who've gotten out, a few months, a year at most and they were dealing. Me, I'll be out in few weeks. Just wait and see, Babe."

"Don't Babe me! Better be!" My mother wasn't convinced. She started shrieking at him again, then began a wailing the likes of which surprised even us and pretty soon the guard came in and ushered us out. She explained to us between snuffles on the subway going home that before she met Daddy she had a boyfriend who used to smoke a lot of pot and sometimes would give it to his friends for money and how they put him away and she never did see him again.

Well it didn't take long for my father to have his hearing. He said he was assigned a lawyer named George who looked about fourteen and had just graduated law school. He recommended something called plea bargaining but Daddy didn't trust him and wouldn't go for it, insisted he was innocent anyway. He called Daddy an idiot, but Daddy poured his heart out to the man, told him all his difficulties and how he was a family man had gone to church as a boy in Costa Rica, had even given some money to a man on the street with a cup at least once. He hoped he'd get off for being a good citizen because this was really his first arrest, and things were looking up. On the day of his hearing though George had looked distraught like he had come down with some sort of fever but he wouldn't tell my father why. It turns out Daddy had gotten the most unlucky judge around, some sharp nosed woman, and they said she would send somebody away for ten years for chewing tobacco. After making a lot of nasty comments to my father, she said no bail and told him she thought he'd be getting two years that maybe it would teach him a lesson, slammed her gavel down and stomped out of the room. We were all there naturally and mother had been expecting maybe six months, that's what George had expected, and the minute Mother heard that she shouted about what the judge could do to herself right at the judge who was just disappearing into her chambers so all you could see was the tail end of her black robe.

The guard lurched towards my mother who was by then running out of the building with us three girls following. Wanda had had a wad of sticky gum in her mouth almost the size of a golf ball which she mistakenly spat out as soon as she'd started running and calling after mother. The guard slipped on it and lost his balance, then fell on to the cement steps outside the building. I guess he just gave up on us around then because when I looked back he was still on the step rubbing his ankle and talking to some woman in a very tight skirt who was also rubbing it.

Chapter Four

So pretty soon things changed a lot more. My father was to have his trial and mother wasn't one to take a back seat as you might imagine. It had been a few weeks by then and no one had the money to bail him out even if we could, so there he sat. It turned out he had two and a half pounds of the stuff and when he told the cop he was just a heavy user himself the man had laughed so hard he'd busted open an old hernia scar and had to be taken to the ER right away. So let's say my father did not find himself on the good side of that policeman nor of the other ones he had any contact with.

Well, mother got us all gussied up that day anyway. She washed her hair which was abundant and crimped it up by twisting it into a bun on the back of her head and then sleeping on it that way. In the morning she had a bunch of blond corkscrew curls all down her back. It was pretty I have to say. Me in my best or I should say my only dress because I had no others, even if we could afford them, I didn't like them. She insisted we all take long baths and wash our hair the night before, then did up my sisters pretty yellow hair in poofy curls with some old hair spray she had, but my wiry red hair she left alone. She scrubbed their cheeks with a plastic scrub brush so they looked as pink and shiney as the kewpie doll my father once gave us. Then the two little ones were squeezed into pink chiffony dresses she'd gotten on lay away at K-mart and they looked like they just stepped off the doll counter themselves.

As for my mother she squeezed into the shiniest dress she had, covered with tiny mirrors."Men are attracted to shiny things, like birds," she explained and how she know this judge was a man and not so old he couldn't look at a woman either. Well I had my doubts about this approach but she was sure, so all I could do was kind of watch things. She had everything so set in her mind she didn't even ask me to help---she was going to do everything herself, had us all gussied up like the dummies in a Macy's window because that's what I felt like, even though she left me alone compared to my sisters. So my mother was pretty much pulling out all the stops you might say in hopes that one of them would help.

Finally she marched us all into the subway but wouldn't let us sit down for fear we'd wrinkle our dresses and she didn't sit either, just stood and stared at us through out the whole trip as if we might somehow change before her eyes if she weren't careful, then she marched us into the court room like some kind of pink Disney parade float with everybody turning to look at us and sits us down right up front. Pretty soon here comes my father, looking completely beat.

Turns out all mother's efforts were in vain. She never knew it but my father had been arrested years before for having a half pound of pot on his person, so the judge did not take kindly to them finding two and a half pounds on or about his person this time. Also the officer who'd had the hernia was there and had no kind words to say about Daddy. So they did sentence him to fifteen months which seemed pretty harsh to me. As soon as my mother heard it she folded over like somebody had knifed her in the belly and gulped, but then commenced a caterwauling and leapt up off the seat and toward the judge who by then was disappearing behind the door of another room. The guards ran up to grab my mother who was whining loud by now about not having enough to eat with my father gone and my father was being led out of the room by another guard with Daddy looking behind him telling my mother to simmer down it, that he'd take care of things, it would all be alright.

She finally screamed as he went out the door, "Maybe for YOU it will, you get three meals a day, how are WE going to get enough to eat!" Then she was quiet and the guard let her go and she turned and walked out of there with all of us following behind like three baby ducks.

When she got outside to the top step she turned and stood there spitting towards the building; it made tiny arcs in the air and landed in small puddles on the step.

———————————•●•———————————

After that Mother's behavior changed. She started to stay out later, then going out at night and coming in very late, and sleeping in front of the T.V. There she would be I guess, until later in the day; anyway she wasn't able to get us ready for school. She told me, now being twelve, I was old enough to help take care of my sisters until my father got home "I depend on you," she told me after a few such nights, "you're my baby, well not really the baby, but the smartest. You can help by getting the girls ready in the morning. Just for a while Sweetie, then things'll be back to normal," she yawned and I noticed how the make up had settled into the lines around her mouth. She was sure that if Daddy stayed on good behavior they'd let him out early and things would be fine from then on. But word had it that my father was not on his best behavior and had even stolen something in the jail, a CD left behind by a volunteer. I don't know what he planned to do with the thing; he didn't even have a player, and the whole thing set him back a bit.

Soon Mother began to bring in some money, most of it she gave to me for food which I bought and would give her the rest--this she would tuck neatly into her bra. This went on for a while but Mother seemed to get more and more irritable; the two girls who were difficult for anybody, were even worse for me. Let's say my getting them ready for school was not their idea of a good time. Mother would be snoring on the sofa and if she woke up from all the noise and screaming she would cuss us all out and if there was a tantrum that refused to wind down, she would drag herself off the sofa in her slip, cause that's what she slept in, and zero in on whoever was yelling with a ferocious slap to the mouth.

Chapter Five

So it was one of these times that first drew a social worker to us like a chicken on a bug. One morning my mother had slapped Wanda and she had a bit of a bloody lip which I tried to clean up but it was still bleeding a little and got a little swollen by the time we had to run outside to catch the bus. This was a mistake. You see, being five, Wanda didn't have much sense and had just yelled out that my mother did it after the teacher asked her about the lip. Wanda's teacher, always was a bit of a busybody, putting her nose where it didn't belong; I know 'cause I had her when I was in first grade and she complained to my mother then that my clothes were too wrinkly, and wrote a note home about it which my mother wrote back to but when I brought it in to the teacher she accused me of writing the note. That's how bad of a writer my mother was. Anyway with Wanda she wasn't about to back down and the teacher sent a note and demanded that my mother come in the next day and discuss the situation. So my mother dragged herself to school instead of collapsing on the sofa, and went out to meet the principal at 10 o'clock.

I had to wonder what would happen that day. We'd had enough to eat in general and enough soap and toilet paper. But things were not good at home. Even though my grades were steady catapulting from the A's they had been, still I managed to pull off C's though I'll admit I was too tired and worried to pay much attention to the teacher most of the time and I figured my teacher might rat on me too.

So my mother tried her best to be presentable the next day and went to see the principal. I did see my mother at the school that day and I can say that she didn't look like most of the other mothers I'd seen in there. I don't think she really washed her face or the rest of her from the night before because she had the same make-up but had put on some more over it and her perfume smell was so strong I knew she was around the corner before she came into sight. I could tell the principal was not impressed.

That afternoon back at the apartment my mother let fly with some of the worst cussing I've ever heard and the gist of it was that they were going to send some social worker down to evaluate our home. The three of us just stood and started to cry cause we'd never seen Mother in such a state while she repeated "evaluate our home" over and over like she was a stuck record. Finally she burst into tears and went to sleep. She didn't go out at all that night.

———————— • ● • ————————

Mrs Gibbon, had a head which reminded you of a shark, all pointy towards the front, ending in this really sharp snout, with a tight little mouth and lots of pointed teeth crowding inside it. Her hair was pushed back into kind of a stiff wedge which stood out from the back of her head almost like a flat tail, unusual for social worker I thought. But she was very clean and neat and always wore a black suit over her really bony body. First I thought she might even be a man disguised as a woman because there was nothing like any type of curve which reminded you of a woman's body. But when I heard her voice I was sure she was a woman. It was so high and unhappy, like a little bird shriek, but not that either because it was very slow and calm.

The first time she came, my mother did not say two things to her. My mother had washed her face for the occasion and was not wearing make up, the first we had seen this for many weeks. She was wearing a billowy yellow dress which she had bought at the thrift shop special for this occasion and had even bought Salada peppermint tea which we never had in the house but which she was going to serve Mrs. Gibbon. "Fancy people always drink tea," she explained. "I know this cause I saw it in some movies my mother got a long time ago. And they stick their little fingers out when they are drinking it. Like this," and she showed us, holding one of the two teacups she had in the apartment. "Now I want you girls to sit real still over there," she pointed to our old bumpy sofa, "while I talk to her. Or else," she added with a threatening look at us, "she's gonna take you away from me, or me from you, I don't know which," she said and began to cry, "and put... put you in some institution or even with," she choked on the words, "some other family." Then she collected herself and announced. "But its going to be alright. I know this. I can feel it inside my stomach, it's kind of, well... a gift, I got from my grandmother." We'd heard that story before but we all sat down and were told it again while we waited for the social worker. She was a little late and my mother began muttering about "These people, they don't think we have any rights just because we're poor. My time is valuable just as much as hers, maybe more," she added with a smile like she was smiling at herself.

After a while longer and no Mrs. Gibbon, mother turned on the TV and we all started playing and running around the room. I guess we were nervous but then just like magic there was a knock on the door and mother made us all sit down again then walked over to it real slow like she was a queen with the best posture I've ever seen and said "Who's that?" and winked at us before opening the door.

The best I can say is my mother gave it her best shot. Try as she might, she hadn't primed the two little ones well enough or maybe they were just too young to really understand the situation. Because after fielding Gibbon's questions pretty well, my mother smiled and thought she was done. She told her about our dad being in jail and her getting a job at night job at a 7-11, but it turned out Gibbon all ready knew all that and she also knew my mother had no 7-11 job. Then she turned to the three of us and as if all that wasn't enough, asked every kind of question you could imagine, and the little ones just seemed too happy to whine about everything, especially me taking care of them in the morning and then hardly ever talking to mother anymore, so that soon Gibbon's face became meaner and redder and those lines around her mouth which was pursed like a prune, were as deep as spokes in a bicycle wheel. Mother's face was getting paler and whiter, as white as our sheets were when they were new.

The upshot of it was Mrs. Gibbon gave my mother an ultimatum. Even though we didn't know exactly what that was back then, we could tell it wasn't good. The choice she told us was things had to improve at the school and mother had to be home for us and whatever she was doing at night, it had to stop. And she had to be the one getting the two girls ready for school so I would be free to return to my studies. She added that she knew I had been an A student and that my grades had dropped. "Dramatically, like a rock plunged into a pond," she added and looked at me, all pity. For her part she would try to get public funds for us while my father was in the jail.

Then she sent us girls out of the room and told us to please close the door---that's when she planned to stick it to my mother. Of course we all leaned up against the crack in the door, one head right above the other, and quiet as the bed bugs we could see at night. We were good at that by then.

"And if you can NOT comply with the demands of our department within three weeks," Gibbon announced in a low angry voice, "the children will be removed from your custody, temporarily of course, until you CAN manage."

My mother was at a loss for any words but finally did kind of sputter at the woman, "For what… I'm a good mother just look at these gorgeous children and Raynelle's even an A student. So responsible. This is not right." Then she began to bawl.

"Raynelle WAS an A student," Gibbon said calmly, looking like she was used to this kind of display and it wouldn't phase her one bit. "But as you know, she is no longer, and you clearly are not fulfilling your role as a parent adequately. In addition, the little ones come to school looking dirty and disheveled and then one had sustained physical abuse."

"But she was throwing a fit, she wouldn't stop, I had to sleep, it was just a little tap anyway," my mother screamed.

This was clearly the wrong approach. "Exactly. What looks like a little tap to you, had to be treated at the infirmary. I shudder to think what goes on here," Gibbon added as she headed towards the door. By then all our heads were hanging out of the doorway and Mrs. Gibbon nodded at us as she left the apartment and everyone began to feel better all of a sudden.

Mother left off her night time forays and we were all kind of feeling like there was hope again. Mrs. Gibbon came back four days later and felt so good about us she smiled. I thought her face might crack though. It looked like it was made of glass. The girls looked half decent when they went off to school and my grades began to creep up again. Gibbon was good to her word and we did have money coming in. At first mother was using it for food and clothes and of course the rent.

One night Wanda crawled into my bed and told me she was just happy. We snuggled there for a little while until she fell asleep and began to snore; she always breathes through her mouth; mother was afraid she would need her tonsils out. So I carried her back to her little bed, really a mattress on the floor and drifted off myself, wondering how long it would be before we had enough money to get that new apartment.

Next week though there was a sale down at Wal-Mart for some kind of fancy computer camera you can keep in your purse and right away mother announced that she had to have one. So there we all were one night in line waiting to get one of those things. It looked like it was so popular they had a line of people waiting there just wanting to hand over their credit cards and there's mother with her cash, for a down payment, she told us, then she'd make the monthly payments out of the money she was getting from Gibbon. I knew it wasn't all that much and while we were standing there I began to worry if this was the best idea, after all it had been pretty nice having enough to eat and still having her there at night. I knew she'd blow up if I started to question her plan so I tried to come at it from an angle. "It's sure nice having you home at night," I told her sidling up and squeezing her hand. "And having food too. And you can pay for your TV again." She smiled at me, kind of impatient then turned back to the front of the line, like she might never get there and just couldn't wait. She just couldn't imagine life without that thing in her hand I guess. She didn't say anymore and I'm still standing there hanging onto her hand which is becoming sweaty and finally I let go and I could tell she was glad I did. Well, I pulled out all the stops then. The two little ones were squealing and running around us and like we're a rotary in a highway and I blurted to mother "Are you sure we're going to have enough money if you buy this thing?"

Well, she looked down at me like I'm a cockroach crawling up her sleeve and shouted "I just KNEW you had that on your mind, always trying to rain on peoples' parades. Just like your father. YES. We will. I've figured it out. So just shut up. Hush your mouth or they won't let me have it." Of course given mother's skills in math, which I already mentioned, this was not very reassuring.

Well for a few days after that everybody was in bliss---mother had her new thing and we all had enough to eat.

She felt so good that week, she was even decorating the girls' hair with bows. It was a while after that that Mother began getting more crabby, just slowly like something you really can't see unless you're thinking about it already. I expected it--- the crabbiness--- it never went away for long--- seemed like whenever she got something new then it would be gone for a few days or maybe even a week or two at the most. But out it would creep again after that, at first like a mouse just sneaking into your kitchen at night hoping you won't see him, then after a while just running hog wild all around the place in broad daylight. So that's how it was with my mother. The middle one began sucking her thumb again, it started to get so bad. We didn't have much food. There wasn't enough money, after all mother had two things she was trying to pay off. She would sit in front of the TV all day, cussing during the commercials, staring at it most of the night, like there was some answer to her problems there if she could only figure out how to get it out. Gibbon had made one more visit on one of mother's few good days and seemed happy when she left. She even told mother she wouldn't be checking in on us again few a few more weeks. Well, I think that was a mistake. It was during his time mother disappeared one night and didn't come back for almost two days.

I had to get the girls ready again and was almost shaking with fear at school, expecting them to come and take us away like I'd seen happen to a poor scrawny dog who lived on the front steps of our building for a while. This was right before my mother took off this time. I used to give him a little of my lunch from school every afternoon. He got so happy when somebody fed him he'd wag his tale so hard his whole body would waggle back and forth, like it was all too good just for an ordinary tail wagging. Well one afternoon I didn't see him there on the step which surprised me because the dog was almost always there. I looked all around but didn't see him. When I got up to the apartment, I heard an awful yelping and crying out my window...there was the little dog, Happy I had named him, being wrestled into a big white truck with Animal Rescue Services in big blood-red letters on the side. I knew this was no rescue and begged my mother to go get him. I knew what she'd say and when

I heard it, it sounded like someone singing a horrible song I could not stand to hear one more time, so I put my thumbs in my ears. "We can't afford no dog," she said over and over as I ran to my room to bawl into my pillow. But then I got up and raced downstairs to tell the dog catcher he was mine, my dog, anyway. By the time I got there, the big truck door had been slammed shut and the man was in the truck revving it up, ignoring my yells. All I could hear was a dog whining inside as he drove away. I knew I'd never see Happy again.

Well that's what I was afraid would happen to us, just hauled away into a truck one day with nobody looking, someone running after us in the street and grabbing us then stuffing us into a huge truck with Child Rescue written on the side and bad as things were, we'd never see our parents or maybe even each other again. So when I saw my mother back again after the two days she was gone then, it was a big relief. She had some money and gave me some just like the old days then told me to go get food with it.

It didn't happen like I thought it would.

Chapter Six

They took us away one day about two weeks later in a fancy white SUV with Child Protective Services written on the side over some small black letters like insects crawling across the door.

We all cried and screamed and they tried to reassure us we'd be back with our mother, "Before you can say Jack Robinson," the kind beige lady driving the SUV told us. But we ended up in a big brownstone building with "The Miss Willoughby House" on the outside. Everyone there was trying to be very sweet. It was fancy place with some other kids who I guess were abandoned by their parents too, and we got lots to eat. Ms. Gibbon came to visit a few times a week, all tight lipped and angry, and with no good news. It turned out mother had flown the coop and they had no idea where she was. Wanda and Ravena didn't take kindly to the place. Food or no food, they weren't happy without Mother. And no one could find her. "We're getting in touch with her, trying," the ladies told us.

"Don't worry the ladies," Gibbon told us, "she'll be back to visit." Well after a few days of this I could see that whatever they were doing to find her, it wasn't working.

When they didn't know I was there lurking in the hall one night,

I heard one therapist say to the other, "They'll be better off without that woman anyway." Bad as my mother was, I knew this wasn't true, especially for Wanda and Ravena. Well, I wasn't just going to sit there like a chicken in a coop. It didn't take long to formulate my plan. I made my move. And that was to get myself out of there late one night after the therapist, cause that's what they were called, who was supposed to be on duty started to snore. That was one thing about me and I decided it was an advantage: after watching grown ups for near twelve years I could tell most of them were really slaves to sleep. How can I explain it? I could wake up whenever I wanted to and still pretty much feel like I had enough sleep, at least act like that way for a while. But most grown ups, if they didn't get all that sleep at night, it seemed like just couldn't make it. So there was that therapist snoring, at first little bitty snores then big blasts like a big dog coughing. She dropped her keys as I stood there watching her and I picked them up. I went out the front door, after my mother.

She wasn't at the apartment, it was empty. I pounded on the door but it sounded hollow inside there like a cave. I walked around the streets and alleys, mostly staying in the shadows the rest of that night. I knew I wasn't tied down to eating three square meals a day either like the adults were. Seemed like they all pass out right there if they didn't have that fried sausage for breakfast or hamburger for dinner.

I'll have to say though around about three the next morning, there I am, sitting on a sidewalk by Wal-Mart and thinking maybe I really do need something to eat when I feel this big hand, big as a ham folded over, clutching my shoulder. I look around and here's this cop wide as a car with a broad smile stretched across his red face. And he seems to know me. "Raynelle, zat you?" he asks.

"No," I say.

"We've been looking for you," he shouts, ignoring me, then slaps handcuffs on me like I'm a prisoner and bam! I'm back at Miss Willoughby's. My sisters are glad to see me but no one else is. They treated me like I'd robbed a bank they had all their money in. They put me on one to one precaution they called it, with a lady assigned to me at all times even around the clock until they could reassess me. Then the owner of the place, Miss Willoughby, called me into her office all smiles and we just sit looking at each other for a while, then she moves her chair closer and asks me why I think I'm there. "I don't know," I tell her.

"Then I'll tell you," she says. "For your own good. Why did you run? Do you know how dangerous those streets are at night?" she whispers looking into my eyes like she's trying to find something she lost in there. I don't know what to say and just stare back at her; there's no way in the world I'm telling her my private stuff, even if I knew it all which I don't.

She just stares at me some more and for a minute I debate having a staring contest with her which I think I can win, but it wouldn't be worth it. "I want to find my mother," I finally say, and feel surprised cause all of a sudden I'm fighting back tears.

She leans back in her chair and takes a deep breath like she's won whatever the contest was and looks smug. I don't say anything, just swallow and the feeling is gone.

"She's gone," she says, snapping her fingers, then like she just realized maybe that wasn't the best thing to say, she quickly adds, "I mean, well, we can't find her right now but we're trying…we'll find her, don't worry." Like she's just solved my problems.

The next day they let me off the watch and the next night I took off again, just like shooting fish in a puddle as my father used to say.

Chapter Seven

At first I was glad to get out of Miss Willoughby's. After apprehending me the second time,they sent me to Precious Moments Rehabilitation and Therapy center, I was happy with anything to get away from Miss Willoughby's where I had just sunk into extreme boredom. I shall now refer to this place as only P.M.,since it really doesn't deserve all those letters, what they are supposed to mean. P.M. had a big picture in the lobby: of a starry sky with a silver fish sailing through it, like the most crazy free image you could think of---a fish can't even get out of the water let alone fly into the sky.

That was just for show though, probably to fool parents dropping their kids off there, because they never made it into the rest of the place where you had to go through at least three locked doors with no windows to get anywhere. It was divided into two houses attached by a long hall. Each house had a central area where group meetings were held and people were publicly humiliated if they'd made really major mistakes like running away. The five villages [jail cells] where the citizens [captives] were kept, radiated from the center like spokes in a wheel; though I never saw the boys house, I heard it was made the same way.

I dreamed a lot at P.M. or maybe I just paid more attention to dreams because the days were unbearable. In one dream I was home in the apartment and things were back to normal, well normal for us, before my father was put in jail and mother started disappearing at night. My father was sitting in front of our old TV playing video games, something that always made him happy and he spent most of his time at home doing, as far as I could tell. I was sitting on the sofa watching him clobber someone with a ray gun and the two little girls were playing on the floor beside him. He would usually shout at them to keep quiet because they messed up his concentration but in my dream he didn't say anything, just had this huge scowl on his face. Then the thing just spread from his face to his whole body like a deep crack through it, then he disappeared into it---just swallowed him up. Scary. Especially since I hadn't heard a thing about him for months and from my mother either. My caseworker at P.M. said she was OK, they'd found her but I didn't believe her, after all she hadn't come to visit me.

At the end of that dream I remember looking out our apartment window, the one that looked down on the main street where the traffic never stopped, even in the middle of the night. You could wake up at two in the morning and there it was, trucks roaring, horns beeping. It made me wonder why people were up then, but it was a little comfortable too, just knowing someone was always awake out there, knowing what was going on. Nobody could sneak up on us that way, I don't know who I was worrying about but I always had a deep feeling in my stomach like a worry or a fear that something might happen at any time and I would have no control. Sometimes it felt like I was floating in the air but not in the happy way of fairies or angels. I didn't know where I was going and had nothing to hold onto. So I had a little of that feeling again in my dream after my father disappeared inside himself. I woke up for just a second or I'm not sure if I was still asleep, it was one of those times you just couldn't be sure. Anyway there I am, feeling all scared and I look out the PM window or maybe it was a dream window, I don't know. But there it was---something, I don't know what, hanging there outside that window just like me floating but it wasn't me. It was kind of oval and had lights, and it just seemed to rest there in the air, almost like it was watching me.

Then I think I kept dreaming and dreamed nothing more or I went back to sleep, I don't know which. But I do know that when I woke up in the morning remembering that thing scared the wits out of me and I just lay there for a while, like to reassure myself. I remembered my mother telling me once to take a deep breath after I told her about my scary floating times, she said that would heal almost anything, that's what she did and it always worked for her. She didn't tell me what it was that it worked for, but that was mother, a closed book she called herself. I guess it was something to do with her early days and whatever she hated her father for.

Anyway I just lay there that morning breathing deep breaths, while I could hear the helpers outside [really our jailors that's what I called them]. They were yelling, screaming at me that if I didn't get up I'd regret it and lose my privileges and REALLY regret it. It didn't seem to me that I had any privileges in that place so that threat didn't scare me at all.

They didn't take my privileges away after all. I had one of the nicer helpers, Taletha, and I told her I didn't feel well so she was all sympathetic.

It was later that next day after I finally got up that I met Mrs. Addel Goonson, my therapist, who made a point of telling me right off that her name was pronounced Go-onson, but I called her Goon, not to her face of course. "I will meet with you twice a week," she told me smiling as though I should be happy about this.

"Why?" I asked. It didn't seem to me that talking to anybody twice a week was anything that would help anybody especially me. All I wanted was to get out of there and maybe to get my family back, that was my only problem, and how could she help me with that? I asked her all this and then she really surprised me. She leaned back in her chair and smiled at me like she was the Chesire cat and knew much more about me than I could ever imagine, but still didn't say anything.

"Well?" I asked her again. She shook her head and smiled at me then laughed a little, probably at me, that's the feeling I had.

By this time I definitely decided I didn't like her one bit and began to wonder if I could change therapists or if not, what I could actually do with my mind when I was sitting there in front of her desk during my therapy sessions. But she began to yak, just running at the mouth telling me about the issues I have and the first step was to recognize this, how with all the losses I've had anybody would have issues. After that she said, I just need to work on them then she says to me, like I'm the one who is nuts, "Why, your grades went down... then you ran away from Miss Willoughby's twice or was it three times. Acting out, that's a problem, wouldn't you agree?"

"No," I said. "I didn't like Willoughby's". Seemed like she had some new vocabulary all her own and I was just supposed to know what she was talking about. So I asked her how did I act out, what are you talking about, I wondered if she was crazy herself and maybe if the P.M. Treatment Center just took people off the street and called them therapists. "How?"

She added,"And you are very angry. You need to get in touch with that anger."

Well that floored me. Here I am minding my own business a couple of months ago then all because of my mother they lock me up and when I try to get out they tell me I'm angry.

"You're the one with issues," I told her. "I just need to get my butt out of this place that's my only ISSUE. How would you like being locked in here?" I sneered, not so politely.

At that point her face got red and she announced, "You know, if you keep talking that way you'll need to be on escape precautions, especially given your history of two runaways. You have no insight, zero," she clucked. In the middle of this ridiculous pronouncement her stomach set up a terrible grumbling, I mean so loud you couldn't ignore it. I guess maybe she skipped breakfast and here it was almost eleven o clock and obviously being one of those adults controlled by three meals a day, her stomach was screaming.

Well needless to say I laughed out loud. Then she got all red in the face with a tight little smirk on her mouth like she was saying you're going to suffer for this and then her beeper went off. She gave a tremendous sigh like somebody had just let the air out of a balloon and answered the page but she kept her eyes right on me.

From that moment on I decided I would get out of there, that would be my first aim. It was just a matter of when, and doing it right. I wasn't going to try some half-baked way like I'd done the last times, then get caught the next day by some overweight cop. This situation called for a whole new level of planning and smartness. It had become clear by then that no one was going to magically appear and let me out, like for instance my father or mother, though I still did have hopes that she would get her act together and there she'd be at last, to pick me up. No, this would demand a whole new level of intelligence to get out and stay out, but something I felt I could carry off very well.

After all, did I ask to be locked up? Bottom line, I hadn't done anything but get A's then get C's and escape after they locked me up. It was like I was punished for getting good grades otherwise maybe they wouldn't have noticed it. Anyway, it was all my mother's fault and my father's to be honest. And I suppose they would say it wasn't their fault, it was their parents fault for their lousy upbringing, and their parents would probably say the same thing and on and on. So I decided it was going to stop here. I wasn't going to pass on this chain of misery from my poor parents but the first thing to do was get the heck out of a place where they had unfairly stuck me.

Even though I was trying to formulate escape plans like I said, I still had these tiny hopes that mother would get herself together and show up to save me. Well a few weeks later these little hopes were blasted away. Maybe it was because of my therapist's complete stupidity, I don't know. Anyway I was being taken to her office by a helper for my session one morning and I heard her talking on the phone in a pretty loud voice from down the hall and I knew immediately she was talking about my mother "...out on the streets that blonde hair... she's earning money out there now being kept by some man, giving him most of it. What a shame, was brought in by the cops but they couldn't keep her." Then she must have heard us coming because she lowered her voice and almost whispered, "But they'll keep trying. Here she comes now I think." The helper looked at me, all sympathy, like how could that therapist be so stupid then dropped me off at her office.

l thought about my mother as I walked into the room to the therapist. How could all of this happen to her? It always seemed like she was smart in her own way and so sure everything would work out. I remembered her again, staring up at the sky outside our narrow apartment window at night, telling me, "Raynelle, you know people don't realize this but they're here already, the beings from space, maybe the Gallations... I don't know which planets for sure but they are already walking among us I can tell you that and they're already helping us, maybe not in ways you would notice yet and they'll help us more, that's one thing they have, kindness, not like most earth people. I've read all about this." The thing is all her talk got me interested and I began to believe most of it myself, and also to believe that things would work out in the long run with or without their help, but secretly I hoped it was true and not just crazy thinking as my father used to say. My mother had strong opinions about him as well. She once confided to me specifically that she felt he was really one of them, that's why he would get so upset when she talked about them. "He's got a bit strange looking head too if you really look at him, those almond shaped eyes, that big head--- but he's done a lot of good for me at least, that's why I first thought about it..." my mother added. This was before my father was thrown into the slammer for dealing pot. But it was becoming clear now all hope was gone about my mother's theories, she had to have been wrong. The therapist slammed down the phone and stood up to meet me.

"Have a seat dear," Goonson chimed. I kind of thought she let me overhear this on purpose, that's the kind of therapist she was. She was trying to get me to distance myself from my parents, accept that I would need to make my way on my own. "Just let go," she had already said a few times. That was fine with me. I had decided long before that I'd need to make my own way but I at least had hoped my mother would be around, like in the background of an interesting picture. Well, I finally did just let that go.

As I sat in front of her, listening enough to nod or smile when she paused, I decided to devote almost all my time to my plans from then to evacuate the place. Twice a week I would go in and sit in front of Goon while she droned on about my problems and how I could overcome them. In reality, I was using this time unbeknownst to her to plot the specifics of my escape. I had developed a great ability to nod pleasantly to her when she thought she was making a point, like a little part of me monitored what she was actually saying in case she asked me a question. I didn't want to miss it or she'd be onto the truth that I was paying about as much attention to her as my mother gave the background music at Macy's.

Chapter Eight

It was a few weeks later that I made my first major mistake at PM. I had gotten friendly with one of the helpers; actually at first to help me get out of there, I figured I had to create some staff trust towards me, that would be key. So I got chummy enough with Taletha to actually end up telling her a few things about myself and one of them being that dream or vision I had of the thing with the lights outside my window. I wasn't prepared for her reaction, though I could tell she was making more of it than it really was. She kind of jumped just a little and raised her eyebrows then tried to wheedle me into talking more about it from that point on--- no more like two friends, she was now keeping a distance, just watching, scutinizing, just squinting slightly with those pale eyes like sizing up a piece of jewelry to see if it's really gold. Clearly she had learned in her two week orientation that something to do with seeing things or hearing things was a big red flag in the wind that immediately had to be grabbed. She looked a little afraid as I talked, looking at me like seeing a strange insect all of a sudden, that she must identify before it bit her. "There's no more to tell," I then told her, "that's it," but you could tell she wasn't convinced. She tried to be nice but after a while her whole attitude changed and her whole body stiffened a little, sitting up a little straighter, on the alert. Well I learned then to keep anything even a little strange to myself, but she didn't keep it to *herself*. Before you know it there I am in front of Goon who brings this up out of the blue in my next therapy session, calling it a vision and demanding how often I have these.

"It wasn't a vision," I finally shouted after she had lectured me for a good twenty minutes about dangers of leaving hallucinations untreated.

"They'll grow and control you," she continued without listening, looking genuinely worried. "Medication will help this symptom."

"It was a DREAM!" I shouted.

"That isn't what you told Taletha. We have very good communication here you know, otherwise how can we help you people?"

"You're NOT helping people, at least not me," I screamed. "I just need to get out of here. I'm not crazy. I don't see visions and I don't need any medicine."

"We'll see Dear," she says. but I do need to refer you to Doctor."

"For what!"

But the session is over and she had begun straightening up her desk, silently.

So the next thing I know I'm sitting in some huge office with a bearded man staring at me from behind a huge desk, wider than a car. At least the room had a lot of windows, it was more light than I'd seen in a month.

He reaches across his desk to shake my hand and mumbles "Dr. Loofah" and stares into my eyes, that same look like he's trying to find something that was lost in there or maybe that he's looking at a thousand piece puzzle strewn around in front of him wondering how long it would take him to put it back together. I look right back at him, straight into his eyes, which I've learned grown-ups, at least the ones here, like. His eyes are moist and pale green like two pools of salty water. "Have a seat then," he says to my helper then turns and looks out the window. "What brings you in here today?" he asks me in some kind of accent, and turns towards me again.

"I don't know. SHE did. Ask her," I tell him. I assume he'll know who 'she' is.

Meanwhile the helper who brought me there is sitting in another chair filing her nails, apparently used to his routine.

"You don't know," he says, not a question, and raises his furry eyebrows. They remind me of the black caterpillars I used to catch on the tree trunks at Prospell Park and I stare at them. I notice his ears which are also big and somewhat furry; they move just a little every time he talks, like they're some kind of small fleshy animals clinging to the sides of his head. I begin to wonder if there are any animals which do this and the glance at his thick fingers which are tapping the table, fast.

"I'm sure you *do* know, Raynelle. Ms Goonson has told me all about you." That was the first time I remembered anybody using my actual name in there, it was usually dear, miss, or hey you. So I looked him in the eyes again.

"She said you had reported seeing visions," he said in a small voice then cleared his throat with a rumbling sound and added loudly, "hallucinations, we would term it."

"I don't see visions and I don't have hallucinations. I was dreaming."

"Oh. Tell me, what did you see then--- in that dream?"

"Nothing."

"Now, I know it wasn't nothing. Please, you can feel safe here." Now that statement was clearly ridiculous. Here I am locked in a building a with a therapist who hates me, a helper I thought I could trust who ratted on me, and they want to stuff some kind of medicine into me and this guy with the big ears tells me I should feel safe? I smile at him, it's all too absurd to say anything.

"So you're not talking. You know you must be able to tell people all about what it is bothering you."

"Nothing," I volunteer again.

"You have so much anger!" he breathes at me. "Very deep, I fear and are so reticent to discuss your issues. Then this vision or hallucination or maybe even a dream as you insist. How many times has this happened.?"

"Never! It didn't happen. It WAS a dream!" I shout.

"Oh goodness you are such a smart girl. Have so much to offer. But an upset girl. My Dear. I don't know what is going on exactly," he tells me, "because clearly you have such trouble speaking about your many early issues and ongoing family stress. We have discussed you in our meetings. We know you have great potential but are unwilling or unable to make progress. Poor Ms. Goonson feels so frustrated, she's a very good therapist you know." He squirmed in his seat and was quiet for a minute or two. You could hear the scraping sound of the helper's nail file against her thumb nail. He sighed finally and said, "How would you feel about trying some medication, only a little to see if it will take the edge off…your anger, make it a little easier to make progress here and of course eliminate the hallucinations or dreams as you refer to them. Sometimes these are symptoms of worse illness to come…if not treated immediately."

"No! I don't want any."

"That is a common response but usually people who are stuck in their progress here are helped by this, for a short time."

"I won't take it."

"Well, you may have to if we can get permission."

"My parents won't give it."

"Well no one will be forcing you… but I believe this will help you. you'll be glad you did," he said and the chair squeaked as he swiveled in it to face the window again. The helper, who understood this meant the end of the session looked up from her nails and put the file away then led me out of the office.

Ms. Goonson informed me in my next session that I had been

made a temporary ward of the state and if the doctor thought medications were needed they would be given." It's just, just temporarily of course, because your parents are presently... not available for you".

Chapter Nine

And so it began. Everyday they would march me down to the nursing station in the morning and the nurse, Ms. Honne, would hand me a plastic cup with a green pill in it. At first it was a silent kind of a thing, no questions, no asking, just them knowing I was going to take that pill. But I didn't and after a while this became a problem; she started to wheedle, praise, then threaten and make disgusted faces at me. I still didn't take it. The therapist said she was disappointed in me, that I would get nowhere and might be in there for years before somebody decided I was better or at least until I was eighteen. Finally they ushered me down to a 'team meeting' where two doctors, several therapists, and nurse Honne stared at me. She asked me if I wanted a shot.

"No way," I told her. The doctor interrupted the nurse's tirade and told her basically to shut up, that they could not do that unless I was a danger to somebody. Then there was silence.

One of the therapists tried to explain that they couldn't make me take the stuff by withdrawing privileges, "This is not our style", she said.

"Well how come I'm always on restriction then?" I asked.

"Your attitude," answered Nurse Honne. "Disgruntled.

Sometimes disruptive too. The medicine can help your attitude, you won't be so angry then get you'll get your privileges, that's just the way it works. Angry people just don't receive privileges," she added as I'm sitting there still wondering who is really crazy.

"Wouldn't YOU be angry if you were locked you up just like that, that's what happened to me."

"When you act out, you receive consequences, that's something you learn in here."

I tuned them out; then they all nodded to me and told me I could leave, that they were making a plan for me.

By then I was feeling hopeless and began to wish I would have more of those dreams or whatever they were. I started to scan the sky outside my window at night above all the brightness of the city, searching for more weird lights. Deep in my heart of course I never thought that was a dream, that circle of lights I saw from my bed. I had finally decided I agreed with my mother: they're out there and they're watching us. The more I thought about it the more sense it made. After all most of us didn't seem to manage very well on our own---we needed help. Question was, were they just staying up there or walking around among us, like my mother said. And if they're out there, were they just in regular bodies or maybe something else, maybe even no body? I'd heard that of possibility once.

After lying in my bed for many nights thinking about all this I began to ask them, WHOEVER they were, to come back and help me, help my mother too. I did this very quietly of course just whispering under my breath so my roommate wouldn't hear me and think I was really crazy. They would hear me if they were out there.

———————— • ● • ————————

In the beginning I felt that this medication thing might seriously interfere with my bigger plan, blowing the place as fast as I could. At first it did seem that being on a higher level would help me with this but then I realized that even if I got outside and ran when we were on some outing they'd see it and send somebody after me immediately. So it was clear it wouldn't matter if I took the medicine or not, as long as I wasn't being watched 24 hours a day by a helper keeping you in her line of vision. So I would again use my skills at not needing sleep as my primary tool, with a building full of helpers who snored at night like buzz saws especially one of them--- this would be my only chance. It wasn't hard to study the habits of those people. It was like having a dog, you think they don't know anything and you're taking care of them but all the while they're watching you, sizing you up, and know as much about you as you do about them. maybe more. At least that's how I think it is with animals, especially dogs.

After our meeting, they switched me over to the liquid medicine. It was an ugly dark purple color like a wizened grape. Naturally I refused this but they kept trying to give it to me anyway. One night they brought me down there again to Nurse Honne and stuck it in front of my face as usual. Of course I said no. Just as I was refusing, the girl next to me started screaming then picked up a chair which she held in the air for a few seconds, like she was deciding what good use to put it to. As I turned to look, I took my eyes off the nurse's spoon and in the slop went, right into my open mouth. Well some of it got down but I pushed her hand away and the rest went flying right into that plexiglass window so it was splattered all over with purple, even some sailing through the small hole onto Honne's face. The girl then promptly decided to throw the chair at the nurse's window. She began to yell, a very high squeaking sound-- then I did too; the more I yelled the more it seemed like I just wanted to yell, that I LIKED the sound even though my whole life I had been mostly always quiet. Not only that, the other girl was still yelling and then battering the window with her fists; it's like we had a duet. I just decided right there, screw it, I'm going to show them some anger; they say I'm so angry for no reason, well I'm gonna show them some real anger. It reminded me of how my father used to say sometimes if one of us began to cry a little: "You want to cry, OK, I'll really give you something to cry about." So for the first time, I took my fist and slammed it into the nurse's plexiglass window then tried get it through the hole to pop Honne who just force-fed me the medicine, right in her nose which I missed, but only by a hair.

Well I continued to scream and by then I was kicking the walls and hitting, like pretty soon this thing I had just decided to do, really took off by itself, like got a life of its own you might say. And it felt weird but a little good. By then I was screaming, "If you ever let us outside to run this wouldn't happen". I don't know where that came from but when I thought about it later it seemed pretty reasonable, obvious even, us all locked up in there hour after hour with no running except now and then to toss some volleyball back and forth in the gym and call it our exercise for the week. So the scary thing was, as I looked back on it, how much I really liked this at the time, going stark friggin' crazy with every body part of me moving, even spitting at people. I guess I got that from my mother. In the meantime the other girl who had been throwing the fit had stopped, like only one person should have the spotlight at one time for a really major act and here was a real pro, and they were all gathered around me just standing back and staring, afraid, like maybe I was a 400 hundred pound gorilla who had just wandered in there. Well you know that couldn't last; in a few minutes there was an overhead page with the operator yelling about a code red in the nurses station. In a few more minutes there were twenty helpers there, men too, something you usually don't see there if you're a girl, and they're all on me, wrestling me to the ground then I see Nurse Honne coming at me with a huge needle, which she slides right into my backside. I don't remember anything else until I woke up a few hours later I guess. I think it was night, though there were no windows. I tried to move and found that my legs and arms were pinned down hard like there's a fat man's rear end sitting on each one; turned out I was all strapped down with leather straps, restraints they called them. And then here comes a voice from behind me, "Ray you ready to settle down now?" She didn't give me a chance to answer. "What happened to you? You always been so quiet," she says like she's really mystified. "I thought you was a peaceful kind of a girl."

I crane my neck to try to see who it is but it's sore and I can only move it so far.

"I don't know," I finally said. "It all started when that nurse just stuck the medicine in my mouth, force-fed me, like an animal. Against my will. Completely." By then I had learned a lot of the catch phrases there, like that one. It seemed like they had a vocabulary all of their own.

"Well I didn't think you could throw such a fit, didn't think you had it in you." It was clear she was impressed.

"They wanted angry, they got angry."

In truth it began to work on me more than a little that I had even been able to just go hog wild like that. They said I injured two people who were now out on leave because of it. That must have been after I blanked out because I don't remember it. They kept me on watch and then Goon wouldn't see me without a helper present. This didn't bother me cause I never said anything important in there anyway. I was hoping they'd assign me someone new but no such luck. Well, around this time it became clear that my plan would never succeed if I kept being branded public enemy number one and kept on their watches. So one day I told the Goon that I decided I would take my medicine if that would help me get out of there.

I never saw her smile like that or actually hardly any at all, come to think of it. She was just beaming away at me like maybe I'd just composed a wonderful poem about what a good therapist she was.

"And now you can really get to work," she announced.

What she thought that work would be I didn't know or care, I just nodded my head and smiled at her, and said 'umhum'. But in my mind I was spinning out a web of deceit. Yes I definitely could see things would improve in there if I took my medicine, or they thought I was taking my medicine, which they began giving in pill form again.

I got away with 'cheeking' as they called it, a few times. The nurse began to rave about what a cooperative girl I'd become, what a change and the therapist bragged about the change in my behavior after I was compliant [that was another key word in there] with the medicine. I got off all my precautions and even went out for a few trips away from the place. What they at that point didn't know was I had been putting the pill inside my cheek and, after a short while so it didn't dissolve in my mouth, then carefully spitting it into the toilet. Unfortunately this device was short lived. My roommate who was a teacher's pet type had to barge into the bathroom which didn't have a lock on the door just as I had spat it into the toilet and ran over just in time to see the pill go down the tube then ran out like the goody-two shoes she was and blabs to the two helpers sitting there playing canasta that I'm cheeking my medicine. Well that was it for me; Nurse Honne told me she'd do mouth checks on me every time, you couldn't fool her, she grumbled. So I'm refusing it and they all decide I'm acting out again.

Chapter Ten

Well I remember when it came to me--- a brilliant idea, a little risky but worth trying.

I'm lying there one night feeling my teeth with my tongue just to make sure I'm still brushing right even though I'm in there, and bam! There it is, that space where I had a tooth pulled. It was my back top right molar second to the end; since my mother usually forgot to take us to the dentist it had become rotten and had to be pulled by Dr. Schwartz our once in a while dentist while my mother stood there crying about how she always tried to get us to brush our teeth. In reality she never mentioned it until I was eight and we had a dental hygienist at our school talking about how you should brush your teeth twice a day at least and preferably three times and floss too. Ever since I told her about this, my mother bought us tooth paste and little brushes and once in a while even dental floss but it was too late for me.

Anyway there was that hole. The idea came to me out of the blue. Of course! The perfect size for one of those purple pills. I just had to quickly jockey it into place with my tongue and hold my head just a little lower when they did their mouth check. I practiced this over and over in my room, when the roommate was asleep, with a tiny plastic game piece someone had lost; I got it down so it took just one quick tongue movement lasting about a half second and there was no detectable face movement to give it away. Of course I was careful when I disposed of it and let it float down the sink drain while I stood between the sink and the door. So things went better for a while after that, staff started raving about my good behavior again and I simply kept taking that thing out back in my bathroom and slipped it down the drain into the sink, no muss, no fuss, no bother. Even if goody two shoes came in she wouldn't see what I was doing cause I held the thing in my palm facing the wall not the door.

After the first two weeks of everybody praising me for taking that pill and especially Nurse Honne who began to give me a lollypop each time I took it, things changed again. It seems one of the teachers, who came in there every day to help us with our studies while we were temporarily out of real school, reported something negative to my therapist. Specifically that she thought I looked spacey or like I had poor focus which in fact I may have had for her stuff, because I was busy with my main plans. It didn't matter to her that I was getting mostly A's, so the team all met once again and there I sat while they all stared at me to determine whether I had poor focus. Nurse Honne piped up that while she saw a real improvement in my attitude, still I did seem a little spacey, "disconnected a little," in her words. Another teacher was there who said that I clearly seemed to lack focus and she had wondered about this right along but didn't say anything because of my pretty good grades. Of course Goonson piped up, adding that she'd always thought I was spacey, clearly without focus. Surely I would do better if my attention was improved, they all agreed. Meantime I'm focusing clearly on each one of them, sure they're going to decide to send me back to Dr. Loofah. After all most of the girls in there as far as I could tell, were on two or three maybe more different pills or medications as they liked to call them like somehow the fancier name made the whole thing more acceptable.

And so they did and there I am again perched on the edge of my chair with Loofah who's looking at me in a disgusted way and asking me in a sweet voice how I'm doing on the medicine.

"Fine… better," I tell him. I don't want to seem overly positive or they'll know I'm faking. Of course I'm anxious not to be on any more of it. I like being off precautions and I have only one hole in my teeth.

"Yes yes of course," he announces, "we knew you would do better. Much less anger Ms. Goonson tells me." I should say here that seeing the doctor was a little like seeing a celebrity because as it turns out, he only came in once a week and in that time miraculously touched base with each of the three therapists about their 'citizens' and saw about thirty kids for medication checks which is what this was called. "But even though you are some better, and now beginning to work on your issues, there may be some problems with your attention… uh focus." Actually I still hadn't said a word to Goon, except to make up some stories which I thought would be the most normal sounding things in the world for a girl in a locked building and which I told her were my dreams.

"She says you are doing very valuable work," he added.

"Yes," I agree and smile just a little at him, making eye contact with his chest; he was portly with a very round prominent chest and I could imagine him being a very fat kid. The stories I told the therapist were about living happily in a clean house with two loving parents and I told Goon these were my dreams, and that I was dreaming about the way my life really had been, pretty much. She would smile and mumble at me that she wished it had really been that way and tell me she was proud of my progress. Once I told her that I dreamed of her, but she was dressed up like the good witch in the Wizard of Oz and was so beautiful, even had a magic wand. Well, she liked this especially, like I knew she would; she giggled and blushed then announced with a sigh that we finally had a therapeutic alliance. The next time I saw her she brought me a Milky Way. But still and all according to Loofah, she was also worried about my focus, especially given my excellent grades in the past and worried that I should be making straight A's in there all the time.

So Loofah asked me some more questions at that meeting about how I felt when I was reading or attempting a difficult task and I told him great, no sweat. But he wouldn't buy it. He was silent and looked over at Taletha who'd brought me in and who was busy knitting. She looked up with a bit of a start, obviously hadn't planned to be consulted in there. "And how does she act on the ward,?" he asked her, misnaming our particular locked area, which was of course supposed to be referred to at PM as a village.

"The ward?" Taletha responded, with a confused look, laying her knitting down on her lap. "OOOh, you mean our village. Oh fine, she's fine." But then seeing his dissatisfaction at her response, she added, "well, except for the times she's a little off,

I guess."

"Off? You mean with poor focus?"

"Yes, I guess that's what you might call it," she smiled at him then picked her knitting back up.

"Yes. Well that's the way it seems I think. You know Raynelle, you have made such progress on this medicine, I would like to see you really do as well as I think you can."

"I don't need more medicine," I immediately told him. "I need to get out more, move around, get outside, run," I said honestly for once pulling out all the stops to avoid more confrontations with Nurse Honne.

"Well I'm not in charge of all that but I'm sure you get some exercise here, even outside time."

"Hardly ever," I pouted.

"Well I doubt that just that would be enough to make a real difference anyway." He then picked up a piece of paper while mumbling about getting some testing and began to write. This he handed to Teletha who had put her knitting back in a bag and was standing by his desk. "Give this to the nurse," he commanded. The man had made up his mind before I even walked in there

"Yes sir," she says and before I know what happened we're out the door.

Well, now I'm stuck again I realize, as we walk down that hall towards our village. It would take them a while to get their permission to stick me with this stuff though and I decided to use that time to get a new strategy. It was clear to me I didn't need this stuff, the reason I was spacing out in the teacher area was that it had a window and staring out of it actually helped my thinking process, to plot my escape. I decided I'd pull up my grades completely before they got permission for the new medicine, maybe that would show them I didn't need it.

Before I got too far into this approach one of the girls in my village told me she'd heard-- [people talked there, even the so called helpers]-- about my new prescription and how it really helped her. This is what she said in front of the two helpers playing gin rummy in the hall that afternoon; but in the next minute she pulled me into her room and shut the door

"Leave that door open at least a little," one of the card players yelled down at us without looking away from her cards or vacating her seat.

"You got to take this stuff!" the girl told me in a loud whisper, "it really, really gives me a buzz. I used to buy it from a kid at my school and now they're just handing it out to me. Not only that it really does make you focus I can finish my homework in about twenty minutes---it used to take an hour. And if you don't want it, cheek it girl, and give it to me, you'll figure a way. OK?" So I had to think about it, consider it as they would say there. I had to admit that some of those wacko kids seemed much better after they took whatever crazy potion Nurse Honne was handing out to them. I saw their behavior when they refused and some of them were climbing the walls, literally, until they got their drugs. But I reasoned, that was THOSE kids; I didn't have their kind of problems I was just in there, an obvious mistake that no one had discovered yet. And yet-- if it did make you think sharper and faster for someone who already thinks fast---well then, I'd come up with a plan, a good one, fast. Plus I hadn't figured out how to keep it in my mouth along with the other pill and I liked keeping my privileges and that was easy--- easy, once I'd figured out I would be blowing the place, to just chill and hang with it until the time came to make my move. So bottom line, I would take the pill right after I'd stuffed the other one up in my tooth hole, I'd actually swallow this one.

There was no preparing for this one. An hour after I had it, I was flying so high everything seemed possible. For a while it didn't even seem like I ever wanted to break out of PM-- hey, if they were going to give me this everyday who needed to get out? I raced through my work at school then sat there asking the teacher for more, believe it or not.

I got the most improved student two weeks running and all I did was smile, even got to go to a special lunch for the honor students with as much steak as I could eat and two desserts. The problem was I was beginning to lose my appetite and kind of had to force myself to eat; even though I'd always been the master of my appetite and was thin, this was ridiculous. I complained to Nurse Honne about it and they weighed me. I'd lost three pounds. They started double portions. Then they gave me a vitamin but it made me throw up and I almost lost the first pill I had tucked in my teeth so I refused the vitamins and they didn't care about that. Then I noticed another interesting thing. I began to need less sleep so I was getting to sleep later and later but as soon as I swallowed that pill in the morning, it was full speed ahead. I was beginning to feel like there was a motor inside me and it was always on, even when it was idling it was going, fast.

Believe me, I would have stayed on those pills forever. I liked having all that energy and even having to eat twice as much. Also because by then I had almost complete control over my sleep, well not so much getting to sleep because that had become a bit of a problem, but control over staying awake. Where I'd been easily able to do that before, it now became a complete habit.

I wasn't prepared for what happened next.

Chapter Eleven

I got to know the late night habits of the helpers very well.

There was one helper who actually didn't ever snore so I'd never gone into the hall at night to take a peek at her. I finally caught a glimpse of this one and it looked like the reason she didn't snore was that she slept so deeply all she did was breathe quietly through her nose, where the others would wake themselves up now and then with an earth shaking rumble and look around quickly to make sure nothing was wrong. Not Alice. Once the other helpers had left around midnight and they put up the cards she would sneak into the kitchen in our village for a little snack, something the girls had left over that day, then bring it back to the desk in the hall, eat, make one last round of the five rooms in our village, sit back down, yawn and blink a few times like she's struggling just to keep those eyes open then she's out, just like somebody turned of the light in her head and she folds right into herself so she's there almost bent over on the desk but her belly is keeping her head and shoulders up and she's out. Then there's the breathing, real slow and regular but not deep, she's a real throat breather; her chest doesn't even move when she takes a breath. If you do hear her begin to breath you can be sure she's about to wake up which she will do, then she'll look around and maybe get up and check us like she's supposed to but the minute she sits back down the chin goes down to her chest and she's silent breathing and out for at least an hour, sometimes two. So I know all this due to the close observation I've been able to conduct in the middle of the night. It just so happens our room is adjacent to the staff desk so I figured a way to wedge myself behind the door and look through the crack next to the frame where I can see just about everything that goes on at that desk and the cushiony chair they made the mistake of letting the helpers have. Maybe I was good at this because of the practice I had back in our apartment looking through cracks in the door, though at home we usually used the front side by the door knob. So I was pretty well able to figure out how I'd blow the place. Alice would be my real helper so to speak, the only hard part was getting a night where she was silly enough to place her keys which were heavy and probably cut into her round belly, on the desk. Some nights she would foolishly just toss them in front of her. Course she wouldn't do this loud so anyone would hear but real soft like a feather on the desk and before long that chin would go down, she'd fold into herself like a pillow and the breathing would begin.

Well since I now had everything figured out, I decided to just bide my time a little. I was enjoying that pill and every day I would get some new prize or honor. Looked like I was headed from being public enemy number one to one of the top girls. But it didn't last; who knows-- if it had, I might still be there today at the age of eighteen and they would have to blast me out of there.

It happened at school--- about three hours after I'd taken the usual morning pill and washed the other down the sink as usual. I thought I heard someone call my name and it was a real loud voice, like jarring my whole body, which was pretty thin by then-- but I couldn't understand what it was saying. So of course I looked all around but there's no one there, for sure no one calling my name and the teacher who was by then my great admirer, was staring at me a little strangely, like oh no, is my best student going back to her old self. So I ignore it, tell myself it's nothing but my imagination---after all I don't hear voices--- and it went away. That night though, when I'm about to make my approach to check things out from the back of my door, there it is again.

But this time the voice is much louder and for first time it calls my name and I freeze. There is absolutely no one in there that the voice could be coming from. It's a male voice booming and heavy and it's threatening, like accusing me of something I have no idea about. I jump then run out, I'm so scared, and there's Taletha out there tonight, just sitting reading an 'Us' magazine. Well at that point I didn't care if it was crazy or not, I'm going to say what just happened. I sat down and mumbled something about it to her.

"What! Hearing voices!" she shouted like it's good news, and so loud the others wake up, "Oh NO! It's all coming back, only WORSE!" She's frantic but also seems kind of excited in a not unhappy way, to have this happen on a what had been turning out to be a pretty boring night.

"It's not coming back. This never happened before," I told her sternly but quietly. I didn't want all those other girls up staring at me, but they were up anyway staring from their doors, like just standing there watching some really entertaining TV show. She called the nurses station but naturally Nurse Honne had gone for the night. By then I was frantic and Taletha, in spite of ratting on me that first time, finally realized there was no other help, takes me back in my room, wrapped me in her arms and rocked me, then believe it or not started to sing to me, a real song, low and comforting so the other girls who were sent back to their rooms can't hear and my roommate was snoring by then. I felt like pushing her away at first but something stopped me and I had to admit it was very soothing. Well finally I got sleepy and fell asleep right in Taletha's arms and she must have tucked me in because that's the way I was when I woke up in the morning, tucked in. Needless to say, the day after that the whole of PM knew about my problem and everybody was trying to be nice but you could tell the ones who weren't completely off themselves thought I was totally loco and kept their distance.

It wasn't long before I was back in Loofah's office--- that next day in fact-- he just happened to be there for a meeting. Well, in I go, feeling like this time I really do need help, I mean this was serious. I would have taken anything the man gave me if I could be sure I wouldn't hear those things again. So he makes me tell him exactly what happened, not leave a thing out--- he was careful, I'll give him that. As it happened I hadn't heard any more voices yet that day but it was like my body was so pumped with fear I was flying and not in a good way. I was so wired I had forgotten to tuck my morning pill away in my teeth.

"So these voices… you must tell me about them. Inside or outside your head?"

I had to think about that one. "Outside." Of course, why else would I have been frantic, looking around to see who was talking to me. "Outside," I say again louder and noticed both of my hands are trembling.

"You have been doing so well after your first unfortunate visual hallucination, and on the stimulant so well in school, we must not take any of these medicines away. We will increase your first pill, clearly you need a higher dose of this. It is primarily for hallucinations though it also does help with anger. Actually you have been tolerating your medicines very well; even your weight, though you did lose three pounds, is now holding steady and you are growing at the normal rate. Your sleep, it's still good right?"

Now here I had to pause, bad as I felt, I did not want him to take away the extreme advantage I had over my sleep all other things being equal. I finally nodded to him and said yes.

"Well then our path is clear," he said and I noticed a slight lisp as he said 'is' and for some reason my mind focused on that and wouldn't let go. I began to laugh. "Well, well, so what is so funny my dear girl, these voices aren't talking to you now, are they?" and he began to look worried. "Yes you are on a very low dose of the Peacemak and we have plenty of room to increase it if needed, just a bigger pill." He smiled as if he'd unexpectedly just solved a difficult problem and began to turn to the window, "Of course the stimulant itself can occasionally cause psychotic symptoms such as voices but I doubt that this is what is happening here--- you had your visions before after all," he said apparently to himself.

"What!" I shouted and he jerked his chair back around.

"The stimulant very occasionally may cause psychosis, maybe hallucinations, as I know you were told before you started it. I know you were told about sleep and appetite, Nurse Honne always educates the children about any side effects," he said earnestly, staring at me.

"Nurse Honne didn't tell me *that*!"

"Well I doubt it is what is happening here anyway. Remember you had hallucinations before, Raynelle."

"No--- only a dream." But it was pointless to argue with him. It always seemed like he had his mind made up before he even laid eyes on me. I guess he would say if he did that's because of the close communication he had with the staff particularly Nurse Honne, to psych out your problem before you even come in. "So why did you even bother to see me?" I blurted before I had a chance to catch my tongue.

"Now, now, look at yourself yelling again just like you did in the beginning. You must work on expressing your anger appropriately. As you have been doing." At that he swiveled back to look at whatever it was he liked out the window. "And don't worry, the dose will be increased but it will still be just one pill, no need to swallow another one. The helper Alice walked out behind me still staring at the soduko puzzle in her hand.

By then I was in a complete quandary about what I should do. I was sure the medicine was causing the voices. On the other hand I liked the medicine otherwise, and knew it would help me when the time came to spring the place. On the other hand I kind of liked it there by then, eating the best food I'd ever had and getting to stay up late not only because I was by then one of the top kids in the place at least among the girls, but also making my own hours with the help of that little pill I took every morning. On the other hand, those voices had been the scariest thing I could remember but then, since I knew now what was causing them, they were a little less scary. I decided I'd try taking both pills, just to see what would happen.

Now this slowed me down a little in the morning--- that one that I'd been putting in my teeth was obviously a downer. I was still getting a little buzzed but nowhere near where I'd been before. So I came up with an ingenious plan. I'd ask Nurse Honne if I could take the one medicine at night and the other one in the daytime; this would provide me my usual high and since I had figured out the specifics of my exit strategy, I could actually use the extra sleep at night. Well this scheme worked very well in general. Nobody was able to topple me from almost the top kid position in school and that I liked, though I knew in a real school I'd still be low on the hog you might say, well, my mother would say. Anyway I decided to stay through Christmas; I knew being a ward of the state, they couldn't depend on my parents giving me any presents so they would have to ante up.

Chapter Twelve

I hadn't wanted to go to any holiday dance, that's for sure, but the other girls began talking about nothing else since around about November. They would all go in these fancy dresses the PM company had bought; they spent hours arguing over who was going to wear what. Word had it that PM also owned a chain of department stores and were able to get this sort of fluffy plastic stuff dirt cheap. In the meantime, my medicine is actually going pretty well; even though I'm sure I don't need any, it suits my purpose in there and I'm going along with it. And the best part was I still had my energy during the day and wasn't hearing any voices.

A few weeks later in early December Goonson told me there would be a surprise for me that week. I wracked my brain for a few days and couldn't come up with anything but figured it must be some special present they were giving me early. I was wrong.

When Taletha pulled me out of school one morning and told me there was someone special at the front desk to see me, my mind raced and I started sweating, sure it would be my mother. I started rehearsing what to tell her, basically a lecture about taking care of us better the next time but I didn't want to come on too strong and have her dump us again. And of course I was hoping she'd be taking me home---then and there, that day. I ducked into the bathroom on the way down the hall to make sure my face was clean and my hair relatively neat, as neat as you can look when you have wiry red hair going out four inches in all directions from your face. So finally I get to the lobby and look around. No mother. Just some PM kids decorating a plastic Christmas tree and a kind of overweight man sitting in the corner just kind of looking on at everything. He was smiling for some reason and he had very friendly eyes but like they were just taking everything in. He looked at me for a second and smiled a bit wider but his gaze seemed to scrutinize everything and I looked away from him; he was probably some father come to visit his kid and thinking everything was fine there--little did he know. My head swiveled as I quickly surveyed the room--nothing, no mother. Then I saw them: two little blond heads on the other side of the big sofa:Ravena and Wanda, sitting there all scrubbed and bigger, in clean new looking clothes. I ran over of course and they jumped all over me screaming. I sat down with them and noticed they'd grown and looked thinner, really kind of wispy. They were pink and pale too, like worms, like they never saw the light of day anymore. "Aren't you eating?" I asked and Ravena nodded yes but didn't say anything. Wanda looked at her feet and didn't move. The lady from Ms. Willoughby's squirmed a little in her seat, like that's a touchy subject. I say "You need to eat," to them but I'm looking at her, straight in her eyes.

"Where's Mother?" they asked me in a pleading voice. It's clear they haven't forgotten about her and there's no other subject they are interested in.

"I don't know," I said honestly but then added, "but I know she'll be back---soon. She's probably looking for a good place for us this time. Don't worry--- I know she's coming back." But I'm lying through my teeth and my face is taking on a deep shade of crimson, I can feel the heat. They both look at me and Wanda started to cry.

"Your face looks fatter," Ravena says out of the blue, "sort of like a pumpkin."

"It's like you're somebody else," pipes up Wanda through her tears. The staff member Taletha looks at me, then everyone looks at me. I touch my cheek; it feels hotter and maybe it *is* a little fuller, kind of sticking out where it never did before.

All of a sudden I feel ridiculous and then my mind wanders. I remembered Loofah saying this medicine that helps me sleep can cause weight gain. My thoughts scramble--- what was my weight last time? I knew I hadn't lost any more. I didn't remember but I probably gained weight, more than I had before---was it all going to my face? Then I thought I remembered Honne commenting to someone at the nurses's station, "Well it's not a problem, she's growing," when I was there to be weighed. That was me she was talking about---all the while here I was thinking it was somebody else. I touched my other cheek and looked down at the girls. They were still staring up at me, at my fat red face. I felt humiliated and vowed right there not to take that second medicine. "It will go back in my teeth," I said under my breath.

"What?" Ravena said anxiously, "what about your teeth?"

"Nothing."

"You keep touching your cheek, do you need the dentist, is that what's wrong?" said Taletha, always on the alert for trouble.

"Nothing's wrong," I snapped and the two girls jumped a little.

I tried once again to be pleasant and asked them how things are going. They had almost nothing to say which seems a little odd to me especially because Ravena is almost eight.

So I sat there with them silently for a few more minutes, maybe fifteen or twenty until I guess we all decided we'd had a long enough visit. I hugged them good-bye though I'll admit I felt a little bummed at Ravena and as soon as I got away I raced to the bathroom to study my face. She was right. It was fatter. I was beginning to look like

Porky Pig, at least in the face; my clothes were a little tighter too but not so you'd really notice.

———————————●—●—●———————————

The Winter gala dance was coming up the next week and I decided to go, to just kind of check out people. I'd never seen most of the boys. We had two separate buildings and you can be sure the chances for us crossing each others' paths in any casual way were slim to none. Word had it that there used to a lot of fornicating on the premises so they built a new building and stuck the boys in there. Legend had it that one girl had become pregnant right there in the room across from mine several years before, due, they had said, to collaborating staff who just stood outside their door and then let the kid out to sneak back to his room in the middle of the night.

There *was* a hugely pregnant person in our village at the time, one of the citizens, but she had come in there pregnant; nothing like that happened at PM any more. She was very quiet and pretty much stayed to herself, unlike a lot of the other citizens.

So I had begun cheeking my night time medicines and every night would study my face in the mirror. It was beginning to deflate just a little like a pink balloon you're slowly letting the air out of it, bit by bit.

I didn't want to look fat in any way at the dance which I decided to go to but I definitely wasn't decorating myself up ridiculously in one of those flimsy day-glo plastic gowns either. The other girls reminded me of badly decorated Christmas trees with too many bright lights and tinsel; so I put on my best pants and the only good shirt I had, and just for kicks my roommate's eye make up even though I definitely wasn't interested in any boys. I'll have to admit I looked pretty good. The way I saw it was that I had my own decorations with my kinky bright red hair, my dry white somewhat flakey skin like the inside of a boiled potato, and my eyes which are so dark brown, they're nearly black. Still the staff gave me a hard time for not dressing up. "It's like you don't even care," they whined.

"I don't," I said, and they pouted, but they couldn't keep me away from the dance for that. It was like they wanted to see me all pimped out and looking like a freak.

The night arrived and I just tailed along behind the parade of girls ahead and up the stairs, listening to their dresses rustle and their complaining about each other taking up so much room on the stairs and jockeying around, trying to be in the front. They pranced into the multimedia room which they've got all gussied up with balloons and streamers and there was some guy in the corner behind a big computerized machine who said he was going to play music for us.

But where were the boys? A general hubbub of anticipation began and with the anxious words 'where' and 'not coming' or 'we're early' rising above it like so many helium balloons. I sat down, ready to just watch the action if there ever was any. In a little while there was a rumbling and a stomping on the other stairs then in comes the first boy, with a big grin on his pimply face and what my father used to call a buzz cut. It looked like he met up with an army recruiter; then the next one tumbled in, then the next. 'Tumbled' because they didn't walk in like normal people, they almost fell in, like their feet had been going so fast up the stairs they were almost out of control. Must have been at least thirty of them up there, all manner of kid too, skinny, pimply, tall, short, blond, black, laughing, scared and leering, but most making snarky faces. All of them were eyeing us, well, especially the other girls, like they're in a store and somebody gave them a choice of one thing, one shot at it, and they wanted to get the very best---what would it be? I just sat there watching the whole scene like I was watching television. No one came up to me. I knew they wouldn't and didn't care. I was never interested in any boys and didn't intend to be for a long time. I'd seen close-up where all that will get you. And besides none of them were my type. Unlike them, I did not need to come in to PM--- I had no big problems, it was all a fluke. Clearly from the monkey way most of them were acting then, they were stuck in there for good reason.

I decided to get some of the punch from the big plastic bowl on the table, filled with some frothy pink liquid and thin slices of lemon floating aimlessly on the surface. As I helped myself to it, the music started blaring from the speakers around the room.

"Loud isn't it?" came a voice from behind me. I turned.

"Yes," I said and took a deep breath. Where had this one come from? I hadn't seen him with the others. He must have snuck in after the rest. I'm no admirer of boys or men in general but I had to say this one was alright to look at. He had tan skin and dark grey eyes with a little slant to them. I stared at him for a minute than looked across the room toward the D.J. Too loud. I looked back at him. He was still standing there like he wasn't part of the big chase to get the best product. Didn't seem to me that he felt he needed anything at all and I wondered why he was in PM.

But I didn't say a thing, just stood there. Pretty soon he started talking, not saying anything I was really curious about, like why are you here and where did you come from, but just talking about nothing like grown-ups do all the time: what a nice night it was out, what nice decorations, the music wasn't too bad. There was no one nearby then so I guessed either he was completely nuts or he was talking to me. It occurred to me then that he had some kind of a accent and one I'd never heard before.

I turned to him. "Where you from?" I asked him. I wasn't going to participate in any dumb chatter.

"Oh not this country," he said smugly, in his clipped accent like that was secret information.

"Well, I can tell that. Where'd you come from then, France or India?" I figured it most be someplace far off where the accents are completely strange.

He looked at me for a minute like he was trying to decide if I was worth sharing any crucial information with and since he didn't answer, I turned away from him and looked across the room.

"Ethiopia," he said finally, with a sharp determined edge to his voice aimed like an arrow at my back. I wasn't quite sure he was telling the truth, it seemed like he had fished for an answer and just then decided on Ethiopia.

I turned around. "Oh--- I never met anybody from there before. How'd you get over here?"

"Long story. You want to hear it?"

"I got nothing else to do."

"I thought you would have many boyfriends…let's sit down."

"I'm not interested in boyfriends."

"Smart girl."

So we sat throughout the dance with the others prancing and twisting trying to do the dirtiest dancing they could with the staff watching and carping at them if people got too close or tried to sneak down one of the stairways. After a while one of the girls peeled off her underpants and threw them at a male counselor who immediately caught them and apprehended her, then took her back down to the village, with her underpants under his arm. Another girl, who had begun to imitate the first one, saw what had happened and pulled hers back up in a hurry.

"Silly, aren't they?" said the boy who called himself Omar.

"Completely," I agreed. Well I just sat there while Omar rattled on about how he got there. I didn't know whether to believe him or not. "My father was deported from your country," he said. "They accused my father of colluding with terrorists after we got here, when I was little. My mother was allowed to stay but feared she would also be deported and missed my father. She wanted to go back to Ethiopia---I had run away from home at about that time, I was afraid I'd be sent back too if I stayed home and I didn't want to go back. Well they found me and brought me back to Mother but she put me in a special school where I did something stupid and then they put me in here, for treatment, if I wanted to stay in America, which I did. I've been here for two years."

"What'd you do?"

"Stole some cigarettes from a teacher, then smoked them in the boys' locker room---pretty stupid. They accused me of starting a fire with them but I didn't." I wasn't so sure if I believed any of it but went along with it. Sometimes it's smarter to just keep your mouth shut and wait for things to unfold. If someone is lying it will show up eventually, that's one reason I never lie.

"Yuh. Smoking too. How you get hooked on that?" I asked, taking it all on face value.

"Best friend got me started. Then I couldn't stop."

"You still smoke?"

"Oh yeah," he says mysteriously, but it sounded a little funny with his accent.

"Well, how are you getting 'em in here? There's no way."

"That's what you may think. How long have you been here?

"Almost three months---of torture."

"I've been here two years. They tried to discharge me after a few months but I did something so they'd keep me. No matter what, I want to stay in this country. My mother went back to Ethiopia, she goes back and forth."

"What'd you do?"

"Stole some cigarettes again, from a helper, she had them locked up safely in the staff room, she thought," he smiled.

"But HOW?"

"I have my ways," he whispered, then didn't say anything for a while and we both just watched the other kids act like fools. But I was in no hurry to move. There was something about Omar--- it just felt comfortable sitting beside him like he knew something I didn't or was just ahead of everyone else. Or maybe it was because he was the first kid I'd met in there who just wanted to stay there at PM, I don't know. What he did the next week completely blew my mind.

Chapter Thirteen

Nine nights later something woke up me up from a deep sleep.

I looked toward the light in the hall.

There was Omar, standing at my doorway at 2 a.m. "What you doing in here?" I asked him, "How'd you get down here anyway?" It turned out he had a friend among the night shift staff members who would let him out now and then to scale the fence around the PM property and go buy cigarettes at the 7-11 down the street, then he'd come back and smoke them with the helper when the others were asleep. Well that night he'd talked the staff member, who knew he didn't want to leave, into giving him his keys for a little longer to buy cigarettes but then he snuck down to see me.

"I have a friend," he told me. "I stay in the shadows. Your helper was asleep. I've been here long enough to figure out the schedules of all the so called helpers. And I know Alice. She used to be in our village last year, sleeps like a log."

"Yuh. Alice. She'll be out for another hour." So we sat on my bed and talked. He had his ways that was for sure, definitely the coolest kid I had ever run into; he even had the helpers, at least one of them, fooled.

It got so he would come down every week or so, since he knew our night time helper schedule and managed to arrange it so he'd get there each time when she was sleeping which was inevitable around two in the morning. "What if I DO get found out?" he asked me, shrugging his shoulders, "So what, they'll just keep me here longer, it won't be your fault, you can say you don't even know who I am." I had to admit he had the system figured out, for his purposes.

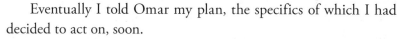

Eventually I told Omar my plan, the specifics of which I had decided to act on, soon.

I would take Alice's keys on one of the nights that she laid them on the desk foolishly, at the beginning of one of her sleep cycles. She generally stayed asleep for an hour and a half each time and only then would drag herself up and check the rooms, and didn't pick up her keys which she didn't need for her little forays. With any luck at all this would give me almost two hours after I snuck out the back door, before they even realized I was missing. It was clear Goonson's plan was to keep me in another six months or a year and even after they decided I was ready to go, it would probably be another six months before they found somewhere to put me, almost for sure not with my mother.

Omar listened carefully to my plan but I could tell he wasn't interested at first.

After a couple of weeks though it seemed like he did think it might be a good idea and maybe not just for me, but maybe for him as well. It allowed him the perfect chance to get his freedom and hopefully not be sent back to Ethiopia. Bottom line, soon we began to make plans for our escape together and Omar, getting excited about this, limited his risk taking to just sneaking down to my room once a week, no cigarettes, which I think he held like a prop anyway just to look cool. With him on board, I wouldn't even have to take Alice's keys and that might give us a while longer to make a break for it. Meanwhile I think part of his plan was… well he was four or five years older than me but I think he was kind of getting to like me and not just as a friend. But he knew better than to try anything because that would have ended it all right there. I was not interested. It seemed like there was a big empty space inside me. Maybe it had something to do with the feeling I had in my floating dreams…. but I wasn't about to let any boy try to fill it. I could tell, even back then, that this would not work. Maybe I'd heard so many warning tales about my mother, of her feeling so alone and hopeless and then taking up with this, that, and the other boy; they loved her blond hair and called her Barbie or Doll she told me proudly. But what happened is they always dumped her or were up to no good and left her feeling worse than she had before. She even got pregnant with one of them when she was thirteen but had a miscarriage. "I didn't know what to do," she had told me, "I felt so guilty years after that…. I still do, it was like I willed it to happen, I don't know why I feel that way…. I just couldn't do it. I was almost out on the street then, well I was …that pain was horrible like your period times a thousand" and she trailed off and wouldn't say any more. The period part I couldn't relate to since mine hadn't come yet--mother thought I was purposely willing myself not to have them, since she herself started at age 10, "I grew up early, had to," she would tell me mysteriously.

But it was a big confession for mother the day she told me about that pregnancy. Like I said, she usually did not like to say anything about herself, though she did like to brag about all the boyfriends she had. "Until I met your father," she would sigh, "and I gave everyone else up--- then and there. *'Yuh and look where he got you,'* I thought to myself the last time she told us about all this. "And three beautiful children, that's the best part," she added, all pink in the cheeks with excitement. I had to admit that part was true, maybe except for me. So there was no way any boy was touching me until I figured out about that empty place.

As the date for our blowing the place got closer, I started getting more nervous.

Omar liked to be called O and that's how I will refer to him from now on. I did realize by then that if what he said was true, it would set me back months maybe years if they caught me. I'd be stuck in there forever.

So a few days before the escape, I was really getting scared. O wasn't going to come until the night we had it planned, in early January.

It was a week after New Years eve as I was lying there in my bed listening to everybody in the hall making noise, that I heard it again--- that voice, this time just bellowing at me about what a fool I was--- and there was no one in the room. At first I wondered if it was an actual message from someone out in the hall or maybe in another world, trying to warn me about my escape. But then I remembered the words of Dr. Loofah, who I had decided never to see again, and I decided to stop that energizing medicine right there. So the next morning I stuffed it between my teeth and at night also put the other one there. I wasn't so good at it then maybe because of the nervousness I was feeling and the pill dropped right in front of Nurse Honne the first morning; she told me to pick it up and handed me another which I graciously took and successfully tucked between my teeth. I noticed a difference right away. On the good side I didn't feel as anxious and after one or two voices in school that afternoon I didn't hear anymore,ever. On the negative side, it seemed like I was moving through something very thick at first, like honey, which slowed me and my thoughts down quite a bit. That night I conked out immediately and didn't have a chance to stake out the village in the middle of the night; I hoped Alice hadn't changed shifts with someone else on the night we had planned; this occasionally happened.

Well with me just dragging through the days then, I attracted a good bit of attention and curiosity. Nurse Honne wanted to know if I was sick, and I told her yes I was--a mild virus, not to worry and asked for a tissue to blow to dry my nose. The teacher was sure I needed a higher dose of the stimulant on the third day of my avoiding it. She pulled me aside after school and asked me in a whisper if I was alright, "because your work production has slowed down a lot," she frowned.

"No I've just been a little tired lately," I told her honestly, trying to avoid being foisted back onto Dr. Loofah who would of course increase my medicine and then it would probably be in two pills in the morning which would be impossible to get rid of. I stared at her earnestly trying to make optimum eye contact, which always made adults believe you.

"Well I don't know. Would you like to see Dr. Loofah again?"

"No!" I shouted, then when I saw her look of alarm, I modulated my voice and added in a steady low voice, "No. Let's give it a little while longer, I just have a virus."

This seemed to satisfy her. She sighed, then patted my shoulder and whispered, "Well… we'll see then dear." I was glad I'd be out of there the next day.

Well that night, January 15th, needless to say, I was scared, in fact shaking in my sneakers. Naturally I planned to put on all my layers of clothes in order to peel some off when I got out of there. That was rule one. Everybody knew they'd remember what you were wearing "like a yellow sweater and blue pants," they'd tell police who would not be looking for somebody in a red shirt and grey pants, which is exactly what I would peel down to. The biggest problem was of course my hair which being so bright and electric looking, would be a complete giveaway, like a red flag. So in my pocket of my second layer of pants I had carefully folded a dark knit cap which would neatly cover my hair.

Well around about one thirty that night I'm lying there on my bed just listening for the sign that Alice had sat down and gone to sleep. For some reason though, she took longer with her snack than usual and it was past two when she finally sat down. Well, about that time, I really began to worry. I hadn't heard O sneak in the side door of the village, a sound which I had become very good at picking up by then. I finally heard Alice settle with a big groan into that fat chair so I got up then and began to check out the hall from my room. I saw that she was asleep, all folded into herself, a good sign of deep sleep. I got out into the hall and here comes O sneaking along the walls like Spiderman staying in the shadows and creeping towards my room. I signaled a thumbs up to him and we're just about ready to make a break for it when there was a loud groan, then a wail coming from Samantha's room down the hall.

Then we heard a scream from a citizen there and the staff, namely Alice, ran down the hall, taking all her keys with her. Everyone in the other rooms rushed groggily into the room where they seemed to think Samantha was acting out and Alice called for emergency staff to restrain her. All of a sudden there's staff everywhere thick as fleas on a dog and O was standing behind my door when I ran to the doorway of Samantha's room who was, by the way, the one who was now humungously pregnant. Staff from other villages were running in and one was carrying restraint leathers because they're still thinking Samantha was just acting out and she began screaming and hitting at staff in all directions. Well about the time they begin to put her into the restraints all the other citizens were crowded around her room and I ran back to O and we scooted out the back door of the village just in time to hear Alice scream, "She's in labor!" and we were out of there. So we flew out the door and just got a gift of probably two or three hours before they'd figured out we were gone. The staff who had given O the keys hardly ever stayed up to wait for him to get back, that's how much he trusted the boy.

Chapter Fourteen

The night air was so cold and bright, it blasted right into my face and I had to catch my breath. I stopped for a minute to look at the stars which were brighter than I'd ever seen and I hadn't seen them in months. O grabbed my sleeve and jerked me along the road where I peeled off my top shirt and realized I'd left my jacket behind. I was so cold I left all my bottom layers on. It dawned on both of us around that time that neither one knew exactly where we would go and knew nothing about the area. O started to cuss in some foreign language and I was hoping he'd come up with a plan. After all he'd been out in the area, at least to the 7-11, many times. So for a minute we both just stood there like rabbits in the headlights wondering which way to go. Nothing was open and there were hardly any cars on the road.

"The sun'll be coming up soon and we'll be like fish in a barrel," I told O, who said he had never heard that saying.

In a second he dashed into the middle of the road to flag down the only car around which didn't stop. I wasn't sure this was the best plan and began to warn him not to risk it again. Next thing I know, here comes a car full of teenagers who pulled over by us and all of a sudden we're sitting in the back of their car. The one driving is smoking and offers O a cigarette which he takes while I'm sitting there worried that maybe I should have stayed back at PM. Pretty soon we're racing along the interstate on 87 north; turns out the three boys up front had hot wired a car from a used car lot a few minutes before they picked us up and figured they could dump it and melt into the woodwork up in Albany.

When I woke up the boys were pulling over by a sidewalk in some neighborhood in south Albany. O was holding another cigarette but pulled me out of the back seat and we walked off in the other direction from the boys who were headed to a relative's house across town. One of them had a girlfriend up the road and seeing her was the motive behind stealing the car.

Around this time it dawned on us that we were hungry and didn't have much money. We went into a little supermarket on the edge of town where the owner, who had a wizened yellowish face like a sun-dried apricot on top of a muscular overworked body, followed us around the store. We bought a carton of whole milk which we thought would have the most calories, and some beef jerky---anybody knows you can live a long time on that.

Sometime around then we decided we would head west, I mean really west like to New Mexico or Arizona. O suggested it but it seemed like a good idea. I'll admit I liked the decision because of my mother. One of those rare times when she would feel like telling us about herself, she had said, "Sometimes I just feel like taking off and living in the desert. There's something so beautiful about the desert, those cactuses as tall as houses and all those different shapes, and arms that go out, and that sky so starry like white lace, you know because that's how clear the air is there. And the rocks. The whole place is just magic, I know. Even though I've never been there, because I've seen so many pictures." I wondered if she would ever go and doubted it but the description stayed with me. It was probably the strongest I've ever heard her talk about anything, with the most feeling, maybe even the most love. It stood out with her because she'd never said anything like it before and she had a real soft look on her face then and her eyes were like she was just staring through the wall of our old apartment beyond into that vast desert. So it was Omar, who has to take the credit or blame, whatever, for that move. Turns out his heart had been set on it. Actually I didn't have any other better idea, only maybe to go up to Canada but that was clearly a bonehead notion because we would have to go through customs and we'd need warmer clothes. The reason for his decision became all too clear later.

O had decided to disguise himself with a wig which someone had given him at one of the Halloweens he spent at PM. It was a long brown do with curls, so he looked a little like a girl from behind, or considering his skinny hips maybe like a serious rocker, anyway not like himself.

We got another ride and were finally headed off on route 90 going west not far from Utica. Now this was a long road, long and cold. But we were let off at dawn and as the sun rose we could see farmhouses and barns from far away kind of taking shape in the light flowing down into the valley of an immense hill; they looked like toys from where we stood. But it was so beautiful just watching the sun come up shining on those tiny white buildings and then there was a river at the very bottom of the hill, looked just like a little stream from where we were. So we decided to go down there. It took us a while to find the road but we did. Some of the Christmas lights were still on and it reminded me, as we got closer, of the way I would imagine growing up if I could have picked my place, there in one of those little white houses with the Christmas lights still on the fir trees in the snow, with some thick patches of it still the trees from the last snow fall.

There was one place that kind of stuck out in that town. It was big and looked very old like if it had been in New York City it would have been torn down long ago. Behind it was a big barn, which we snuck into. There was no one around and the house was still dark inside. We went up to the hayloft on a wooden ladder against the wall and found piles of hay. We decided we'd stay there a couple of days, just sneak into the town for food and get some real sleep up there in preparation for the next part of our trip. I'll admit I was exhausted and not only from no sleep and running away. It felt like my body was still readjusting, kind of dropping back down to where it used to be, before I had those upper pills. So we slept there in big pile of hay--- must have been twenty four hours. After all that sleep, we snuck down the ladder figuring to get some food, but just as I'm reaching the floor, there was this voice behind me saying "Harumph." And O above me starts hustling back up the ladder but stopped when we heard what she said. It was a woman and there was something reassuring about her. We jumped down and stood there staring at her. "Well lah de dah, two kids. And what are you doing in my hayloft, pray tell?" She smiled, almost like it was no big surprise, maybe happened quite a few times and didn't really bother her. She reminded me of the good witch in the Wizard of Oz, holding a pitch fork instead of a wand. There was quite a silence while we both tried to come up with something that would fool her; after all we weren't so far from PM that we couldn't be turned in.

"We're trying to get to our parents," I finally said. "They're out west…in Arizona and we…we're tired and we need to earn some money, we're broke." I wondered as I spoke if they' had put out an APB on us-- probably.

The woman's face softened. "Well how'd you get way out here then?" she says in kind of a musical voice. Her breath is coming out in blasts like thick white ropes straight out of her mouth. We didn't come up with an answer right off, though I ran plenty of possibilities through my mind as we stood there. "Well anyway, come in the house. I can see you two are cold, and look at you young lady, no coat--- in this weather."

"I *am* cold," I said but couldn't come up with anything else to say. We also didn't know what else to do so we followed her into her kitchen.

It was beyond my wildest dreams in there, like it just wrapped us in coziness, so warm and sweet smelling of something delicious, which I found out later was gingerbread. Also there were painted ducks of all shapes and sizes in there, some walking across the cupboards, some wooden, sitting on the counter and some even woven into edges of the tablecloth. The woman liked ducks. And it was so clean, I'd never seen such a clean place; it sparkled almost as much as the decorations on their Christmas tree. There were Christmas decorations of every type in there too, little trees on the mantle all with their little lights like real trees and sparkling silver and gold angels and stars hanging from some of the cupboard handles. And when she opened the cupboards there were the neatest stacks of red and white dishes and red cups with pure white hearts in a circle around them. Everything you could imagine together was with its same size, not like my mother's cupboards which were disorganized with every bowl or dish we had kind of tossed in there, you never knew where to find anything--- no offense to my mother, I know she tried.

There were two little kids playing in her living room by their Christmas tree which had lights of all colors. They looked about as clean and scrubbed as the rest of the place. We just stood there, O and I, taking in the whole scene almost like breathing it in through every pore. It seemed to be the exact opposite of almost everything I had ever known, like people DO actually live like this, warm and happy, cozy where everything seemed to have a place and be happy there, even those two kids. I'd seen this type of thing on Christmas cards but figured it was just make believe. The woman who said her name was Emma made us sit down at her little kitchen table which was covered with a red table cloth surrounded by white ruffles and on the table there were gingerbread men with raisins for eyes and white frosting buttons, in a huge red plate there. This also reminded me of home and how my mother once got a cookie maker, supposed to make cookies in all kinds of Christmas shapes like trees and wreaths and Santa and how excited we girls were about this when Christmas rolled around. But then she never did use it, in spite, or maybe because of our nagging, she would always get mad and say she had too much to do already to prepare for Christmas even though it looked like her time was still mostly in front of the TV.

In a few minutes, Emma popped down some pancakes in front of us. "What a thing!" she tells us "We just happened to have extra this morning probably because I made some for Harold as usual, just wasn't thinking, cause he's out of town for several days. Up to Albany, on business. So," she says after giving us a bottle of maple syrup, "tell me what's REALLY going on." This woman is smart I'm thinking, she knows bull when she smells it. I debate telling her the truth--- maybe if I could say it in the right way she wouldn't turn us in. So I finally piped up because O for once is speechless, just gobbling the pancakes, he was so unprepared to ever be in such a place I guess. I doubt he even saw Christmas cards of places like that.

I decided to pull on her heart strings. It was just a hunch that anybody so clearly happy must have some kind of a wish for others to be happy too---they don't need anything, including for other people to be miserable, like a lot of people seem to. "Well," I began, and the two of them looked at me like they were both curious about what would come out of my mouth, especially O. Emma looked up at me and O just sat there with his mouth stuffed full of the pancake, a little dribble of syrup under his bottom lip and his eyes wide open. Really I liked that moment; couldn't remember anytime when what I was going to say seemed so important to two people. In the meantime the two little boys had come over and were told to sit at the table and listen, which they also did. "Well," I continued half expecting her to grab the phone in the next moment and then O to high tail it out the door, followed of course by me. Emma took a sip of her coffee and smiled at me, in no rush, I decided. She had pale skin and red cheeks with light brown hair in a thick braid down her back; you just don't see many women like that anymore like she was really living in another time. I wondered if she could even knew such a thing as treatment centers for bad kids exist. She continued to smile in between sips of her coffee; her teeth were white and almost round like pearls.

"Anyway," I began, still having said nothing, "We're from the city." That part was true.

"Yes?" She said, raising her eyebrows.

"And our parents…they're not there, they've left us," I blurted all of a sudden surprising even myself, and as all my coolness and planned statements left me, I almost began to sob. It was true. Was I just realizing this for the first time? How pathetic I thought, trying to choke back the tears.

"Where?" Emma frowned.

"In jail. Well my father is in jail and my mother… she just disappeared. I know she's around but I don't know where." At that, I realized that this information actually did apply to me, lost control and began to truly blubber--- tears I never knew were in me. I'd always thought my mother's disappearance made no real difference to me; after all I was now twelve. Emma stood up and gave me a tissue then wrapped her arms around me and kind of leaned against me like she's propping me up. And I'm leaning against her trying to stop crying but those tears just keep pouring out like I'm a spicket somebody left on by mistake. I'd never been a cryer. In fact I despised girls who resorted to tears to get their way. I'd seen it done by others, even by my sister Ravena, who still didn't get her way. I guess that's how I learned not to do it. In fact it never worked,none of us ever got our way. So I'm just bawling there and trying to stop while O at first looked panic stricken and I could tell he was debating just jumping up and leaving me there with Emma. Then in a minute I guess he sees the reaction I'm getting from her and sits there with a little smile across his mouth like 'Oh yeah, this is gonna do it, we're alright now'--- as if it's all a fake, just to get her. But it wasn't and when I finally gathered myself together down to those deep gasps and gulps you have after you've just stopped really bawling, I gave him an angry look. He looked down at the table at his plate with one large piece of pancake left and pushed it into a tiny puddle of syrup then swallowed it in one gulp, like a wolf. Emma drew back from me finally as her two quiet kids were still sitting there staring and one blurted, "Is she alright Mama?" and I was sure they've never seen anything like this before. Even though it should have been clear that O and I probably didn't have the same parents, she didn't pursue the subject anymore, looked like my outburst was convincing enough.

So that did it. I never actually said why we were going out west. I guess she decided we had relatives out there. It was like, given my first response, she was afraid to delve into anything more. "Well you two are welcome to rest here for a while on your trip. Raynelle you can have the guest room and Omar you can stay on the sofa in the den if you don't mind. It's large and comfortable and private. You can close the door. I know it's not what you're used to but I hope it will do," she said. Well, that was the truest thing: it definitely was not what we were used to and that was fine.

Chapter Fifteen

My room seemed like a princess's castle. Maybe it was reserved for the little girl Emma hoped to have some day. In the meantime it looked like she had used it as a sewing room, with pieces of bright cloth and patterns around the small sewing machine in the corner. There were ruffles on the pink bedspread and decorations everywhere and not just of ducks. There were only a couple of them up there, on the closet door. There was a little cabinet and when you opened the door--there was a doll house with tiny furniture and a tiny doll, all just a tidy as Emma's real house. And there was a thick pink rug on the floor so thick it pushed up through my toes when I walked barefoot through it. And when you looked out the window you could see the barn and the field beyond on a slope where their two horses and the cows were let out. All in all I felt like I had gone to some enchanted land, a girly heaven. But I wouldn't let myself get too comfortable because I knew it would end. O was happy with his little den where they also had a TV and since my room was over his I know he had that thing on late at night, every night. He wouldn't tell me what he was watching though. Also we did have to do chores in those several days we were there. I had to baby-sit the little boys and O had to help out in the barn, feed the animals and also clean after them which he thought was definitely the worse end of the deal. He sulked about it the whole time when Emma wasn't looking. About that time I noticed that the accent which he seemed to have before had somehow disappeared. Maybe now that he knew me better he was more relaxed and let it go. But I didn't mention any of this to him.

I liked to watch Emma when she was in the kitchen. I would just sit there at that ducky table while she was preparing dinner and do whatever she asked, peeling, beating, whipping. I'd never done any of it before---my mother was not much of a cook. But Emma was extremely patient. She was always trying out different recipes and she seemed so organized like nothing ever happened that was a surprise to her. Her clothes were always clean and smelled of spring flowers. She would sit at the table with me sometimes and thumb through her cookbook just taking her time; when she turned the pages she licked her finger just with a smart little lick, like a cat cleaning her kitten, then flip the page over. I wondered how she ever got so in control of her life and if there were any other people like her around. I'd certainly never met any. Then I'd fantasize about just staying there forever, just soaking all this up, becoming that daughter she hadn't had yet. As for O, he seemed in a constantly grumpy state from the time we got there maybe because his chores were harder than mine, but maybe also because of how late he was staying up watching whatever it was on TV every night. The sad thing was I knew it all had to end. So I shouldn't have been surprised the afternoon that Emma told us her husband Harold would be home the next day. It had just seemed like we had been there so long, even though it was only about a week, that I thought we should never have to leave. It gave me a little start when she said that, and though there was really nothing bad about her tone of voice, I could tell things would be different when her husband got back.

So that night I was lying in bed, a little anxious again, wondering what this Harold would be like and when exactly he would get there.

The house was very quiet that night; even the barn was quiet--- there was absolutely no noise from the cows or horses like there usually was. And there was no creaking in that house like there had been and like Emma had told us old houses just do---that's the way they are, releasing a little energy from years of being used hard. "Maybe houses talk a little, they've seen so much, how could they keep it all in?" she laughed. And looking back on it I think everybody knew a little something, me, O, the house, the horses and the cows.

And Emma.

I had just drifted off to sleep that night when I was awakened by what seemed like a slamming sound. I listened. It didn't happen again and I went back to sleep. Then again there was the same sound. I got up and walked to my door. Voices--- first soft then very loud and they were coming from Emma's room. At first I thought she must be talking to the children---maybe they'd gotten up in the middle of the night and made that slamming noise. I snuck down the hall, telling myself maybe she was in trouble and I would help her. But when I leaned my head against her door, there it was, another slamming sound and a man's voice, loud. He was yelling at Emma. I wondered if it was an intruder, but no---she was calling him Harold in a low kind of cowering voice, like at first she didn't want to wake us up, then she was just afraid. I went to my room to put on my clothes then stepped back into the hall. I could feel that dread in my stomach--- I'd had it before from time to time--- like the first time my mother stayed out all night. He was yelling and not just about anything. He had gone into his den, he told her, to check something on TV after he got home and there's this kid, O of course, watching it. Then he learned I was here too. That was it for me. I got what I had and put it into a cloth sack Emma had given me.

I snuck down to O's room and told him to get himself ready before realizing that he was dressed and had all his stuff together. I still don't know if he was planning on blowing the place without me. He told me Harold had come in and when he saw him, had just about blown his top. He screamed so loud, O told me he wondered how I didn't wake up. Then he slammed the den door, hard. That's when I woke up. "That's all it took," he said, "I got myself together then and there."

"Do you think we should call the police?" I asked O who said nothing and we stood there by the front door for a few minutes listening to Harold shout about how it was his house and what these kids were doing here, he had enough mouths to feed already and why did he marry her anyway. At that point I ran upstairs--- I was that ready to just barge in on him. But then I thought, what if they're naked? Who could tell? So I pressed my head to their door again, I was so ready, while O was standing at the bottom of the stairs saying in a loud whisper, "You are crazy. You do what you're going to do but I'm getting out of this place." At that I heard some crying--- Emma ---and I leaned towards the door again---she's asking the husband to forgive her, adding that "those kids" will leave the next day. And then next thing I know they're talking to each other all sweet and romantic even and I guess she was rubbing something because the last thing I heard before tumbling back down the stairs was him groaning about something feeling good. I decided they're both crazy and wondered if this was something they always do, like some kind of strange routine. I decided to leave her a note on which I printed:

WE BOTH THANK YOU EMMA. WE HAD A
NICE REST HERE AND THINK YOU ARE A
VERY KIND PERSON.

BEST OF WISHES TO YOU,
RAYNELLE AND OMAR

It was in kind of a scribbly printing because I was in a hurry--- who knew what would happen next? On our way out of the yard I asked O what it was that got the father in such a dither after finding O watching.

"Doesn't matter," he said irritably.

But I kept prodding. It had to be something, didn't it? "Come on! What was it?" I wheedled.

"Porn. The raunchiest kind," he said finally. That ended the discussion.

Chapter Sixteen

We started heading down I 80 south, figured to get out of the north country as fast as we could. Well, we hadn't gone too far into the morning---the sun was just coming up on one side and the moon still hanging in the sky in front of us, when someone screeched to a stop up ahead about 10 yards so we figured we'll risk it--- what choice did we have? We ran up to the truck, an old white Dodge with paint missing on the doors. A middle-aged aged man is sitting there revving his engine in the cold air and we climbed in. He has a grizzly blond beard and kind blue eyes. "Couldn't let you kids stay alone on this road, and in all this cold. Where you headed anyway?"

"Arizona," O pipes up.

"That far? Well you do have a ways to go, guys. Where you from anyhow?"

"Uh, Albany," I said, thinking that might make the most sense.

You can tell he wants to dig a little and maybe ask us some more but we're both sitting staring straight ahead with our mouths closed tight and he didn't. There was a faint smell of cow manure in there which I had become quite familiar with, given where we were just staying. O coughs and I can tell he's smelling it too and doesn't like it a bit, considering his recent close experience with it at Emma's. I asked the man if he minds if I open the window a bit and he says, "No, you hot?"

"A little bit," I say not wanting to offend him.

"Tough kid I guess. You don't even have a coat," he says looking at me. "Well I'm going as far as Pennsylvania. Got to go down there and look at a piece of equipment, I believe I can get cheap. For my farm."

"What kind of farm?" I say to make conversation because O who is sitting next to him is as silent as a stone.

"Sheep farm but I have a few cows too." Clearly, I think, and can't come up with anything more to say for the next half hour. By then the man whose name is Ronald announces that he's hungry and wonders if we are too. Of course we both say yes but I'm wondering who will pay the bill if we stop somewhere because we have hardly any money. I begin to wish I'd stayed a little longer at Emma's to give her the chance to give us a little cash like she said she was going to. But that was before Harold came home.

In a little while the man's stomach sets up an awful rumbling and he gets a little red in the face especially his nose. I believe he was truly embarrassed by it and pulled off at the next exit. He spotted a diner down the road about a quarter of a mile and yelled out happily and in a moment we're all bundled in the diner sitting in a booth, me and O on one side, Ronald on the other. He orders double everything: coffee, eggs, sausage for himself then looks at us and asks, "What'll it be kids?"

I explain we have only a couple of dollars and he laughed and says, "My treat, looks like you kids have had your share of problems." Little does he know, I think and order a Swiss cheese omelet, with everything on it. As I'm eating I look up and see someone kind of perched on one of the seats looking in our direction. My first thought was that he was some cop after us. But looking closer I saw his rumply clothes, overalls with a faded plaid shirt--- no cop could be dressing like that. In a flicker the man turned back to his coffee, but the look in his eyes stayed with me for a few hours---it seemed so suspicious.

Ronald let us out in Pennsylvania that night and we were on our own again. I remember thinking as I climbed out of his truck that there were sure some nice people up there in western New York state. Maybe it was the country air.

Chapter Seventeen

The strangest thing about New Mexico was the air. The warmth seemed to seep into each pore and lift me up like a helium balloon as I stepped out of the mini-van that had carried us there from western Pennsylvania. It seemed like every part of my body was lightened after sucking up that air. After so much clammy cold, the hot dry air was like a dream come true. But we wanted to get to Arizona. We heard it was even warmer there and that's the place my mother had dreamed about and O was determined to get to. So once again we set out hitchhiking. We had been able to mooch off the people in a mini-van for a couple of days, not stop at restaurants but to feed off the stuff they had brought in the van: canned peas, pork jerky, dried fruit. We would all stop at the rest area and if it was cold, we'd just eat there in the van. It was a mother named Sheila and her two children and they were very nice. Every time we stopped to eat, the mother would make us bow our heads for a prayer; that was alright with me, though I'll admit I didn't know much about the praying stuff since I'd never done it and neither had anyone in my family, to my knowledge. I was respectful and bowed my head like she asked. To be honest the idea of someone looking out for me hadn't occurred before and I liked it. But O wouldn't participate. He made a point of looking out the window or setting up a loud fidgeting every time. To be honest, I thought the food kind of tasted a little better after the prayer, which I told O but he wasn't having it. "It's just food anyway," he said and the matter was closed. But it was kind of like the price Sheila wanted for us riding with her. She said she knew we were both lost sheep and didn't have to know anything about us other than to look at us to see that. I thought she was pretty smart and did listen to her advice which she repeated over and over and which I thought made sense. She said we will reap what we sow and to love God whom she said resided inside of us as well as all the other places around. That at first sounded a little strange to me but then I remembered once thinking about God after seeing a preacher yelling about religion on TV and so I asked myself where is God then--- but it was like a boomerang--- the question just went out away from me and then came right back to me. This happened exactly twice, both the times I asked myself this question but I do remember them because it seemed so strange. When we got out of her van, Sheila insisted on praying over us, her and her two teen-age kids. Well I was a little embarrassed standing there on the sidewalk with her holding her hand up and mumbling over us but I did it. After all, look what she'd done for us. Omar just kept shuffling his feet and looking off towards the mountains. So there we were, brought all the way from New York and only a few hundred miles to go.

We had a little money, a few dollars between us because Sheila also gave us three dollars. We started west on route 66 and it wasn't long before someone pulled over. It was a youngish guy in a beat up silver Lexus, but he wouldn't let O get in first--- he insisted that I get in beside him. Neither one of us liked the smell of that so we waved him on. He was not happy and revved his engine then sped away, churning up some dust and stones in our faces. We agreed at that point that we'd probably been real lucky with our rides so far and weren't going to risk anything with some jokester specially since we only had a few miles to go relatively speaking. Finally though we did get another ride with a charitable looking sort of lady with a large stomach wedged in behind her steering wheel and with wispy gray hair which was gathered into a long pony tail twisting down her back. It was nearing dark and as she opened the door to her old maroon Dart, she told us she couldn't bear to pass us by, that something just told her to stop

"Though I do know better generally---you never do know who's out there," she mumbled after we got in, all the while looking at us suspiciously. She pushed the debris in her front seat to the floor: some old Womens Day magazines, a few crimped recipe cards, and a half eaten Twinkie and I sidled in there. She let O get in back. So then of course she starts asking about us: where we're going and where we're from. It seemed like these questions were part of the routine for giving someone a ride. Since O was always silent when the questions started up, I had developed quite a knack for answering them. It was always a different story that I tried to gear to what the person might like or expect. In the meantime with this one, I was trying to keep my feet off the Twinkie and the old recipe cards; I thought about picking them up but decided if she wanted them off the floor she would not have put them there. So I just kept my feet pressed close together by the side of the car door and told her we had gone on a skiing trip to the northeast after we had won a contest but that our skiing gear and our bus tickets home had been stolen by some deranged rock musician who then just disappeared. We called the police but they couldn't find him and of course our parents were too poor to send us more money. Then I looked to see her reaction. She raised her eyebrows and looked at us, until I was a little nervous about the road ahead. Her eyes looked weepy and her nose was red and round at the end like a jacks ball. I looked in the back seat. O was staring straight ahead but he had the tiniest grin on his face, just barely visible in the darkening car.

"My word! You can never trust anyone anymore," the woman said then paused as if to reconsider her own wisdom about picking us up. To be honest I started to feel a little ashamed for making up all these stories but was sort of surprised at how easy it had become. Then I began to worry that she might just drop us off.

"Nice car," I said, trying to change the subject.

"Oh thanks, it's old but it does the job. Like me," she smiled and I breathed a sigh of relief. "Well how far you two going? I'm going down to Phoenix, then I'm stopping. Got relatives there. I'll be stopping soon though, to get a bite to eat."

I was hoping this was an invitation and said, "Well then... we'll go along with you, to Phoenix if that's OK," hoping that would include some free food along the way.

"Great," she muttered and soon was pulling over at a rest stop. "Care to come?" she says as she started moving toward the building. This wasn't the kind of food I was hoping for; all that was inside there were machines with gooey looking overpriced stuff which she wasn't even offering to buy us anyway. I was hoping for something more along the lines of what Ronald had gotten us. And she didn't offer to buy us anything at all so O and I spent half of our remaining money on two doughy stale Danishes and were hardly satisfied. The woman spent several dollars on jelly doughnuts which she gulped down fast then swilled two cups of coffee with cream and sugar while we looked on munching slowly on our pastry, knowing that would be all we'd get for a while. It was shortly after that when we pulled into Phoenix and she let us out with many warnings about hitch hiking and staying safe.

We reassured her and I thanked her twice which seemed to satisfy her but O shut the rear door with a bit of a slam. "O!" I yelled at him as she pulled away. "She gave us a ride, we'd still be walking if it wasn't for her."

"She could have bought us some more of that lousy food."

"You could see she doesn't have much money."

"She has enough to support that big belly."

We were both in extremely crabby moods as we headed out of Phoenix--- what could we do there? We flipped one of the remaining coins we had to decide if we would go south or east. It was heads, my choice, and east it was, which put O into an even worse mood.

By then it was good and dark, and pretty cold as well, though nothing compared to New York state. He was walking along looking at the road and I was following behind with my eyes on the stars. To be honest, that's a habit I've had since I saw that light in the sky, maybe before then, that's the reason I saw it to begin with. O had begun to complain at that point that he should have stayed at PM---that at least he got three meals a day there. "I was due to get out soon any way," he added.

"That's not what you told me before," I reminded him, and mentioned his story about being abandoned by his parents who he said were both now in Ethiopia. He didn't answer me, just said a cuss word almost under his breath so I heard it loud and clear.

"Oh well," I said, "it was your choice to come. I didn't force you." As I said that, I looked farther down in the direction we were heading in and saw something looming in the dark, coming toward us.

It looked to be moving, extremely thin and very tall, likely a person, not my imagination. It didn't veer away, but just kept coming straight at us, and I could see by then it was a boy, maybe fourteen or fifteen, with a turban on which is why he looked so tall. "What the..." I said.

He stopped about three feet away from us. We stopped too and I was wondering if he was maybe a ghost or some kind of extraterrestrial, as weird as he looked, maybe he was even from those lights. For a minute we all just stood there like three dogs sizing each other up but without the sniffing. "Jose," he said finally reaching out to shake O's hand. Omar, not used to such behaviors, let him have it and the guy who appeared by then to be an actual person said, "Hungry?" Seemed like he knew exactly what to say.

"Yes!" I shouted before O could mutter a word. And we all marched off together after him into the blackness.

Chapter Eighteen

Little did we know that cave on the mountain would be our home for quite some time. This was because Jose, who owned the cave, in a manner of speaking, had been living there for a long time. And there was a lot of stuff in there, mostly as it turned out, stuff that he had lifted from various department or convenience stores in the area, some as a result of pick pocketing. Jose, in spite of, or because of, his impoverished condition, had become quite a sleight-of-hand artist. He told us that when he was small in happier times in Mexico, his father who had been a skilled magician, attempted to supplement his farming income from this and had taught Jose several secrets of magic. The bottom line he said was that the hand was quicker than the eye particularly if you set up appropriate expectations with people, who are geared to expect certain things, not what you are doing. Jose was using this as way to stay afloat in difficult times, until he could make some money and send a lot of it back to his family in Mexico. "I thought you were from India," I said that first night, pointing at the turban.

"Oh this," he said, deftly unwrapping what was actually a large white bath towel, "it throws people who are looking for a Mexican off. Also because of the added height of course, because they don't expect this height from a mere Mexican," he sneered, "but of course it's a towel."

Meanwhile that night I was just wondering why on earth he started talking to us, not to mention immediately taking us back to his home you might say and why we even followed him, sort of like it was all preordained.

Later that night I got up the nerve to ask him about this. "I knew you two were coming," he said. "I'm a little sighted sometimes, can see things other people think are just crazy, I get this from my father's side mostly my grandmother... she made good money telling fortunes. It comes to me early in the morning, sometime around three. If I wake up then I know there's something for me to pick up on, I feel it in my heart, then my head, that's how it comes, a feeling, and usually right," he said and put his hand on his heart. He was saying all this in an accent which is not quite Spanish, but something like a song, thick and different.

"It's Indian," he said. "I have an Indian accent. I picked it up by watching movies with somebody supposed to be from India acting in them, a real exaggerated accent. I'm good at languages."

"Do you speak Indian?" I asked.

"No, not really, just the accent but I speak English as you can see."

"Yuh. So you've got everything all figured out," said O irritably, still apparently wishing he was back at PM. "Then why do you need us anyway?"

"I'm not sure. Maybe I sent for you," he said mysteriously and at that I began to wonder if he was just another crazy person. A tiny fire Jose had started sparkled there and threw off weird shimmering lights against the curve of the cave wall behind it and you could see O's eyes roll at this last statement.

"Seriously. Those things can happen. The world is full of strange undercurrents. Energies we have no idea about."

"Ok," I said, wanting to get back to something more substantial. "So how long have you been here in this country?"

"In this country, three years. In this cave 10 months. It's not bad actually," he said like a proud home owner.

I had to admit there was something cool about it. He had everything organized and it was beautiful--- well not the cave necessarily but outside it. It was on the edge of a short mountain in a long mountain range not far from town. And yet when you stepped out of it you saw no lights from the city, just stars, just maybe a few lights from the convenience stores below the mountain.

"I came most of the way on a train," Jose began again, "but I won't tell you about that, almost didn't make it. It was a miracle I'm even here in front of you now." He's telling us all this baloney, I thought, wondering if that was just more of his imagination.

"My dream is to somehow make enough money to send more back to my parents who have nothing now; even my father's magic is no help. But I have to get legal. That's my plan."

"And how do you plan to do that?" laughed O, snidely.

Jose smiled. His mouth in the dim flickering light looked pursed and round then extended like a snake slowly uncoiling itself across his face. "That's where you two come in and I'm not sure how, I just know it is going to happen. You can't believe how happy I was when I saw you coming. I'd been going out there at night for the last several weeks, just waiting and walking. And there you were, finally." He laughed again and I got up to go outside and stare at the sky. By then I was beginning to think that maybe we both should have stayed at PM.

I lay down there outside the cave and put my head on a soft round bush, probably some tumbleweed. I became a little sleepy and inside the cave it was quiet. I figured O had stopped asking questions and Jose stopped explaining things. In a while I heard O's deep breathing which I knew by then meant he was asleep and decided I'd just rest out there myself for a while. I wasn't at all sure of Jose's motives and thought he might be more than a little nuts.

So I got real groggy out there. It was a little chilly but I was in a sheltered spot between the bushes and a big rock and there was no wind there at all. I believe I finally fell asleep. Things seemed different when I opened my eyes as though I had gone somewhere else. There was something howling not too far away. I thought it was a cayote, but far enough not to come looking for me and I still lay there looking up. The stars were much brighter than before, brighter than I'd ever dreamed they could be. It was like they were huge lights just hanging there, decorating an immense curved ceiling. Now and then one would shoot through the air in an arc and disappear. This I had seen only once before and it held my attention. I was watching this incredible show but all the while, it seemed like, *'You like this? Well this is nothing, you'll see.'* That's was what I imagined the sky was telling me. And I was the only one seeing it. I could hear somebody snoring and the other one deep breathing in that cave. They both were zonked.

In a moment I heard a rustling behind one of the bushes and turned my head a little to see what it was. Just as I did that, I my eyes caught it.

Well, you could hardly ignore it.

Chapter Nineteen

There they were again, just sitting there in the sky, just like they had before.

I was steady staring at this thing because it was a bunch of lights just all together like it's definitely lighting around something. And it makes those stars I was raving about a few seconds before look like tiny specks. *It's an airplane,'* my head told me, *but it's not moving, it can't be an airplane.* 'It's a helicopter then,' but it seemed so close and it wasn't making any noise. Even if the wind were blowing the other way I would hear something from a helicopter. 'Of course, it's a spaceship,' I concluded finally, 'but no, I can't really see a shape like spaceships are supposed to have, like a saucer or something long and pointy; I can't see a real shape but it seems so close.' And it sat there, hovering, because that's what it seemed to be doing, for a long time. It then began to seem like maybe it was trying to contact me and I began to have thoughts of being inside a spaceship, flying through the universe like princess Leia in Starwars, my mother's favorite movie. In the next minute I became afraid, really afraid, like maybe it's come to get me and I'll never see my family again; even though I had real doubts about whether I'd ever see them again anyway, this idea really scared me then and I got ready to run back into the cave. But at just that moment the lights gradually faded and then they were gone. They didn't disappear in a flash like I've heard space ships do, like faster than anything you've ever seen---just gone. These faded gradually, like in my imagination it was saying,'*Don't be afraid, we'll just take our time. We don't need to hurry.*' I didn't know where these ideas were coming from, but what really freaked me out was it was almost like whatever that group of lights were, they were really trying to communicate with me---it couldn't have been my imagination. Where else would those thoughts come from? Maybe Mother was right all along.

I stayed out there again the next night. To be honest I was mystified about the whole spaceship thing and because I thought it was really special in every way I could think of, I didn't tell either one of those boys. As crabby as O had become, I knew he'd tell me I was crazy. I didn't know Jose well enough to tell him something like that, even though he was definitely on the far out side himself and probably wouldn't think it was a bit weird compared to what was going on in his mind. So I kept it to myself. In the morning I walked back into the cave just like nothing had happened the night before.

"You don't have to sleep out there you know, there might be snakes ...or other creatures lurking in the dark" Jose said as I came in. "I'm not going to bother you and I'm sure you trust your friend O." *Not necessarily*, I thought but said nothing.
"Besides I've fixed up a place for you to sleep here---it's like your own little corner." And he led me over to a place which was like a mini-cave within a big one. There was a bit of a stoney wall between it, and the rest of the cave. Jose had a couple of blankets which he had laid down there for me and a small pillow.
"Not too bad," I told him as I tried it out.
"Maybe we can get out of these dirty clothes," said O. It was true we hadn't changed our clothes since we left Emma's so abruptly that night and were beginning to smell a little ripe, well rotten.

"Yuh," said Jose nodding his head in agreement. "Matter of fact, I've got lots of clothes here, boys stuff of course but the only thing that's really different for you," he said, looking at me, "is the underwear".

O laughed and said "not that different." A lot of the stuff still had price tags on it and looked like Jose had just taken some of it just for the fun of it, maybe just because it was so easy for him.

"I don't even wear half this stuff," he said throwing pants and shirts our way. "It'll probably fit you OK O, but it'll be a little big on Ray." That's what he called me right from the start, even though I clearly told him my name, Raynelle. It didn't bother me though because that's what my father used to call me when he was there and in a good mood. He was the only one to do that.

"How do you bathe then?" said O, in a whiny voice like a kid who'd been raised in a castle with a silver spoon in his mouth. Of course he was older than I was and I guessed he cared more about hygiene than I did at the time, when boys were just not relevant to me. But Jose did look clean.

"I go to the Y," he said casually.

"What?" I asked. "I thought you were hiding out."

"Not from everybody. I've got a friend, works night shift at the Y, from Colombia. He's legal! I pay him a little and he lets me in late once a week to use the facilities, sometimes twice but I don't want to overdo it, he's doing me a big favor."

"Well what about us then?" O whined again.

"Give me a little while, I'll think of something. Nobody's really after you now, right? So you don't have to worry."

"I don't think so," I said. "We've been gone more than two weeks and if they can't find an escaped kid in two weeks then they almost always just discharge them. No fuss, no bother."

"Good, then if you have a little money, I'm sure my friend will let you in there at night now and then. Just to use the showers, no activities or things that'll draw peoples' attention."

"Great," says O and walked outside to survey the morning scene.

I meanwhile was left to take my first good look at Jose in the light. He was clean, amazingly so for a cave dweller, though he had a little mustache growing right under his nose. His eyes were dark and a little slanty and he had a small mouth which just spread across his face like a wave when he smiled, with square white teeth that looked like he went to the dentist every six months.

"You have really nice teeth," I told him. "Do you have a dentist around here too?"

"Not yet, but I used to go in Mexico, took after my mother. Strong teeth and I brush them everyday," and he pointed to a gallon of water by a large mirror on one side of the cave. "This is the bathroom, well not all of it. I use the facilities outside for... you know, then bury it like a cat. Very sanitary."

"I see," I said and could tell the timing of things was going to difficult there, even for me who grew up sharing a tiny bathroom where the water was occasionally shut off, with four other people. I didn't like Jose's arrangement but what choice did we have then? We had no money and no food. I had nothing to go home to and neither did O. Also I kind of liked Jose and thought he had everything figured out at least for a sixteen year old. And I was interested in his strange tales. Although O had obviously decided he was just blowing it out his ear, I thought or maybe hoped, it was for real. Also I had seen that vision or whatever it was the night before, like it had just found me once again, here on the side of a mountain and the magical feeling of it was still inside me sitting right in the back my mind like a really good dream stays inside you the next day. Maybe it was a dream, I didn't know, but I did want to find out.

Chapter Twenty

I had noticed that O had begun to carry a little notebook with him most of the time He also kept a couple of pens in his shirt pocket, like an engineer or politician. Now and then I'd find him scribbling in it or jotting something down then quickly putting it back in his pocket.

I had asked him about it when I first noticed it up at Emma's after we had done our chores.

"Just an old notebook," he told me kind of nervously then slipped it out of sight. "I like to write down my feelings about what's happening, sort of like a diary but shorter. I don't go in for long descriptions," he added. "Only facts." I was curious and asked to see it.

"Not now," he told me, "maybe sometime. There's nothing much to show right now anyway. You wouldn't find it interesting." I knew O was smart, that was clear, and very mechanical, though I figured a lot of that was because he was older, now almost seventeen. But I became more curious again in Jose's cave. Seemed like he would whip it out every time he had a spare minute by then and lots of the time he would be just staring at it like he was trying hard to figure something out, to come up with something, just focusing all his concentration on that little white page. Even Jose finally became curious about it.

"What you got there, man?" he asked O the third day after we arrived.

"Nothing, just some scribbling. I like to draw sometimes."

"Yuh, I used to do that when I had time in Mexico. Now I'm too busy."

"Doing what?" O asked.

"Planning, things spinning in my head all the time, truth is I imagine what will happen or what I want to happen then it will manifest...sooner or later. How do you think I got so much stuff?"

"You still have to hide out most of the time?"

"Well that's a big problem, but its going to be solved sooner or later. I have ways."

"Yuh? What?"

"You'll see. One other thing though I do, is I always rehearse things in my head before I act on them. Almost always. Like there's a stage in there and I can see what I'm going to do, just feel myself doing it and then I guess what people will say, even under different conditions, maybe different answers, and I plan what I'll say back to them. I cover any possibility that way. like rehearsing for the future, that way I stay flexible, always land on my feet like a cat," he laughed.

"You've got everything all figured out," O said in a sarcastic tone.

"I know," Jose answered calmly, completely oblivious to, or just ignoring the sarcasm.

After O discovered there was a library in the area about five miles down the road he was gone a lot.

"Studying," he told me. "World affairs. I'm keeping up with things, even though I'm here. Not going to waste my time, got to figure out what my next move will be. Won't be staying around here in some dirty cave much longer."

"Ok," I told him and it was clear I'd better do the same. But where was I going to go? There I was, pretty much dependent on this Mexican with a turban and an Indian accent and a hand quicker than almost anybody's eye. And he did bring home the bacon. He would be out a few hours each day to go to different stores or maybe some days just go to the same stores and shop ---like a valued customer---with the money he'd got from pawning the stuff he'd stolen a few days before. He seemed to know where he could steal and where he would need to have cash, usually the cheaper stores which were more on the lookout for thieves. Sometimes Jose would take off the turban and wear a New York Yankees cap, backwards. A few times I went with him, not walking beside him but just staying behind or around the vicinity, just there in the background of the picture. He didn't want me right up next to him. He said he figured an Indian guy with a turban might be easy enough to forget but an Indian guy with a turban next to a young girl with bright red hair that stood on its ends wouldn't be so easy.

So I just watched from the periphery, he wouldn't let me do it more than that. "They'll begin to associate you with me," he explained, "in their subconscious mind, there'll be me and then you, somewhere by me in their minds like a wild dream, then they'll find it easier to remember if the time comes, which I hope it doesn't. It will be like a red flag. The mind is like an iceberg, you only see the top of it you know, the rest of it is down there below, huge, but beneath the surface,we just aren't aware of what's it's doing. Or what it can do," he added.

Jose had a lot of theories and he didn't doubt any of them. He had explained it to me, "That's what happens when you are raised by two parents who are well... I won't say better, but removed from the common mind, the usual ways of thinking. I absorbed it and of course I was probably born with some abilities, most of them, like gifts. Got to have something when you're poor. It's only fair."

"Yuh," I said this because it all seemed completely reasonable at the time. But I did know about myself that I generally found any opinion reasonable when someone took the time to argue it. It could be the exact opposite of something someone else just argued, which I had also completely agreed with. My mother told me that was the sign of a peacemaker, but I don't know. I had decided many times that I needed to watch myself about this because it could lead to trouble.

Chapter Twenty One

So this last time I went with him, Jose was looking for big things in an appliance and jewelry store, expensive stuff like gold watches, silver cigarette boxes and fancy clear-colored stones like diamonds and rubies all around, some lying right out on the counter. I was poking around a few counters down from him, just pretending to look at the watches and trying to follow what he was doing from a distance, but not to be too obvious about it. I happened to know that he had debated picking somebody's pocket in there or just lifting something but he decided against the pick pocketing--- it wasn't crowded enough. So I'm staring at him and can tell he's checking something out and is timing it from watching what the salesperson is doing. Also he managed to get himself at an angle where he was just out of sight of the big curved mirror at the end of the room. I was staring at him when a saleslady walked over and planted herself right in front of me and then I couldn't see O. "Can I help you?" she says suspiciously with quite an irritable voice.

"Oh yes," I said to throw her off, then amended it a little. "Well I'm looking for something for my mother, she's been sick you know." I looked up and see the sales lady is looking less irritable and even a little interested. Then I was inspired ...I went on. "Yes she's had some condition...her memory is fading a little and she's had trouble keeping time really well."

The saleswoman suddenly is completely sorry. "Oh," she says, "so young! She must be so young for that."

"Oh, not really," I said seeing the possible problem there. "She had me when I .. or she was quite old...I was the last one and I'm actually older than I look. She's fifty."

"Oh, but still so young," she sighed. "Well dear don't let me stop you. Just go head and look. If I can help you let me know." And she walked off, sniffling a little.

I'll admit I felt a little ashamed to lie like that but then decided I hadn't done any harm and when I was older I was going to do something wonderful, I mean I'd already decided that long before, that it would help everyone, even her. In the meantime I had a clear path again to see Jose who was by then chatting happily with a sales person down the way. I stepped somewhat closer and could hear his Indian accent, loud, from where I was and that happy soothing voice; it sounded like music. I guessed he had convinced the woman that he had a lot of money which he did actually but he wasn't there to buy on that day. She had put out seven or eight necklaces on the counter that he's ogling, occasionally touching, like he was trying to decide which one to buy for his aunt, I heard that loud and clear, because she had just come over from Bombay he was saying and he wanted to give her a present, something gold to make her feel at home, at one point affectionately touching her hand, just briefly. So there he stood a few more minutes just chatting amiably about the homeland and I guess he picked a saleslady who looked like she would never have gone to India. Then before I know it, he turned and bid her a warm goodbye, says he's got to discuss which one to purchase with his mother who will be in the store later or the probably next day.

Well by the time we left out of there I figured he just changed his mind. I asked what happened after we got a few yards away from the store.

"Nothing." And he didn't say anymore until we were close to the cave, then he reached way down inside his pants and pulled out a long gold necklace with a diamond in the center.

"What!" I yelled. "How'd you do that? She was standing right in front of you. You'll be caught you know. Besides it's not good to steal."

"No I won't. She was so distracted by the talk and the many moving and glittering necklaces, and my hand movements, especially the little touch, she was actually in a state of semi-trance. That made it easier--many people will be like that. Then again some you think will, actually turn out not a bit like that and then you must depend on your skill, the quick hand. But the first is much the greater skill and more fun. She was very relaxed, enjoying the whole thing.

I could tell, the pupils dilate, the breathing slows, the voice becomes soft. It's a much more valuable skill in the end, because it can be used in many ways. That will partly answer the second comment, that is, it's bad. I know that, but I am supplying some very poor people, myself and my parents, with money and when my dream is fulfilled I will do much more than that. I will use my skills to help people---and get paid of course."

"Like a doctor?" I ask.

"Of course… or a doctor of the mind. You'll see." From what I had seen of Jose at that point I had no doubt about that.

Chapter Twenty Two

I spent my first days there off the mountain getting to know the lay of the land. There were some quick stop stores along the road by the mountain and after following Jose those few times I could imagine myself taking up his game---stealing. That is, I saw opportunities for doing it; but I wasn't yet desperate enough to try anything like that. Jose was supplying us with food from his 'earnings' and we had it pretty comfortable in there though I was getting to miss television and I wanted a cell phone but though Jose had lifted several of them he only got one on a month to month payment scam and was still working on a way to get on the internet, given our lack of electricity and connections up there.

I was particularly unskilled in any mechanical or computer ways for my age, so was designated the laundry person and made my way down to one of the two laundromats in the area twice a week. All in all, I had plenty of time to think and, though I was anxious to see my family again, I decided it would be smart to just lay low for a while. After all, I would just be stuck back into the same situation I had before back there. For sure my father would still be in jail and mother wouldn't be living in any respectable self-supporting way. In short my rear end would get slammed right back into that

PM center or maybe something worse, if such a thing existed and I figured it probably did. So I occupied my time with roaming about, not too friendly with anyone in the area and making up alibis when people wanted to know anything personal about me. At this, as I have already said, I was quite proficient ...at misrepresenting the truth and became even more so after a few weeks. It got so I was hoping people would ask me stuff so I could come up with stories and just gauge their reactions. I had to be careful though because being in a fairly small area, people might talk, so I made my stories interchangeable emphasizing some things to one and other things to another, so they didn't really contradict each other. Also I took up Jose's penchant for disguise--- he had some hats which I usually bundled my hair into and he gave me some money to buy myself some make-up for women with dark complexions. This made my skin which was cloud-white like my father's a little less noticeable. So I also got a wig, that is Jose bought me a pretty believable black wig with two long braids and with my make-up on, I looked like a an Indian maiden. I had always liked Indians and especially liked this disguise. I also circulated around, didn't go to the same store twice in one week and most people ignored me.

It was at one of these places after a few weeks that I saw it.

I was looking around in a little convenience store, the one closest to us and Jose had given me money to get myself one of those ready-made cheese sandwiches, which I loved, in the refrigerator case. Just as I was fumbling in my pocket to get the two dollars, I glanced down-- then jumped about a foot off the floor. There it was:

O's face, bigger than life, staring up--- from the front page of the USA Today on the rack next to the floor. I picked it up. Yep, there it was… maybe a couple of years younger and before he started sprouting the whiskers that were growing on his jaw by now, but it was definitely O staring right back at me from some other time and place. It gave me a very creepy feeling, especially as I started to read it. The man at the register began to look at me strangely after a minute so I put back the cheese sandwich and bought the paper then walked out of the store. After going down a couple of blocks, I leaned against a shoddy apartment building behind me and read it carefully, each word was an incredible discovery.

WEALTHY MASSACHUSETTS COUPLE DESPERATE TO FIND THEIR SON, the headline screamed.

I kept reading.

"It's been a month and two weeks since Omar, son of Computer Foundations magnates Earlene and Carl Brigandian, disappeared from school, the Precious Moments Center in Castov New York where he had been an exemplary citizen according to the headmaster there, who stated, "There is no way he would have run away. We are sure someone engineered this disappearance, knowing about the fortune of his parents." It said they were among the founders of Computer Foundations and resided in a posh gated community in Brookline Massachusetts.

"We are distraught," his mother is reported as saying, "and are doing everything we can to find him."

'He was our pride and joy," said his father hugging two younger children as they gave the interview. "In spite of not yet receiving any communication from anyone, we have refused to believe he could have simply left the place voluntarily. He was so happy there, also we felt he was receiving a fine education--he didn't want to leave." After becoming overwhelmed with tears, the couple terminated the interview and hurried back into their large home. The article said, "The state attorney general is looking into the details of this strange situation."

It went on: "Omar's father one Carl Brigandian is the son of wealthy Estonian parents who came over here in the 1950's; the younger Mr. Brigandian, not to be out done by his parents, started the Brigand Computer Services in his twenties, a computer repair service, which metamorphasized into the sprawling international Computer Foundations with its tentacles all over the world,' the article continued. 'The younger Brigandian's wealth soon outstripped that of his parents. Mr Brigandian apparently met his match in 1985 when he married the estimable Abigail Bockchok, the daughter of Finnish heiress Madeline Bockchok whose family owned a very profitable fish processing company in Helsinki. The two met when she was visiting Boston on a brief sabbatical to Tufts. They were married and it is said she never has returned to Finland. It is rumored that the young missing Wolf Omar Brigandian who goes by the name of Omar, likes to pass himself off as Ethiopian. In spite of the overwhelming sense of loss the parents have expressed, it is said that the youth had given the two of them a run for their money with multiple behavioral problems which landed him at the well respected PM Academy, in fact, a locked treatment center and the second institutionalization this lad has had. It is noted by reporters on the scene of the parents' press conference that young O, as he prefers to be called, in fact somewhat strangely bears no resemblance to his red headed father and blonde mother."

I'll have to admit that I was feeling a little dizzy after I read this story. My first suspicion was that it was actually someone else, another Omar who looked exactly like the one I knew. But no--- even to my twelve year old mind that made no sense. So why did he lie---telling me he's an Ethiopian and his parents left him long ago? I was determined to take that paper up to the cave or maybe the library since that's where he spent most of his time by then and lay it on the line with him, just demand an explanation. So that was why he was pretty happy just staying at the cave, he KNEW they were after him. It wasn't until I'd sat there for many minutes, because by then I was sitting on the curb, that I realized it---they hadn't even mentioned me. Obviously PM had just discharged me after a week since they knew I had nobody. But they were keeping that to themselves; otherwise, it would have been obvious that he was just a runaway, a mistake due only to the silliness of the entire PM staff.

Still feeling a little dizzy, I got off the sidewalk and trudged back to the cave.

I didn't mention any of this to O for a few days, just tucked the newspaper under my blanket where I knew he never went, but I would mess with him a little, like a cat just toying with a mouse before it attacks.

"Well O, your parents must miss you a lot being all the way off in Ethiopia like that," I told him after a few days.

"I doubt it," he said.

"Why?"

"They're just over there, trying to scrape out a living. It's tough over there you know, not like here where everybody's got a silver spoon in his mouth. And I know they want me to come with them, they're just trying to get enough together to get me over there. But truth is I don't really want to go. I like it here."

"Yeah...I don't know that much about Ethiopia. What's it like?"

"Well I know it's beautiful and the people are very smart like me of course, but its not like I grew up there or anything." He looked up at me a little strangely with his forehead wrinkled, like why should I be asking him about the place anyway? "Why you ask?" he finally mumbled.

"Oh no reason." Well at that point I just couldn't stand it any more. I went to my blanket and got the paper which had already begun to look a little yellow and faded. I set it down right there in front of him that night by the fire so he could see the thing clearly. "Look at this," I said. "What about that? Isn't that you?"

He picked it up and took his time answering; by then Jose who had been quietly counting money in a corner became interested and came over to look at the paper. "Hey that IS you!" he shouted.

O said nothing.

"Why'd you lie to us then O? I trusted you. Ethiopian. Right," I said.

Jose just sat down and watched him like he's at a concert or something.

You could just tell O's brain was spinning, trying to come up with the right excuse and wasn't sure about which to pick. He probably thought I'd fall for anything but had to take his time because Jose was no kind of pushover. I couldn't believe he didn't have something all ready, obviously being well acquainted with the ways of liars.

Chapter Twenty Three

O left out of that cave then and there without saying another thing. Jose and I both thought he was gone for good, probably back to his rich parents. It was a little odd, me being there alone with Jose. I must admit having O around had kind of taken the edge off just being with two guys; it was like he was just a friend. But I didn't discuss this with Jose, first because I didn't know what else to do- -- after all I had no choices. Second, because Jose didn't seem at all different from how he'd been before, still the same whether O was there or not. He always had only one thing on his mind and that was making money and becoming legal maybe not in that order.

I guess neither one of us were prepared when we woke up a few days later and there's O just as big as life lying where he'd slept before like nothing had happened. Jose just said hello and went back to planning the day ahead like he usually did. I, however, wasn't about to take this without learning what had happened.

"You know I really don't have to tell you," he says. "It's my business."

"But you lied. I thought you were my friend."

"I am."

"It's hard to trust a liar."

Space

"Then you don't have to trust me. I'm not marrying you. Take me at face value."

At least he didn't deny being a liar. "So why'd you come back then?" I prodded.

He sighed. "It doesn't matter."

"Yes it does."

"Ok, they're after me, even more than after Jose. They've put a reward out for whoever finds me."

"How'd you find that out?"

"Simple. On the computer at the library. It's also in the paper. Bottom line, you're the only one who can just go around freely now but as young as you look, it's surprising they haven't nabbed you already." He wrinkled his smooth tan forehead. "We need real disguises." After that he turned around and lay down for the night. I decided to drop the subject for a while. It seemed like it took all of O's energy just to talk about it.

So it almost knocked me off my feet, when one night about two weeks later, O finally decided to come clean. I don't know what made him do it. Maybe it had all kind of been boiling up inside him like the corned beef and cabbage my mother made sometimes in her old pressure cooker days. But he finally exploded.

Jose was out; he'd had a long day and went out to the Y late where he said he was going to swim twenty laps. First thing I heard that night was O kind of groaning and I went over towards him. He took one look at me and began this low sobbing, then almost a wailing which I had never heard from anyone before except maybe my mother when she was very upset and even then not as bad as this.

He began to look embarrassed and tried to stop. But he couldn't.

"They're liars, all of them!" he shouted at me like I knew what he was talking about and was somehow responsible. I backed off.

"Sorry," I whispered.

"My real father IS in Ethiopia, he's not that creep Brigandian. He's a REAL Ethiopian and so am I".

"So what are you here for? Why aren't you with him then?"

"I never met him. He doesn't even know about me. Nobody knows where he is. I don't even know his name, only his first name, Omar".

"Why?"

"My mother. She's a crazy person. Took off from her family in Finland, then just took off around the world. She had her credit cards. Ended up somewhere in Africa, first south Africa then Egypt. She met my real father there... he was a tour guide I know that much about him, I think he'd been a soldier," he sobbed, "then she left him, I'm sure he would have wanted to stay with her or at least to take him with her... but NO she got on her high horse and next stop New York then Boston where she frittered around and met Brigandian at some party for big wigs. Her parents never would limit her shenanigans in any way. Also she was good looking, very good looking, still is, for somebody in their thirties. So she meets Brigandian and likes to brag about it was just love at first sight. They were married a few weeks later, then my mother finds out, well what do ya know, she's pregnant and no one knows who the father is. Brigandian is of course thinking it's his but my mother is afraid it's that Ethiopian as she started to call him. I guess she was pretty tense there for a few months wondering whether the baby would be a blonde or red head like Brigandian or dark like my real father. So anyway around about the end of her pregnancy she became so overwhelmed with worry and the baby was due before it should have been, she told my father the truth, looked like it was the Ethiopian got there before Brigandian. Ha. Tough darts. Well Brigandian, the story goes, was so mindlessly in love with my mother he didn't care. But when the baby arrived, he was still hoping it might be his baby and there I am darker than even she remembered her Ethiopian to be, they were aghast. They didn't tell me all of this but I could figure it out."

"How, what did they tell you?"

"That my father was this Ethiopian. That she came here with

me, that they didn't care, they loved me just the same. I know it's not true, and I'm sure it did take some TALL EXPLAINING to all the grandparents. Well not to her parents... they knew she'd been in Africa and knew her too well. But to his parents,sure they invented some stupid story about her having an Indian uncle and me taking after him. They told me to tell people this too. Well that seemed to satisfy everybody. Everybody but the husband Brigandian. I guess he just couldn't stand the truth, that my mother hadn't been a virgin until she met him, probably she had told him she was. It just ate at him. Every time he looked at me I knew he saw my father who of course he'd never really seen but just imagining it, somebody tall, dark and handsome, made it that much worse. Maybe he tried to like me. He gave me tons of stuff, computers naturally, phones, games, expensive toys, anything I wanted, I got it. Even though my mother became pregnant not long after having me, then again right off the bat, and then he had two genuine Brigandian sons who looked exactly like him, short, squat and red headed, it still didn't matter. I could see it in his eyes every time he looked at me which he tried not to do--- after a while, I guess even he knew it was a complete give away when he did it."

"How? Sounds like he liked you, at least he tried, to me. I never got anything like that from my parents, just coal in my stocking."

"I'd rather have had that and some real acceptance, some real love. You could just tell every time he looked at me. He hated me and was trying to fool me and maybe himself with all that stuff.

"Around the age of ten I decided, well... screw this. I began to run away. They'd get calls late at night that I was down by the Putt Putt Gaming Center, or walking down the road, miles from their mansion. They'd always bring me back and he'd give me the fish eye and tell me they loved me, he'd never say *he* did though, and why was I treating them this way. Then my mother would cry and threaten. Oh they were a mess. I finally began to steal. Yup. Just like Jose maybe not as good, but pretty good, cause at first no one suspected me, I looked like such a rich kid. But the worst thing was

I began to tell people the truth that my real father was an Ethiopian. This, Brigandian could not stand, that people would know she had somebody else before she met him. Nobody else seemed to really care, but he was completely wacko, so possessive. He's nuts, completely nuts, after all she was twenty two when he met her, what did he expect? One night I heard the two of them in their bed room arguing, I knew it was about me and stood by the door for a few minutes. Long enough to hear Brigandian say "It's that Ethiopian, I knew the kid would come to no good." Just then the night maid comes up the stairs and I had to run quietly back to my room. The next day I didn't come back from school, just took off to a teenage gamer's apartment I'd met at Put Put. Stayed there a few days till he kicked me out, told me he couldn't afford to feed me and I needed to go back to my rich parents--- but I didn't. Just took off down the road, it was spring and pretty warm. The cops didn't find me for four days and they didn't take me home. They took me down to some detention center. By then I was eleven. My parents told them they couldn't control me any more. Next thing I knew I was at the Saving Lives Center in Iowa. They figured I wouldn't escape out of there because I didn't know the area. Well they were right, and you were under some guard's nose all the time and the place was triple locked. You thought PM was bad, it was like heaven next to that.

"So how'd you get to PM then?"

"They decided I'd gotten everything I could out of it there and after a while recommended step down to PM. Truth is, I was fine at both places because my freedom seemed like a small price after having someone look at you everyday like he can't stand the sight of you and pretending he loves you."

It must have been an hour that I sat by O as he went on about all this. I didn't notice it at the time but somewhere along in there he stopped crying and started talking in a very low voice like he might talk to a child he was trying to punish or describing a snake he might have seen at some point---a poisonous snake. As he was talking, all of it about his parents, that is, his mother and fake father, my mind began to wander and images of my own parents floated by. I remembered one Christmas in particular when my mother had kept telling us how good Santa would be to us that year--- that was when I still had full confidence in this man and the particular gifts he was going to drop down on us from above. Needless to say we were all exited, even my sisters who were only two and three at the time. Well Christmas morning came and we all got up to run to the plastic tree my mother had carefully picked out two years before at Kmart. She shuffled in after us all bleary eyed and smiling but guess what--- there was nothing there except for the stockings which each had a little candy and some cheap toys from the dollar store. My mother looked hard at the tree and rubbed her eyes then she ran to her bedroom screaming "Horace!", then to the closet ---empty, except for her clothes. She kept screaming for my father but there was no answer. He wasn't there. So we all hunkered over the cheesy stocking presents while she made pancakes with sugar and margarine which was a treat for us, still mumbling about our father the whole time. He didn't straggle in until later when we were still gathered around the fake tree and heard him fumbling at the lock. She opened the door and he crept in like a dog with his tail between its legs. I never did see him so apologetic even when he was in the jail. She told us kids to go to the bedroom while she was pushing her pancake battered hands against his chest like she was determined to not let him back in the apartment ever again. We took off to the bedroom obediently where the little one sat on her bed and wailed and me and Ravena peeked through the door crack to see what was going on. "Where are the toys?" my mother hissed at him real low and serious. You could tell she meant business.

"I had to use them," he told her.

"USE THEM? FOR WHAT! FOR WHAT WOULD YOU WANT TO RUIN YOUR CHILDRENS' CHRISTMAS? USE THEM!" she shrieked.

"To make it better, I had a great chance. I just needed a little money, it could have got us set, not just this year, for many years. So much, We could have had everything you want."

"You PAWNED them, didn't you! To gamble didn't you? How could you! I had those things on lay away at K Mart and now we still have to pay for them and they're gone, GONE! And you ruined your children's Christmas!All for your stupid gambling addict friend!" And she collapsed into the sofa and picking up a shred of wrapping paper off the flour began to blow her nose on its white side. "Monster!" she shrieked.

My father slunk into their bedroom mumbling about how he only tries to do right and closed the door. We didn't see him again until two days later. By then they were all lovey-dovey again. That was the memory that stayed in my mind the strongest when I thought about my parents letting us down, though I suppose there were many other times, especially later when my mother seemed to change and spent nights away from us and him in jail. And yet I thought, as O blabbed on, we always knew they loved us. They just never seemed to be able to get it right. I thought of the time at PM when I heard one of the staff describe my parents as totally inadequate. But yet they weren't totally inadequate because we knew they loved us. It seemed like just the opposite of O's situation and to be honest I preferred my family. Course if somebody looked at my life without being a part of it, like they did at PM, I guess you could see there were some real problems. "Sometimes I wonder how she's done as well as she has," my counselor said about me to the nurse, right in front of me. "I fear for those two little ones though, this one got the best of whatever good parenting those two could scrape together before they went completely off the deep end." Yes, she said this right in front of me like she was giving me praise and I ought to be happy about the whole situation.

Anyway, finally O sighed a deep sigh and lay back down and told me to go to my bed or somewhere away from him, because he was going to sleep.

I must admit by then I had begun to feel very sorry for him. It was a lousy situation for any kid to grow up in, I could understand then why he had wanted to stay at PM, and made up all that about his parents, it was probably the way he wished they were. And he'd never even seen his real father and I felt so sad for him too, never to have seen his handsome son. I wondered if there were any way for O to find the man whom he said was Omar but he had no last name---that's where O got his middle name. I'll admit I felt so sad for all O had been through and his needing to lie about everything even to me, who as far as I could see was his best friend--- he didn't have any others at PM--- that I began to cry myself that night after I got into my bed, real quiet because I didn't want him to hear me.

The next day O acted just like nothing unusual had happened, either him leaving out of there the way he did or crying and bawling about his life afterward and telling me all that stuff. In fact he seemed even busier than ever. He took my black wig and one of Jose's baseball caps and went out everyday, back late at night.

I was so curious about his night time forays that I followed him one day, a week after his confessions. He took off down the mountain, kind of hunched over, keeping his face down then trudged along the backstreet but ended up at the library, but took the wig off before going in. The next day he did the same thing but as he approached it he jerked around and yelled at me for following him. I came up to him so he wouldn't have to yell and attract all that attention. "What are you doing?" he asked me.

"What do you mean?" I say innocently.

"You're following me, you think I don't know it, two days now, what's going on, you after me too?"

This last statement really got to me, that is, I felt all sorry for him again. I had been thinking about him a lot. I'd never liked any boys and didn't want to start then but I guess I was beginning to feel really sorry for him, maybe more.

"I just didn't want anything to happen to you...you know."

"If they get me, they get me, so? There's nothing you can do to prevent it." Then he looked at me sadly like I was too young and uncomprehending, but he stood there just looking at me for a few seconds as if there was a light going off somewhere inside him.

"There isn't?" I asked, sensing some opening somewhere. He was silent.

"Well maybe there are ways you could help me. I think Jose likes you better than me. Get him to get me a light wig, brown or blonde, something like that, you know, and some of the light make-up. That way I'll fit in better. They've got a reward out for me you know, ten thousand dollars, chicken feed for my mother, you can tell she doesn't really want me back, but for some of these rednecks around here that's some major money. Jose would probably turn me in himself if he could get away with it. Unfortunately that would reveal his identity too."

"He wouldn't do that."

"You're just an innocent Raynelle, you don't understand what people will do for money. He wouldn't do it because he CAN'T do it."

"So why are you down here everyday at the library anyway?"

"There's a girl there."

I'll admit I felt just a little disappointed when I heard this but it also surprised me. I thought he had hid mind on bigger issues. "A girl? Pretty?"

"Yes pretty, very, but that's beside the point, she helps me out. Lets me use the computer to get on the internet there, when her supervisors aren't around. She knows I'm on the run, but thinks its from some physically abusive Mexican father in L.A. I'm not telling her the real story, at least not now. Maybe someday though," he mumbled and looked off into the distance. "Anyway," he said turning abruptly back to me. "There might be other ways you can help me. I'll have to think about it."

"I'll do anything," I blurted, against all my better judgment. Just the very idea of his father being in Ethiopia and never even knowing O existed, with all the while O longing to see him, it just made me want to cry each time I thought about it.

Chapter Twenty Four

Meanwhile Jose was continuing his occupation and trying to accumulate more money. He had it stashed in various places around the cave, places I'm sure we would never think or know to look. And why should we? He was very generous with us because, for whatever reason, it was clear he wanted us to stay there. The problem was I had to spend it for O who didn't look really convincing in the light hair and pancake make up, more like an escaped clown, so he had to abandon that particular disguise and work on something more believable. I was the one, being the only one who people wouldn't be actively after, who did most of the shopping for the both of them by then.

On one of his trips to the pawn shop Jose got much more money than he had planned and decided to buy a guitar. So he put on one of his best disguises and went into the big music shop in Phoenix where he got a second hand Gibson guitar with one string missing and a book to self-teach.

From then on it was as though the three of us were energized. Before the guitar, we were just three kids I guess I would say now, tossed together by fate after some pretty rough times and just kind of hanging out on the edge, together by necessity. Well the minute

O saw that guitar he started laughing and grabbed it away from Jose. Then he started playing the thing, I mean like an EXPERT, like somebody on MTV and there was Jose just standing there amazed, the first time I've ever seen him anything but smug and cocky. So O is playing and it's like magic, just playing and laughing and one, two, three songs later he handed it back to Jose. You can throw that thing away," O tells him pointing to the teach yourself guitar book. "I can teach you in a week," he bragged, "somebody who's as good with his fingers as you, maybe sooner."

Well I was mystified.

"I thought you were abused," I said, "and never got anything from those parents of yours."

"I was... but like I told you I got all kinds of *things* and learning to play the guitar was the best thing, really the ONLY good thing they ever gave me. I took to it fast. I think I get it from my father, I mean my real father Omar. I wanted to play music as long as I could remember and they let me take lessons---went into it in a big way, for a while it was like my escape from them. I asked my mother if my real father was a musician as well as the other things but she said no, not that she knew of. But later she told me that she just had a sudden memory of Omar playing the piano at a night club they went to. He just kind of sidled up to it she said and started playing while the band members were on break. "He was good, very good', she said, 'I guess that's one of the reasons I liked him so, right away." Of course Brigandian wasn't around when she told me this and she looked a little sad when she was telling me, like she really missed my father. I'm sure he was much better looking than the fat squat sausage-eating Brigandian. But she had never mentioned him before except that first time when they told me someone else was my real father, she couldn't ever really say anything for fear of getting old Brigandian in a real stew. But he was out late that night. She looked real guilty then like she was embarrassed to even be talking about him without her husband around, like she was breaking some cardinal rule, but I asked her then what he looked like. She looked at me like she was trying to decide, am I really going to cheat and tell him something? Like it was cheating on her husband or something, especially if she said anything positive. But finally she sighed and said, "He was very handsome ---- tall and thin… he looked so much like you,'" then she began to weep just a little and I could tell she was doing her best to hold back tears and she turned and went back downstairs to wait for Brigandian to get home. But then I knew the truth--- he was handsome, and right there it was clear she still loved him. But things were still the same after that even though I had hoped the next day she would come to her senses and leave him and we'd both go back to Ethiopia to find my real father. But afterward they were still the same, all loving and happy full of themselves with those two boys just clones of their old man, who still looked at me coldly like I was some kind of lizard that just happened to crawl into his house for the warmth and his wife wouldn't let him kick it out."

Then O looked at me. "Well it may seem cold to you Raynelle but I think that even made me dislike my mother more because then I knew the truth: she loved Omar and still left him to come over here and marry that keyboard-punching toad Brigandian. And she already… had money already, lots of it, it wasn't like she needed him for that." He looked at me like I might have something to say in the matter, like I really knew something about people; but all that came to me was a huge ache right through the center of my body, in my heart and then my belly then up into my throat where it stuck like a ball of cement, I guess for all O had gone through.

I wanted to say something that would help him, or at least make him think I was smarter than your average twelve year old, but all that came out was. "Parents are weird." But after that night especially on the nights he would play the guitar, I would cry a little before I went to sleep, and hope that my feelings might somehow help his situation.

Pretty soon Jose could play that old guitar almost as well as O who bought himself another one, a little newer, from one of the other music stores in the area, and they would play almost every night, after O had studied the latest scribblings in his notebook and Jose had counted some of his money. As I said he had different piles of it and he would count one or two of them each night like to be sure no one had taken any. He kept shifting the piles from place to place like a squirrel storing acorns in there to throw us off I guess, if we became greedy. It was clear by then he didn't trust either one of us. So after these rituals the two of them would pick up their guitars and jam and believe me they began to sound pretty good. The new guitar was bigger and had a lower tone to it and between they two of them they began to sound like professionals. As for me, I would just sit there and listen and soon I was feeling pretty much out of it but they began to get closer and closer--- you could see all that music was bringing them together. It was like playing music together has a way of just going right underneath thoughts,even emotions, just uniting you in some strange way, connecting your unconscious as my counselor would have said, in a deeper way than words can do. At first they played out of a song book Jose had me buy then another more complicated one he had lifted. Pretty soon Jose started composing his own songs and they would play these. One of those nights, O put his guitar down and announced, "You need to do something too Ray," because by then he had taken on Jose's habit of calling me Ray.

"What? I don't play any instrument," I answered. "My family isn't musical."

That wasn't good enough for Jose. "You can sing then, we need a third someone to sing the lyrics, beside us, definitely would be good to have a girl too, higher." At first this didn't appeal to me at all. Number one, I couldn't see myself singing, after all I'd never even done it at all. Number two, singing seemed way less cool than what they were doing, playing instruments. Yet I didn't think I could do that either. So at first I objected and the two of them said "OK, suit yourself," and began to play some more of the song Jose had just written. I sat there feeling like a little kid and a failure. So with the next song, one I'd heard a million times from the Rolling Stones, I began to sing too, softly. They looked at me kind of surprised then both smiled so I kept right on singing, but louder. What surprised me was a while after I started, my voice just seemed to flow out from the middle of my chest and my belly somewhere, like it had a life all its own and had just been waiting all those years to escape.

"Where have you been!" O shouted at me after that first song. "You've got an awesome voice, specially for a pip squeek, a little off key at times but we can fix that."

"Unbelievable," says Jose. "Now we've got a trio."

"Yuh, but what can we do with it," says O, "it's not like we can go out in public or record music."

"Something will come along now," laughed Jose. "This is it."

Chapter Twenty Five

O treated me a little differently after that night, with a new respect. He looked at me a little different too, I could see there was admiration in his face where he used to think of me as a kid. One night when he was looking in his notebook by the fire and Jose was still out, I asked him again what he was doing with that notebook and the library --- there had to be something.

"Just whittling the time away, nothing special."

"I don't believe it." I had changed a little too, become a little more assertive. Not only because he had been treating me different but because by then I was well into being twelve. As an almost teenager I deserved more respect and O knew it. There was a lot of quiet in there that night except for the fire O had started earlier which was burning very low and crackling just a little.

"It's been building up in me a long time," O said quietly like he was telling me the most important thing in the world and I was quiet. "Maybe I can trust you. I need to talk to somebody about this. Can I trust you Ray?"

I was so happy he was talking to me like this, that I could not speak and only whispered, "Yes!"

"The truth is I need to get back at my parents, especially

Brigandian. I'm not going to just sit by my whole life and forget the way he treated me--- like a dog, worse than a dog. At least people like their dogs usually."

"Yuh?" I said not wanting him to stop talking to me this way, ever.

"I'm going to do something---I'm still not completely sure what. But I've had several strategies I've been reviewing. It's like a cat and mouse. He doesn't know where I am but I know where he is. I can see him, sort of, with the computer. I can even get into his e-mail. I learned one of his passwords when I was living with him."

"Oh," I said, beginning to feel a little afraid of what O could be planning.

"At first I had plans to just get rid of him. I won't go into how I could have done it, but it would have been easy. But I decided no, that would make my mother unhappy and she would never be able to see my real father again. I'm sure she wants to. And she's the only one who knows enough to help me find him. If I can just help her understand what a dweeb she's married to she might come to her senses."

I was a little relieved to hear that. "Then what?" I asked.

"Well, after my studies, I found that the major site of operations for Computer Foundations is ...guess where? LA ---how convenient. A huge corporate headquarters. that's why he was always flying back and forth across the country. It's his pride and joy, like the power cell for all the rest of his offices, the smartest people, the latest innovations, the most expensive lay-out, like the Taj Mahal, all made of gold."

"Really?"

"No." He looked at me again in the old way and I felt like a stupid kid again. "But everything is so high end and extravagant it might as well be made of gold, probably worth more than gold. I'm going to blow it up," he announced matter of factly, like he was forecasting rain for the next day.

"What about the people who work there?" A jolt of fear shot through me, straight to my heart. I felt my face get red.

"I've thought of that. It won't hurt anybody. It'll be late at night or way early before anybody gets there. Just the first floor anyway, that's the most disgusting part. You'd agree if you saw it. It's got a big fountain with real diamonds embedded in the base, Brigandian used to brag about how it makes the water sparkle, and actual velvet carpeting down on the floor there believe it or not, a special blend, it gets replaced every six months, Then there are some real gold plated fixtures in it, twenty four carat. It's so ridiculous, but he loves it, considers it the flagship for his other branches. That's where they have all their meetings, where they get together with other corporate big wigs and try to figure out how to fleece people out of more of their money so they can get even richer. From all over the world. Meanwhile people in countries like my father's are starving. I've researched it, don't worry there are no mistakes or exaggerations here. I want that fountain he's so proud of to look like a pile of rubble--- to be reduced to what it really is---junk."

"Oh you'll get in trouble O." I could imagine him being carted off to jail, then I'd never see him again.

"I don't care. It would be worth it. Besides I won't. I'm getting it all figured out down to the last detail, as long as..."

"What?"

"You or someone like you doesn't blow the whistle on me. Actually it would have to be you or someone you tell because I haven't told anyone else."

"Why do this, really? I don't think it's such a good idea," I muttered trying to think of what some really smart adult might say.

"Can't you see? After all he's put me through, this is going to show him what all his stuff is really worth, ashes,the stuff he treasures the most, in LA. He spends half his time there you know."

"And then what?"

"Then my mother will see what a weakling and a fraud he is,

'cause it's going to totally bowl him over. She'll see that it's his stuff not her that he really cares about."

"I don't know. It sounds like he really does like her... to me."

"No. That's another thing. I think he hopped onto marrying her because she's rich. Rich and could help him expand his empire, strengthen the Scandinavian ties."

"I thought she was pretty and he was already rich."

"She was, but not THAT pretty and to be honest, not very smart, I can't see somebody with his tricky evil ways really going for her. She's got to know the truth. And yuh, he was rich but that's the thing about rich people, they have only one thing on their mind usually---getting richer, that's all they really care about."

"I don't know, O. My mother used to say violence doesn't solve a thing, that was one thing about her. She was smart in some ways."

"Yuh. And where is she now? I don't want to be mean but you don't even know--- that's where all her theories have gotten her, probably out on the street from what I've heard from you Raynelle. She's probably no smarter than my mother. No hard feelings."

That did hurt, I'll have to admit and yet it was true. Where did all her theories--- because she had quite a few--- get her? Still, I thought it wasn't a good idea.

"I don't know, you need to think this over."

"Girl, I've been thinking about this, since I went into PM---- almost five years and why do you think I finally took off with you and suggested we go west? It wasn't just an impulse. It was all a part of my plan. I have ways. You'll see. You're not going to rat me out are you Ray?"

"Oh no," and I meant it. Just sitting there by him was by far the most happy I had ever felt in my life, like I didn't want to be anywhere, anywhere, else but by that fire watching him or be with anyone else unless he was right there too. I don't know when these feelings started; I didn't have them before but they kind of crept up on me and boom! all of a sudden, there they were. It was like heaven to me maybe. To be honest not only had I never felt that way before,

I'd never even known anybody could feel that way. I thought of the songs we had been singing, most of them were about love and being in love. I wondered if that was what this was, but had no clue. "I would never do anything to hurt you," I told him sincerely and he smiled at me like he already knew this. Then he did something amazing. He reached out with his pencil hand and touched my cheek real soft with his finger tips then he smiled again, turned away quickly and said good night.

That feeling was the one thing I knew that night. I didn't know if what he was doing was good or bad, or justified or not. And even if it was justified, did that make it good? I was confused. But I did know that whatever he needed from me, whatever, even if it didn't sit just right, I would go along with it. I was sure of my path and that was to help him. He didn't deserve the hard treatment he'd gotten--- every time I thought of it I would get an ache in my belly--- but it wasn't an ache of hurt or sadness--- it had become an ache of love like I was attached to him and never wanted to break that tie. I wondered again as I began to fall asleep how I could never have noticed the strong way I felt about him before, how had it escaped me all that time at PM and traveling out west when he was right there beside me. Well, I figured sometimes maybe these feelings kind of sneak up on you out of the blue or maybe the seed of them had been there and just needed something like hearing about the hard times he'd had, to uncover them. And he was so handsome, how had I missed that?

The next morning O told me he'd had a dream about his mother that made him sure she was not happy with Brigandian. He saw his mother in the dream with his real father, an unbelievably handsome man he told me, a soldier, and O was right there with them but a little behind, giving them space. It became so clear to him then he said, that they were meant to be together to be united again and he would be there too. Every time he thought about the dream he felt he was re-experiencing it, like real life, like he was actually there, at a later date. He thought she might even have another baby with his real father---he could tell that from the dream. But he had to hurry. "That was where they both belong," he said and now after the dream he knew it for sure. Her present life with her husband would be forgotten like so many dry leaves blowing away in the wind O said. But it was up to him now to make her see that.

"What about her two other kids?" I asked, remembering how my mother seemed to love her two youngest children, maybe even more than me.

"She'll forget them," he said, "as soon as she sees my father it will all be clear, I'm sure of it."

"She might want to take them with her," I said, still not at all sure about his plan but not wanting to upset him.

He gave this some thought then told me, "Maybe. But they are so much like Brigandian, like little clones, I don't think she'll really want them."

I didn't know what a clone was but kept my mouth shut at that point. You could tell he was single minded and getting a little impatient with all my questions.

Chapter Twenty Six

It may have been that evening or maybe the next one, I can't say for sure. What I do know was the weather was getting warmer especially the nights and sometimes I liked to lie outside the cave just to breathe in that clear air and watch the stars. It was also nice to get away from that teenage boy smell that I had begun to notice after the two of them had been living there a while, it's a little like a goat, the father goat, that I once saw and smelled on a visit to our cousins out in the country when I was about seven. I can still remember my mother saying "That smell---it's that awful male goat!" then my uncle got mad and yelled at her about that being a natural goat smell and if she didn't like it she should go back to the city.

But I must have fallen asleep one night there outside the cave because what happened seemed like a dream. The truth is there were lights, those same lights again. I thought my eyes were open and I was my real self, only I was kind of floating, not really flying but almost and I could go where I wanted to. So naturally I went towards the lights, they were certainly the same ones I'd seen a couple of times before. When I got up there I expected to find a space ship or airplane, something of that sort, but all that was there was more lights, like thousands of tiny lights just hovering there over the desert, not the mountain. Then I was inside all the lights, that is inside the space they made, not the each actual light. I tried to touch one because they seemed beautiful and extremely weird, all of the strangest colors, which I had never seen before, and I was attracted to them like they were magnets. I expected something there---I don't know what exactly, but probably someone to talk to me, some actual space being with a head shaped like a wedge and huge oval eyes, and a silvery skin, something like the space alien toy my little sister used to play with, maybe with a strange metallic voice like a robot. But no one was there inside all those lights that I could see and no one spoke. It seemed like I was just there for a few minutes I don't know whether sitting or standing but I did feel a somewhat new really peaceful feeling that I couldn't remember having before, somewhere between happy and patient, like there was really all the time in the world to do anything. So I just stayed there a while surrounded by all the lights which, getting close to them, I discovered were just the same size as when I had seen them from the mountain, not bigger which you might expect but much brighter. Finally it seemed I woke up there again outside the cave. While it had seemed that I stayed up there only a few minutes I learned I was wrong, that the sun was coming up behind the huge pine trees to the east. It startled me--- I must have been there several hours. As I lay there unable to go back to sleep another memory about my mother came to me, the time she told me about the day she had read in USA today about a strange event happening to some of the astronauts up in some space capsule. She had showed this to anybody who would look and especially my father, hoping it would win him over to her line of thinking about space. She told me they said they had seen angels up there for a little while, like they were hovering around the space craft, "beings" she had told me and you could tell how excited it made her just to talk about it. It was like if the astronauts had seen it, that won the dispute even if they weren't in a space ship. She said Daddy had laughed at her and said they had just run out of oxygen from being up there and were seeing things. She didn't have an answer for that but felt like she just knew it was true and kept the article which she sprayed with some plastic to preserve paper and put it in her drawer.

I myself felt a little strange the rest of the day after being up in those lights, not really quite myself but not a bad feeling either. I wondered if they had anything to do with the angels my mother read about. Anyway I now tended to agree with her about space beings where I used to have quite a bit of doubt about the whole thing, being generally of the belief that my father had more sense than she did. And where I was used to feeling very well rooted to my body, the day after my experience, I felt just a little lighter and not so worried about the things I tended to worry about.

Primary among those then of course were my feelings about O. Ever since that night when he confided in me, my thoughts hovered over him like the dust over one of my mother's sofa pillows when you punched it, but they didn't go away. He said no more to me about his plans, it was almost like he regretted ever mentioning them and seemed very happy and carefree, as though there had really never been any worries on his mind. Also around then he began to be out more, sometimes even skipping the music playing at night which Jose and I had really gotten into. When O was gone we just shrugged it off and played by ourselves. Though I still had strong feelings about O, whatever they were, he didn't seem as concerned with me. So it was on one of those nights after he just excused himself from us, that I politely excused myself from Jose a few minutes later and told him I was going to lie outside the cave that night, that I just felt the urge. "Ok," he told me, "but you need to be careful out there, with the weather getting warmer, you know, there might be snakes or maybe something worse that might just smell a tasty meal and even come after you for no reason. But generally the snakes won't do that, they'll leave you alone unless you happen to lie on one of them," he laughed. That was one thing about Jose, you couldn't really get him down---no matter what you did he immediately adjusted to it, like one of those big clowns you keep hitting and can't possibly knock over. So he didn't care if O was gone that night and then me, he just kept playing.

Chapter Twenty Seven

I'll admit the snake comment made me think a little about my habit of sleeping outside but it didn't occupy my mind on that night because I actually had other plans. When I got outside the cave I stopped and listened. There was no sound but the whistling of a breeze through the pines but in a moment I could hear O tromping down almost to the base of the path and whistling a little. So I set out after him--- yes, feeling ashamed to sink to this, but also thinking that maybe I would be able to help him or even save him from doing something stupid.

The strength of my feelings for him was quite overwhelming to me by then, I'll admit I was powerless before them. I had been used to my deepest attachment being to my parents who were clearly bumblers which frequently would strain my feelings toward them a little. And of course my love for my sisters, but even that got sapped a little because it was usually so clear my mother worried more about them than about me. I suppose it was because they were younger. But deep in my heart I always suspected it was at least partly because they were blond like her and pretty, and let's face it, my hair looked usually like a red scrub brush and my face embarrassingly white. Also my mother always depended on me to do things for her like an adult, there wasn't much cuddle time for Raynelle. So what I'm saying is, much as I loved my parents and they were the closest people to me for twelve years, still my love may not have always been whole-hearted, where it was finally clear no matter what O would do I would love him with my whole self, every bit. Whatever that was, I had it for O. It was a little like a really overwhelming pity for his story and part admiration for his strength but also, lets face it, he was very handsome, even an almost thirteen year old could see that. So there I was, against all my better plans and knowing better in spite of my maybe half-baked parenting, following this seventeen year old down the hill, to somewhere. I was surprised at how easy it was. He had no idea that anybody might be following him out there on that dark moonless night and as far as I could tell, he was so absorbed in wherever he was going, he didn't even look behind him once. So I took my chances and stuck a little closer to him; I wasn't about to let him out of my sight. By the time we got to the end of the strip of desert surrounding the mountain I couldn't have been more than 20 yards behind him. But I stayed close to the cactus which were huge and some wider than I was, and touched the ground in my sneakers so delicately, first my toes then my heels so even I couldn't hear my footfalls. As he approached the road I began to feel a little cocky and came closer, then tripped on a small rock which made quite a loud noise in the silence of the desert. At that moment, he started to turn around; I fell flat on the ground behind him like I'd seen people do on TV, all the while worrying about the snakes that I might have fallen on and that were probably squirming underneath me. But he turned back and went right out into that narrow asphalt road, against the flow of traffic. I set out after him a few minutes later, but there with no cactus and with the occasional lights of cars, I kept a greater distance, maybe fifty yards. I had an alibi if he happened to turn around unexpectedly and see me: I would say that I missed him a lot the nights he went out and had just come out after him that night with the aim to catch up to him, nothing more. I actually surprised myself with my skill in tracking him and ability to be really, really quiet. I decided it was the Indian heritage my mother used to brag about in her happier moods, that Cherokee blood she claimed in some distant ancestor long ago, and wondered if I should become a professional tracker---there had to be somebody who needed those skills and it would pay me well. As I pondered over this, it became clear that O was heading towards the library and by the time he walked into it, I was but a few yards behind him, silent as a stone.

But when I got to the door, I was presented with a real quandary: go in, walk away or stare in the window which was possible from almost any angle since it was a one story building. I didn't want to leave after all that trouble but was afraid to go in, so I decided to just peer in the window, changing windows every few seconds so no one would see me. I saw nothing in the first window but the entrance to the library. In the second window, which I had to climb on a rock from their garden to see into, I saw the inside of the library and there was O, talking to some girl who I guessed was the one he had mentioned. I moved to the next window with my rock where I could see even better with the advantage that it was around the corner from the entrance so people going in and out probably wouldn't see me and report a peeping tom. There I was, really pretty close to the two of them, close enough to see the color on the library girl's cheek get pinker as she talked to O and her smiling at him almost constantly. I thought her face was going to crack from all that smiling and I wished it would. Then somebody came up to the desk and checked out a book, and her face got pale again as she turned away from O and took care of the customer who was glowering at her a little, though I couldn't hear what either one of them said. Then the woman walked away and up came O again. The girl then looked across the room, laughed and pointed toward the huge clock on the wall at the end of the room. She looked at O again and went over towards what I guess was the main library lady at the other end of the counter. This lady was old with skin as wrinkled as a prune but from what I could tell she was all smiles, excusing the girl from her duties for the night. The girl talked to her some more then gestured to O and the old lady nodded yes. I expected them both to leave the building at that point and got ready to run myself but to my surprise the two of them turned and disappeared into a big room that had a sign over the door: MULTI-MEDIA ROOM, and closed the door. It was eight o'clock and the library closed at nine so I wondered what they had the time to watch in there. I went to the next window where I thought I could see what was going on there, but the only thing I saw was that someone, I think it was the girl, had gotten some tape or CD of some movie and the two of them were sitting on the sofa pretending to watch it, but I couldn't see anything unless the light from the movie flashed their way. The movie was Gone with the Wind I think, something I knew O would have completely no interest in. I stood there a while looking in and now and then catching a good glimpse of them. I could tell they were certainly sitting very close even though the sofa they were on was long. Just at the point I figured that I'd never learn anything from all this and to give up, the light flashed on them for a half second and I saw they were kissing, then it flashed off and I kept trying to see what else was going down. I had my nose pressed flat like a pig nose against the window, that's how hard I wanted to see what was happening but there was nothing. It seemed like just a few minutes after but I guess the clock had turned nine because I think someone knocked on their door then opened it just a crack like they didn't want to intrude and the two of them sprang away from each other, then the door opened completely and the library lady walked though it smiling and telling them it was time to close. I saw them get up and walk slowly towards the door after the girl had stopped the machine. At that point I jumped off the rock, didn't even carry it back to the garden, and began to run home. As I got half way down the block I could hear the creaking open of the big library door then its slamming shut and some laughter and friendly shouts. Well you can be sure I was high-tailing away from there by then. I definitely had no excuse if he caught me at that point. Fortunately I had always been fast for my age and I don't think O was in any hurry to get back to the cave. When I reached the desert, I hid behind a cactus and just could make him out way down the road walking slowly, looking around and up at the sky like he's some dreamy owl watcher. Looked like he was in a trance to me, nothing like his usual impatient worried self. So I just darted from cactus to cactus, kind of quiet and down low. By the time he got up the mountain I was lying there pretending to be asleep, breathing in and out very deeply like I thought a sleeping girl would do and I heard him chuckle softly to himself as he passed back into the cave.

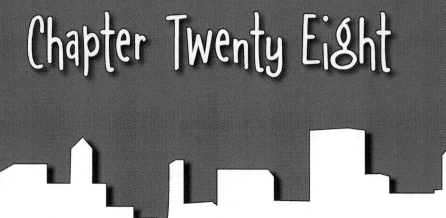

Chapter Twenty Eight

You can bet I thought plenty about what I'd seen the next day. At first I decided, well that's it, he likes her a lot and that's his choice and I need to just leave the both of them alone. But then by the afternoon my feelings got the best or you might say the worst of me and I convinced myself that he needed my help. After all who knew if he had told this girl his somewhat crazy scheme even though I completely sympathized with it. Who knew how she might mislead him? She was clearly just one of those really pretty girls who hardly ever think of anything or anyone but themselves. She was wearing plenty of make up too; must have taken her an hour just to put all that on right, I knew because that's what it took my mother to really do it up right, even after all her years of practice. How could that girl think of anyone else really, when her mind was occupied with all that, then she had her library duties which she managed to do and I was sure she was still in high school. I knew all about those pretty girls, my mother had been one. They never think of anyone else and there would be no way she was going to really think about O's situation even if he had told her and maybe he hadn't yet. Maybe she would even turn him in if he did tell her---who could trust her? The one thing I wasn't admitting to myself at that time was I was jealous, just flat out plain amazingly painfully jealous of this imposter, his new friend, who had actually kissed him and probably plenty of times. After all I couldn't see what they were doing most of the time and I realized with a start he had been visiting the library for many weeks, though only recently at night. There was only one thing crystal clear to me that night and that was I owed it to him to monitor the situation.

So it was clear.

I would sneak back there that night and find a way to get in that room before they did. I'd find out what he was telling her, what was going on even if I had to risk being found to do it--- but then I remembered--- no one was after me. If he didn't come that night I'd keep going there until he did. It was easy a quick run for me. So I played a little music with the boys that night, but Jose seemed tired which he rarely was and O wasn't at all inspired.

I figured he probably was just waiting a while to go down there. So I excused myself to sleep in another higher area there by the cave, I told them, one that was secluded by trees and you really couldn't see if you were just walking by, and since it was higher wouldn't have been so appealing to snakes, then I disappeared out of the cave. They listened but both seemed so preoccupied with their own thoughts that they didn't really appear to take in what I said which was fine with me. So the minute I got a few feet away from the cave I began a trot down the hill and was at the library within twenty minutes.

The old library lady smiled at me as I walked in and I wondered if she was going to interfere with my plan. I pretended to be looking for a book and took pains to ask her where Mark Twain's section was, explaining that I had a school assignment. She was very helpful and instead of just giving me directions, actually walked me over right in front of the correct section so then there was no way I could appear to be just wandering around in there. I thanked her and told her I also was looking for something else. I shouldn't have been too surprised when she wanted to help me find that too, so I told her I didn't know exactly which book I was looking for and would need time to just look around. After she considered this a moment she smiled and told me that made perfect sense, that she was like that too. "Some people just like to browse," she announced. "We get such pleasure from books… its like browsing through an expensive gift shop but its all free here, that's the beauty of it," she said in a loud voice; I felt somewhat surprised and wondered if she would ever go back to her desk. But just then the little bell at her station went off and she almost trotted back to her post.

At first I hadn't seen the girl but she must have been in the back room because as I was wandering around the shelves trying to position myself closer to the media room door, I caught a glimpse of her. She walked by me taking two books to the section I was in. She was pretty alright, prettier at close range than far away and it made my stomach ball up just looking at her. She had those curls that just spring from her scalp and drop down in perfect order, each one exactly the same size as the other. I was sure she didn't even have to curl them. And she wasn't wearing so much make-up, maybe none at all, but her skin was as clear as if she'd never eaten anything but cream and strawberries, and her cheeks so red, with that mouth with no lipstick already shaped in the two hills at the top that my mother used to spend at least ten minutes creating like a painter with her lipstick brush. I felt disgusted, beaten. She was the type of girl I had heard of at PM who just jumps out of bed in the morning and already looks like that, like she's spent an hour putting on make-up, though I'd never seen one of these girls before. Well O had found one. That made me so depressed I felt just like walking out then and there. But I considered the big picture again, O's plans and who knew what the girl was actually like, she was probably a real trouble maker being so pretty. Instead of leaving I decided I would continue with my plan and when the old lady's back was turned and the girl was in the back room behind the desk, I sidled right on into the media room which was dark, went to the old sofa and lay down

under there, ready to roll. I would just do this once, just to listen and
see if he had told her anything and see if she was an OK person. If
I thought she was, I vowed I would not come back---this would be
it. So there I lay for a long time. It got so I could here the big clock
on the wall in there ticking but no one came in, just clicking when
it passed each hour. It had to be almost nine o'clock and where was
O? I was just about to crawl out and sneak back toward the shelves
then out, when the door opened and someone came in. but it wasn't
O. It was the old lady carrying something which she seemed then to
be arranging on one of the desks across from me. Needless to say I
was terrified and immediately began spinning mental excuses in case
she saw me. I then tried to imagine myself as small as possible and
shrunk down into a almost a ball shape as close to the back of the
sofa as I could. Then I imagined myself surrounded by a dark light
which someone at PM had told me to do if I wanted to be invisible
from the helpers there. But in the meantime my mind was spinning
and when the old lady's long high heeled feet moved over closer to
the sofa. I came up with something. When she sat down and seemed
to be counting something, I quickly reviewed what I would tell her
if she discovered me. What I would say was that while browsing the
shelves, I had come upon a book which reminded me ---a Grimm's
fairy tale-- of a very scary episode in my life and naturally I looked
at it but because I was abused by a nasty step-mother like a witch
and the only thing for those moments of anxiety was to find a dark
place like under a bed which I had done in the past to get away from
her, and then the scary feelings would go away. I was sure she would
buy that and relaxed a little, she was clearly pretty nice--- why else
would she be so respectful of the girl and O's behavior which anyone
could see were shenanigans and they were up to no good. Almost
as soon as I had concluded what my alibi would be, she got up, very
spry for her age and turned off the light then walked out the door.
Well I heaved a big sigh of relief and crawled in the dark toward the
door then looked around, hoping the girl would again be gone by
that time which she was, and that the library lady was out of my

line of vision, which she was not. I waited a minute though and she disappeared behind a shelf and soon started turning lights out, I then ran as fast and as silently as I could out the door which I close very quietly and disappeared into the night.

Chapter Twenty Nine

The next day I vowed that I would never engage in such foolishness again, that it was definitely beneath me and it was all a lost cause anyway since the girl was so pretty and didn't even spend time putting on make-up. But by the afternoon after spending some time singing and laughing again with O, my game was on again. I just had to protect the boy, he didn't know what he was getting into. It was absolutely imperative that I give it all one more try. I knew he wouldn't be spending much time away from her, since they hadn't had any fight or anything and he would certainly show up there that night. So soon after dark, when the boys were still both there in the cave playing the music, I told them I had so enjoyed the last night in my special nest that I planned to stay there again and to get there early. They asked my about it like they hadn't even heard me the night before and once again I explained myself.

"Kooky girl," O laughed and hit a few low notes on his guitar.

"Just watch out," Jose said.

"I'll only be a few yards away," I told him.

"Snakes don't care. There are all kinds of animals out there," Jose reminded me.

"They say snakes know heart," O said.

"What does that mean?" I asked,

"If you're pure enough, bad animals won't hurt you. Haven't you heard that? But you have be pretty darn pure," he laughed.

"Then I'm sure she's in trouble," said Jose, joining in the laughter.

"Yuh," I said to dismiss them both and left out of there to make my way down the mountain.

Well once again I greeted the library lady in a friendly relaxed manner and once again she asked me if I wanted her help though she seemed slightly disappointed when I said no. She began to say something. then I told her I was supposed to do this project by myself and she bit her tongue and said, "Well just let me know if you need anything, dear." Once again the girl wasn't in sight and was probably in the back room primping for when O would arrive. So I smiled and turned back toward the shelves closest to the multimedia door which I could see underneath was dark inside. It was about seven by then which gave me plenty of time to position myself under the sofa. As I edged towards the door I noticed several more people come in, all of them interested in books and occupying both the old lady and the girl who had been out of the back room for quite some time. I used this as my chance to run into the multi-media room which I did swiftly over the silent carpeted floor and quickly quietly shut the door hoping neither one noticed anything. And they didn't, at least I don't think so, because in about thirty minutes I heard loud giggles from the girl and the throaty voice of a teenage boy in heat: O. I snuggled against the wall behind the sofa and was quite certain even if they turned on the light they wouldn't see me unless they were actually looking. Soon in they came and she started the movie by the light of the library since they left the door ajar. But after that O closed it firmly and they both settled down in the sofa.

Once again the movie was Gone with the Wind and it was clear neither of them was paying any attention to it all. But I was listening---I couldn't help it. Just as Scarlet the main character I guess, started a rather loud angry speech, O asked if they could turn it down a bit.

"Sure," said the girl who he called Priscilla. "I've seen it before anyway, it's one of my mother's favorites, that's because it was one of my grandma's favorites. She played it ALL the time. I practically know it by heart. I certainly could answer any of Elaine's questions if she asked me just to check up on us, but I'm sure she won't. She's one of my grandmother's best friends, that's how I got this job in here. That and because I'm an honor student."

"You are good at EVERYTHIING," O said, "that's why I like you."

"And I like you," she said and there was a silence which I could tell was them kissing.

"Ooohhhh," said O then, like it was all just too wonderful for him which disgusted me and I felt myself start to heave a big sigh then cut it off---I was afraid they'd heard me.

"But I still don't know anything about you, Omar." He had at least told her his name was Omar not O. "I really want to know more about you, not just meeting you... um in the library like this. I'd like you to meet my mother, and my grandmother."

O squirmed in the sofa and she appeared to adjust her seating. There was silence. Obviously O had told her nothing. After all, what could he say? 'I'm a fugitive from a locked treatment center?' The goody two shoes honor student probably wouldn't take kindly to that.

There was silence again and I held my breath. I could tell O was disappointed and probably just wanted to keep on kissing her and whatever else, without going into any details about himself.

"I am Ethiopian," he finally began grandly like he was announcing that he was some king in exile like we read about in English history.

"Oh," she said, impressed.

He went on. "My parents are in Ethiopia, they had to leave here a while back." There he goes again I thought, he can't possibly tell the truth. "They want me over there but I wanted to stay here." Yes, it all sounded very heartfelt, if just a little crazy like it had when he told me the same story. "My father is very handsome, a soldier, they want me there but now I just want to stay in this country, there are things I want--- no I NEED to do here. They try to get me back there which is why I had to take off from the east and I now I am living here in hiding, in a house I cannot tell you exactly where. I do wish I could". Another lie. "Believe me I would like nothing better than to meet your relatives. Right now I cannot." His accent took on a slightly foreign sound as he said all this maybe to support some notion that he had lived in Ethiopia a few years as a youth. "I do miss them very much though," he said. "This is very hard for me but I will be going back there I just don't know when exactly." There was silence. The girl moved on the sofa apparently closer to him then came the sound of kissing for several minutes.

Suddenly O blurted, "I love you, Priscilla."

She began to weep. She got up in the dark and went to the desk across the room where she seemed to be getting Kleenex and came back to the sofa and blew her nose very gently. She finally said, "And I you," like some movie, "and I you", then more kissing in between her snuffling. Finally she pulled away I think and murmured so low I could hardly hear, "But Omar I must be honest with you. And you with me... I will still love you."

'Oh oh,' I thought somewhat delightedly and I could almost sense O's body stiffen above me.

I saw it coming.

"What?" he whispered.

"Omar, I watch the news at night, believe it or not, I'm a night owl. I study until eleven, from nine to eleven, when I get home and then I watch the eleven o'clock news, sometimes."

"Why, what did you see?"

There was a pause and I could hear someone take a deep breath. "You. Of course. Don't you know it's all in the news at least it was for a day or two... that was before I met you but I'd know your face anywhere, you are so handsome, it was you and it said your parents were very wealthy computer people in Boston who have been looking for you for weeks, that was several months ago." She sighed.

"Why didn't you say something then?" he asked angrily.

"Oh I so wanted to, that is a part of me did, but I wanted to get to know you first and you seemed to want the same with me. I wanted to wait, didn't want to scare you away."

There was a long silence. Then she added, "And it said you came from some treatment school or other that they thought someone had taken you or you had escaped. And it had been a while back, maybe I was wrong, confused".

"I escaped," he said quietly, then he truly amazed me. There was in a few seconds the sound of crying, so hard it was absolute bawling, and I thought it had to come from Priscilla but I soon realized it was coming from O. It was so loud the library lady came to the door and opened it a crack to see if everyone was alright,

"It's OK," Priscilla hastily said, "he was just touched by something from Gone With the Wind, Scarlet coming back to Tara, so sad, he's so sensitive," Priscilla said.

"That is such a touching scene," the lady agreed as she closed the door softly.

"Oh Omar," said Priscilla imagining they were alone again, "you...you are so passionate, I didn't want to hurt you. I don't want to hurt you. Oh how I do love you," and she ran across the room to grab the tissue box. "Oh please forgive me." By then it was about eight thirty and I was wondering how Omar was going to wrap this thing up in a half hour.

"It's alright," he finally said. "I'm so sorry to have to lie to you. I will never do it again," and the next thing you know they're kissing again or whatever because I could tell from underneath them that they were both by then stretched out on the sofa. I put my thumbs in my ears. I just didn't want to know what was going on then but the sofa seats were moving up and down and there was plenty of moaning especially from O. In a few minutes they sat up and O began to talk. I mean the words were just pouring out of him, no accent,you could tell he was talking from the heart. He wasn't lying this time. And he was telling her everything, that is everything he had told me that night about his parents: his hatred, his suffering which it seemed he added to somewhat, and his plan for revenge and Priscilla just sat listening and sighing and weeping a little by then and blowing her nose very softly. All she said after he finished and sat waiting for her response was, "I don't blame you, honey, I had a real hard time with my father too. I never see him." There was no criticism of Omar for anything, no warning nor surprise about the lies or even his plans for revenge on his fake father. This amazed me and all I could think of was this guy is so loved by girls that they'll put up with anything from him because, looking at it objectively, that's what was happening. And I had hoped that all this would scare Priscilla off and that she would think he was crazy or at least dangerous but no, there she was at almost nine o'clock kissing on him again, mumbling about how wonderful it was, and how much she loved him The old lady opened the door a crack but the two of them didn't even try to stop smooching.

She stood there a minute and actually smiled at them and then like she didn't want to disturb them, said softly, "Priscilla, Honey it's quarter past nine, your mom will be worried." At that Priscilla jumped u, straightened her skirt and hopped over to the machine which she shut off and they both left the library yelling cheerful good-byes to the lady, who I could see was back among the shelves again. I appeared just as she was coming out of them.

"Oh my dear," she said to me. "I didn't even know you were still here. I almost bolted the door with you inside. Where on earth were you?"

"Oh way back in the shelves," I told her." I saw something very interesting and just had to pick it up and read, something about Moby Dick. I don't have a library card yet you know," I reminded her.

"Well you may certainly get one tomorrow, we'll see to it, someone who loves to read like you do!"

I smiled at her and took my time leaving there. After I was sure the two of them must have left the library area, I crept out and caught a glimpse of Priscilla next to her car at the end of the parking lot offering O a ride which he finally took and they drove off in another direction from the way to the cave; I wondered where he would get out. So I took my time walking home, still amazed at everything I had heard and wondering what there was about O that had girls so hypnotized they would just ignore the wacko stuff he was doing and do anything to please him

Chapter Thirty

I put him out of my mind for many days after that, that is, I tried to, and just sighed at his comings and goings to the library each night. He looked much happier around that time and was so upbeat he even composed a love song. He said it was for no one in particular but I of course knew different. But it was clear he was still up to no good because he was still hard at work with his plans and wouldn't let that little notebook out of his sight.

After a few days O began to seem like he didn't care that much about who saw him; you might even say he was getting reckless. When I asked him about this he told me, "Haven't you noticed, now I don't even look like I did in that old picture in the newspaper?" It was true--- he looked different. His hair was longer and had turned a kind of reddish brown out there in all the Arizona sun; he had sprouted a mustache although it was thin it was more than he'd had before because he hadn't had anything in the way of face hair. He also wore a pair of black framed glasses which Jose had picked up for him; in short he did look like a different person. "And," he told me "most of all, I discovered I don't really care. Also I never mentioned it but I'm about to turn 18 and soon I can become emancipated if I choose, if they bug me that's what I'll do. They won't though because the truth is they are so delighted that I'm gone and they don't have to mess with me anymore. That's the only reason they put me in those so called treatment centers, was to get me out of their hair. The first one was run by some buddy of Brigandian's, making lots of money. That's another thing---why should child treatment centers be profit making companies, anyone could tell they are going to take every chance to cheese the kid and make more money, that's why there so half-baked. But they're not going to try hard to get me back--- out of sight out of mind. Course little do they know I'm not going to stay out of sight." It gave me a little chill to hear him say that, because I was half hoping Priscilla would talk him out of his plan. At the same time I could understand his feelings and the idea of him busting up some fat cat's fountain didn't cause me much grief. "The folks around here, they're the only ones who would really go after me, some of the rednecks around here---to them ten thousand seems like a real fortune, but I look so different now, I doubt anybody could really recognize me...besides you never even see those posters anymore"

"You do look different," I agreed. "But what about that girl at the library you mentioned?" I asked innocently. "Does she know about all this?

There was a long silence and he got a bit of a dreamy stare on his face. "It's really none of your business Ray, not to be hard on you, I know you're young. But let me just say she is one hundred per cent behind me in EVERYTHING I do. She understands me." And that's all he'd say. So she's still not giving him any flack I thought, remembering with some shame how much I really did know about them.

"Fact is," he said as Jose walked in from his day's buying or stealing---nobody could ever tell what he was up to--- "she has an uncle who has a small bar and he wants us to play for him."

"Us?" I asked. "He hasn't even heard us."

"Wrong. Well, he's heard me, at least. She took me over there the other night. I brought my guitar and played him a couple of our songs, one that I had written."

"What about Jose?"

"What about him? Nobody's picked him up yet. As long as he doesn't seem to be doing anything wrong I don't think anyone will notice him. There are thousands of illegals drifting around here."

Jose, though coming in late, caught the gist of the matter right away and was totally behind it. "I've seen that place," he told O--- "it's tiny but they serve great food in there I've been there myself".

"How do you get around so much, guy?" O asked.

"Money. When you have enough money, no matter where it comes from, you can do pretty much what you want, only thing left for me is my green card and to move out of here."

"Yuh," I told him, I'd gotten a little tired of life in a cave, although it did have its advantages. And one of them was lying out there by the stars at night away from the noise and frenzy going on around the clock at the bottom of the mountain.

Chapter Thirty One

In truth I had gone out there a bunch more times especially when I was feeling under pressure from the wackiness of what we all were doing. I had felt so calm and so quiet that time I thought I was transported up to those lights, it influenced me for days after that. Just a feeling of calmness and kindness, really having no hurry about anything, that all my needs were met. This was something I'd never even heard of before. Everybody was always in such a rush even to do really dumb things like my father racing home to play his computer games and trying to race through them or my mother hurrying so she could watch Jeopardy or get something she wanted on sale. It never occurred to me before that maybe these were dumb things to be in such a hurry about but after all these were my parents and it wasn't just my parents either; the people at my school and at PM, they were always in some kind of a hurry. Even O and Jose--- always in a hurry, O doing whatever he was to plan his attack and Jose trying to make more money and get more things. For a day or two there after sitting in space or wherever it was, all the hurrying just seemed so silly I could hardly believe it. But those calm feelings kind of melted away, especially after the episodes of spying on O. It seemed like the harder I tried to tell myself this was for the best, the more I felt I shouldn't have done it and the worse I felt about the whole thing. So I was not feeling too hopeful about ever going up there or wherever it was again. At that point, I had taken to lying out by the cave and sort of feeling sorry for myself for everything that had happened to me as if to remind the universe or maybe whoever was up in those lights, that I'd had plenty of hard times, that maybe that was why I took to spying on a person who trusted me.

So it took me completely by surprise one night lying out there when all of a sudden I found myself inside the bunch of lights again and looking down at the cave. Once again I began to feel light then a huge calm, like an enormous weight had been lifted off my shoulders. I looked down towards the cave and saw myself, or my body. There I was, asleep, the opening of the cave behind me was dark and the two boys had gone to sleep. Once again I wondered how all this could be happening or was I just dreaming it? I remembered though, that I was definitely awake the first time I had seen these lights, so there must be something more to it than just one of my wigged-out dreams. So I just settled in there you might say and enjoyed the sights. It wasn't long before I was drifting over the desert and the interesting thing was, that happened right after I had wondered about drifting over the desert. It seemed that there must be someone there reading my thoughts and I looked around to see maybe some silvery space being hovering there beside me. But I saw nothing, no one, even though I saw everything else around me as clear as day and especially the lights which still looked brighter than I'd ever thought any light could be. So there was nobody there and yet somebody was certainly aware of my thoughts. I wished, then really focused, on entering into the cave from my bubble of lights and before I knew it--- poof--- there I was inside the cave, and there were O and Jose, asleep, I could hear their snoring, that is O's; Jose never snored that I knew of. So then I wished to be back out again but higher up and what do you know I was there, immediately. *'What's going on here?'* I finally thought, half expecting to get an answer. But I got no answer, that is I heard no words. But I did feel like someone was listening and '*There is someone here with you, thank you very much,*' came to my mind like out of the blue.

So then I said, "Well who then?"

And again I get no answer, just had the thought, '*Antoine.*'

Well, I thought that's an odd name especially for someone I can't even see.

'*French,*' it tells me.

I decided to try to speak because even though he or it could obviously hear my thoughts, they were all a jumble and I was not in control of what I was thinking. I decided I'll just say try to say things, that way it will be clear and it won't pay attention to the wacko thoughts I might be having, like I sometimes do. I'll stay in control. It did seem like I was speaking though I guess my voice box and all that apparatus were down on the ground with the rest of me.

'*Good plan,*' came to me, apparently from Antoine.

Well by this time as you might expect, I was thinking I had either gone completely out of my gourd as my father used to say occasionally about my mother or I had an unbelievable power here. For some reason this is happening to me and I can make this thing go wherever I want, like a bumper car. Course after I thought that last thing, I was a little em*barrassed because of course he heard that too.*

'*No, I'm afraid not,*' came the reply and I had the sense it was amused, not mad like I expected. '*This is all for a purpose you might say,*' it added.

That confused me further--- "What purpose? I'm having a hard enough time just taking care of myself."

Antoine agreed with this and I began to formulate my next question which related to looking in on my mother, but all of a sudden I knew that my time there for that night was up and I was then awake in my sleeping bag by the side of the mountain. I looked up but the sky was black except for a few distant stars and the moon starting to disappear over the western horizon.

Well needless to say, I thought about this all the time for the next few days and went out to the same spot in the sleeping bag Jose had bought me each night. I considered telling O or Jose but then remembered what they had thought at PM when I only told them about the lights---like I was totally bonkers, even the aide that I thought I trusted. So I decided the best plan for then was just to keep my silence, keep my cards close to my vest, like my mother used to tell me about some poker playing ancestor who actually was able to scrape up enough money from his poker to go to Oregon and mine for gold and become very rich. So that's what I did, but sure enough I'd still go out there every night and lie awake for a long time just looking out for those lights, those magic lights. But they didn't come and I began to wonder if the whole thing was just a product of my clearly over-active imagination. It was certain to me by then no one would believe me---they knew how easy it was for me to cook up stories. So I kept my mouth shut and gradually I devoted my energy to other things, specifically getting ready to play music at George's Café and Bar once or twice a week.

Naturally we had all applied ourselves to this task every night before the first show, our premiere. Jose had prepared a set as he called it, of songs, some new, some old favorites, which we had practiced to a 'T' as Father used to say, accounting for his success at a computer game about auto theft.

None of us expected things to unravel the way they did after this.

Chapter Thirty Two

This first night we played there was scary. I was afraid they'd kick us out after a few minutes, or worse. The thing that got my nerves into a real jangle was the sign I saw posted on the door as we walked in: PLEASE LEAVE YOUR GUNS OUTSIDE. "Who ever heard of such a thing?" I asked O quietly as we walked in but he just shrugged his shoulders. After a while we set up on the little stage, that is we sat down, the two boys with their instruments and me with my voice which felt then like it was stuck somewhere inside my chest. We really didn't have anything else to set up because we had no speaker system or microphone and really didn't need any; the place was that small: As I looked down into the audience of about ten or fifteen people, one thing was clear to me: there was a man with a big belly sitting right in front of me and there was a gun on his hip. Not only that, he looked angry especially when he looked at me. So I didn't look in his direction at all as O and Jose were tuning their guitars, just over his head into the audience or what there was of it, while I wondered if I should scream or maybe run out. But O and Jose had also seen him and neither one looked nervous. The rest of the audience were probably all friends of Priscilla and her mother, who were also there, all dressed up like they were at the opera or something, and looked down right friendly. So finally we began, that is O and Jose began 'Stairway to Heaven,' and I opened my mouth but nothing came out while the man in front started to scowl and look really mad. O smiled at me and gave me a nudge and this must have jarred something loose because it was like my voice just popped open and there I was in the middle of the first verse singing like I was Robert Plant, sort of. Well then the man began to smile and watched me almost the whole time. At the end he clapped harder than anyone else.

After we had played there for a month the place started filling up, and not just Priscilla's friends either; all kinds of people and they'd actually gather around us and make requests. Soon another bar a few blocks away wanted us to play. O told him we're busy enough right now but then the new bar owner doubled the price we were getting at George's and we were on. Jose and O began to study new music back at home in the cave and I did my best to keep up with them. Really I was completely happy then, doing this. It was like it opened a new place inside myself that had never existed before and I never would have discovered on my own. I was most happy when I was singing harmony with O because I had a high voice, soprano O told me. Needless to say there was plenty of money coming in. Jose insisted that we be paid in cash and neither bar owner seemed to care about that, "Under the table is alright with me," one said, "keeps the government out of my business and I can pay you more that way." Jose was ecstatic most of the time with all this money coming in which he divided among us. The next step was of course to move out of the cave into an actual dwelling of some kind. And for this once again the services of Priscilla came in handy. As it turned out, her mother as well as her uncle, were very impressed with O, so impressed that she agreed to rent a large apartment for her and her children she informed the apartment manager, as long as we paid the rent which was at that point completely no problem. Fortunately for us the apartment complex was huge and rambling so there was really no one to wonder at the diverse racial appearances of her children. That is one of the reasons Jose, who was always thinking ahead, chose it.

I later learned the underlying reasons Priscilla's mother was willing to go out on a limb and take responsibility for the apartment for the three of us weirdos. Turns out the mother of Priscilla, well, her grandmother, the friend of the elderly librarian, had been a bit of a space cadet herself. Maybe it was par for the course in those times: the sixties, I've heard all about them from my mother who was too young to know what was going on then but remembered what her mother had told her. The fact is Priscilla's grandmother spent a lot of time in a commune somewhere in California where she got pregnant with her daughter, Priscilla's mother, who also stayed in the commune a little while. The mother finally became tired of it and left with her daughter, took courses to finish her college degree and became a secretary at some company. Priscilla's mother was raised in a very middle class neighborhood, like a cozy development with a car in every garage south of San Diego where she grew up in a regular way. But deep down she remembered or thought she remembered her early years at the commune as being really cool and free. She had, according to O, always tried to take care of people who were suffering, even animals, and had adopted three rescue cats.

This generosity didn't apply though, when her daughter was at risk in any way, as we learned later.

I suppose after a couple of months we had all become pretty casual, slack even about the idea of anybody catching us despite the fact that we were runaways in O's and my situations and illegal in Jose's. The fact is, the money was pouring in as we played at the two clubs so we didn't concern ourselves with much else. Those may have been pretty rough conditions, with people totally ignoring the 'Don't bring guns in' signs, the wooden floors covered with pop corn and peanut shells, and all the beer-swilling unshaven men, but the minute we started playing all the talk stopped and all eyes were on us. They inspired us. O began turning out more songs about love and abandonment, then tried to weave the bad times he had had into them; some of them became pretty violent, and I was a little squeamish about them. One in particular described his relationship with Priscilla in the most raunchy but nonspecific terms---he didn't use her name of course. Another talked about using guns against corporate goons, in very specific terms. The crowd seemed just to lap all this up, the raunchier or more violent the better for them. I sang along even though I knew my mother would not have approved of these lyrics in spite of her own tendency for idiotic behavior. But one look at O, who never failed by then to be affectionate to me, dispelled my doubts and on I sang to every wigged out lyric his over-active imagination spun out. And he wasn't the only one writing. By then Jose was earning enough money to give up his career of stealing and sleight of hand, and maybe also not to let O outdo him, had started writing some of his own songs; they even collaborated on one of them, about women.

It did seem though that once on this path, Jose became a bit different. It was as though the digging into his feelings and history, which I guess he had carefully left untouched, presented a whole array of new challenges. This he admitted to me once. He also became more moody and at times irritable when working on one song in particular which he told me related to his times in Mexico particularly when he was trying to make it north on the train. He wouldn't go into any detail about it and told me he probably would never play it, at least not until he had a green card. But I heard him sometimes at night when I was walking slowly down the hall outside his room on my way to the bathroom. He sang something, then sounded so wounded, like a cat wailing, but softly as though he couldn't really cope with what he'd felt. One night I heard him throw his guitar down to the floor, and then I had my ear pressed against his door, then heard him cussing and turning on his radio loud, as if he was disgusted with himself. This all from the person I had never seen any negative emotion from at all for he entire time we'd been there, until he started writing that song. I could only imagine what was going through his head because he really never mentioned it to us. That night, after the guitar throwing, he came out of his room to go to the bathroom and I hurried down the hall to see him, just to check. He acted startled to see me there in the hall and mumbled that he was going to the bathroom but I could see even in the semi-dark of the hall that his eyes were teary and his voice was choked up. But he seemed fine the next day and most days, just trying to work on the green card.

He didn't let this interfere with his daytime activity which related to getting help in getting legal efforts, and unlike O, he was saving his money so I think by then he had plenty of it, enough to hire himself some expert advice in the immigration area.

As for O now, having plenty of money presented no challenge or particular joy since he was used to it. By then he was planning on getting emancipated. He also was meeting with Priscilla almost every night. Sometimes he would take her out after our shows but generally they just came back to the apartment. Sometimes she spent the night. I figured her mother must be a pretty free and easy type not only to help us get that apartment but not to care if she came home late or sometimes not at all. I asked O about this.

"Yes, Ornila is a very cool woman," he told me as if that should explain it all, "but you know Priscilla is a few months older than I am, already eighteen, and she's old enough to take her own risks, make her own decisions." He looked at me like, well that should be that, don't ask any more about it but still he tried to be nice, I could tell that.

He spent a good deal of time in front of the computer he had gotten; Priscilla and her mother had helped him get the access he needed. I wandered in one night after knocking on his door of course and found him looking at some web site for an upcoming gun show. "I'm going," he told me matter-of-factly, it's in Dukork a little outside Phoenix. Priscilla is gonna drive me."

"What are you doing there?" I asked.

"Oh you'll see, don't worry about it." What happened next though blew it all away.

Chapter Thirty Three

One night shortly after that I heard a great commotion and yelling coming from O's room where he was entertaining Priscilla. Naturally I was attracted by the racket. You might think I was just a peeping tom by then with no life of my own. Well fact is, you'd be right or almost right. This is because for the most part I tried to keep out of sight which limited my activity. I figured I'd been very lucky to not be picked up by the authorities by then, given that I had only just turned thirteen and clearly was supposed to be in school. I think the fact that I wore heavy eye make-up during our concerts with a little smudged under each eye helped. This made me look a bit tired and older and the fact that I was tall for my age also helped. Priscilla had showed me how to put on the make-up in a very professional way even though she never wore any herself, bring pretty enough to not need it---but she had experimented with it at my age. So in reality I didn't go much of anywhere and you might say, sort of lived off the doings of my two friends.

Well on this night there was clearly the loudest noise I had ever heard from O's room including when they were engaged in the other thing because you could hear that too if you really tried. I think O took a kind of pride in Jose and me knowing he was really a man,

Space

and could completely snare a girl as pretty as Priscilla. As for Jose I don't think he cared one way or the other what O did, as long as it didn't interfere with him. He always had his mind on something, always set like a stove timer on completing one plan or another. "Take care of each little thing completely and the big things will take care of themselves," he explained to me one day after I had asked him how he managed to do so much and just how he was going to get that green card. So anyway, that night of course, I walked closer to O's bedroom just taking a really long time, trying to seem like I was on the way to the bathroom, in case someone came into the hall.

Well around about the vicinity of O's door, I heard it: O yelling, "How could you do it, I can't believe it!" Then in a lower voice I heard him say, "Pregnant!" This I could not believe either and stopped there in the hall, stunned. The possibility had never occurred to me. I stood just there.

"Its your fault too!" she screamed, "not using anything."

"You said you had birth control," he yelled, "that first night. That must be when it happened."

"I said I had it. I didn't say I was using it then. I didn't expect all that to happen right then. I did after that."

"Great help! You're a big girl, what did you expect? An honor student! You knew what was going on with us."

"I don't know," she said in a lower voice and had clearly begun to cry.

I stood there waiting for something else to happen, unable to move, but feeling guilty.

There was no sound for several minutes, until I heard them both talking softly to each other in a very loving tone. I heard no sound for the rest of the night although I did run into Priscilla later in the hall when we were both really on the way to the bathroom. She smiled at me a little but her eyes looked red.

O received a phone call the next morning after she had gone--he was in the kitchen and took it there. His voice was very calm on the phone -- he only said a word or two but it was obvious there was something wrong. Even though his skin was olive-toned, underneath that it, became white, like porcelain, no life to it and I could see his jaw muscles tighten into a knot. He hung up after about thirty seconds and slammed the phone on the floor. "Believe it or not her mother just called me, like she's some eight year old, she's eighteen for crying out loud," he shouted. Well the gist of the call was, Priscilla's mother had found out and was taking her out of there, snatching her up away from him---"That's right just... just forbids her to see me any more and she went along with it I guess." At first his voice was calm, then a whisper and he tried to smile and act like it didn't faze him; he started to walk out of the room but before he reached the door he burst into tears then just dropped onto the floor like he's a heap of old clothes. I was amazed---I thought the boy was tougher than that, but then all these feelings about Priscilla just started spouting out of him from the floor like a fountain. Of course we both were surprised and tried to be sympathetic.

"She's old enough to do what she wants," I told him, "she'll come back to you." Jose agreed and tried to get O up off the floor onto a chair. But O acted like he wasn't even there, like he was made of spaghetti, so Jose finally let his hand drop and it just fell to the floor with a thud, like he didn't even have any control over that or more like he just didn't care. I, to be honest, could not even imagine caring about someone that much, especially someone my age of the opposite sex, though I did have strong feelings for O. I wondered if he could be acting, just pretending to be hurt so badly, so we'd feel sorry for him and do more of what he wanted. He said nothing for a long time just sat there on the floor. Finally it was like something clicked on inside him and he looked up at us a little embarrassed and got off the floor by himself. "I'm OK," he said and sat back down at the table. I guess he knew it was too late to get to his room and just to pretend to us he didn't have hurt feelings.

"I hope, I hope she does see reason, how much we meant to each other... the baby," he said softly, a subject he hadn't broached with us though I of course knew all about it and Jose caught on fast. "But she was feeling so guilty, like it was all about her mother, letting her mother down, not about me, about us, she's almost 4 months, has to keep it of course at least I'm thankful for that...," he mumbled as if to himself. "I called her three times, before her mother called me---she wouldn't answer. She's gone, just dropped me. Maybe her mother won't control her, but I don't think so, I think she just does whatever her mother says, like a puppet on a string," he mumbled then and swallowed as his eyes started to tear up again. Ridiculous as it may seem I knew right then that he really did have such deep feelings for that girl, feelings I had never even imagined a boy could have for a girl and instead of thinking how foolish he was or how pathetic, I felt so sorry for him, that I was on fire with love which up until then had only been simmering quietly. I wondered if I'd feel the same way if he left me, but then it dawned on me that he really wasn't with me in any true sense of the word, as he'd of course had been with Priscilla. I also realized at the next moment that she was now gone out of his life which was sure to leave a space for someone to fill. I knew it would be me.

The next day when we were sitting in the kitchen, Priscilla did call him and told him that she was really sorry but her mother was sending her to New Jersey to finish school there and have the baby quietly then give it up for adoption to some deserving family. She couldn't see him again, even to say good bye, no, her mother was afraid she'd become overwhelmed by him and they'd both abscond, which is of course exactly what they probably would have done, if O had anything to do with it. So he tried to reason with her over the phone to make her change her mind and stay with him--- he had plenty of money, he said, and would definitely make a lot more, he was sure of it. He ended up pleading with her, begging her, pulling out all the stops. But she was weeping the whole time about how she'd let her mother down, she'd expected so much better for her daughter, what a hard time her mother had had in her life and how she just made it worse. How much her mother had given up for her, she'd been so proud of her, how she'd been a single parent, she hadn't wanted that for her daughter, her future was ruined. He just sat there with the phone a little away from his ear listening with a hopeless look on his face like a neglected dog then he repeated all this to us though we heard most of it anyway--- I didn't eavesdrop. What blew my mind completely was that he even offered to give up all his plans, to go back to Boston and try to get along with his rich parents to keep her. "They have so much money they'd help support a young couple," he told her, they'd like her. His mother felt so guilty she'd probably do anything for him, maybe even for Priscilla's mother, he wailed, grasping at any straw by then. But Priscilla refused.

After begging and trying new angles he finally told her she was destroying him and she'd have him on her conscience forever; his life would never be the same, and neither would hers, he'd be ruined, and what about their baby, didn't she care about him for he was convinced it was a boy. Evidently she didn't, because unbelievably when he told her she was destroying him, both Jose and I could hear some laughing and it wasn't coming from O, then her voice calmly trying to tell him to get a grip, he was being melodramatic, and put things in perspective. It was clear that whatever her feelings were, they were like a drop in the bucket next to his. Well that did it for him ---it was like the floor suddenly fell out from underneath him. "So I guess its all a game with you," he said quietly and just laid the phone down on the table without even pushing the button to hang up.

I had to pick it up and tell her he had gone, "It was too much for him," I added, hoping to make her feel a little guilty. But she had already hung up.

"I was depending on her!" he screamed at us later, like he was totally losing it and blaming us, "I loved her more than anyone, even my real father and I wanted that baby, it's my baby, no one else's!" he screamed. To me he acted like a small child whose mother had just disappeared out of the blue, and he didn't know where she'd gone. I knew all about this because I saw the way my youngest sister Wanda acted-- that same way the first time our mother just left out of our house, like poof, gone;she didn't do it for a long time after that. No one could console Wanda, she just screamed all that day and the next night. My father had to stay home from his job at the 7-11 just to try to help us but especially her. But there was no help; the next day she woke up red-eyed with her white face looking like a cement statue, no movement at all there. Her expression didn't change until my mother came back two days later, and even then it took her a while to warm up. Well that's pretty much exactly what happened to O. He sulked and sobbed all that day and I could hear him doing the same thing that night and talking like he was arguing with her, even though he didn't have the cell phone, until I fell asleep. I wanted to help but there was nothing I could do, just like Wanda, he wanted to be alone. But he kept saying, "You don't understand, you just don't understand," and I think that was probably true but the thing is, I don't think he did either. Two days later he was stony-faced and calm like nothing had ever happened but with a kind of hard edge to his voice and a look I'd never noticed before, a look like his eyes were made of metal.

Chapter Thirty Four

Well, for some reason Priscilla's mother didn't try to sabotage our group. I guess as long as Priscilla was out of there it didn't matter to her. One night though during a particularly good concert at that bar she had set us up with, I noticed a new face in the crowd. He had a sport jacket on and I could tell he had a weapon because of the small bulge under it on his chest, but the main thing was he didn't seem to be enjoying our music at all, just had this sour look on his face, sipping on what looked to be a long glass of water. My voice was particularly strong that night and I began to see if I could make this sourpuss smile or at least look a little happy with my singing, I guess I was singing pretty loud. At one point O gave me a look like what the heck are you doing and then I toned it down some. But I was feeling pretty smug as we got ready to leave that night and took special pains just to look at the unhappy stranger like *'you can see how good we are, why aren't you even smiling?'* So I traipse out behind O while Jose was still there chatting up some girl and the man who was still sitting there sipping his drink casually got up as I passed. Then when we were outside, like in one movement he pulled me over to him. "How old are you?" he says.

"Seventeen," I managed to sputter as my thoughts raced.

"Identification," he demanded, of course.

"I don't have any."

"No I didn't think so," he said angrily and takes me over to the owner. "You got information on this kid?" he demanded from the guy.

"She's a very good singer, don't you think?" says the owner smiling, clearly missing the tone of the sulky man's voice.

"I'm taking her to the station--- she's a minor and a run away, the twelve year old I've been looking for from LA," and he flashed a badge at the owner and took my hand firmly. "Come along," he said, "or I'll put cuffs on you. Your parents have been looking all over for you."

I looked around frantically, then started to yell, "You got the wrong girl! I'm from New York! I'm seventeen!" hoping Jose or O at least would hear but O was gone and Jose was still focusing so hard on some girl that in the hubbub of the bar he didn't hear me. I could not believe my parents would have gone to such trouble to try to find me and for a moment I was flooded with joy that they must be doing that well, to get themselves together and try to find me.

Next thing I know I was in his car and he had handcuffs on me, "You...", I began, "you don't need handcuffs. I'm not a criminal." I told him

He shouted, "Yuh, just a run away," and by then he was not listening. He just turned the radio up loud to some country music station.

"How do I even know you're a cop!" I screamed but he said nothing and I then realize that I'm stuck, sunk, whether he really is or is not a real cop.

"I'm a bounty hunter, girl," he finally yelled back at me and my mind was briefly boggled, wondering how much money my parents could have made to hire a bounty hunter.

I wondered when O and Jose would notice I was missing, "Like they could do anything," I mumbled to myself, "one still illegal and the other a run away too." Before I got too far into my plans for escape he was pulling up at a building, a police station. I was relieved that he was an actual cop of some kind and not some child molester and followed him into the building. He explained his story to the cop there and showed him a picture of some girl which he claimed was me. I saw the picture briefly and everything became clear. They got the wrong girl. You could see some resemblance except for the hair because hers was blonde and straight and mine well, you know. They must have thought I'd given myself a corkscrew perm and red hair as a disguise, but I knew no girl in her right mind would do that for any reason. They were clearly deranged. Well, it must have been almost midnight when they got around to taking me to the Clear View juvenile detention center and locking me up. Needless to say, I was in a pickle since I had thought I'd never have to put up with this kind of thing again. This time too I was behind actual bars, not a room with some addled old lady or distracted girl thinking about her boyfriend outside that I could bamboozle--- one of my father's favorite words, because I guess cause he tried to do it so often to other people. So there I was, led into a square room with bars, a cell, and they slammed the door behind me. The guard was a no nonsense type of woman with dark skin and pinched angry green eyes. There would be no getting on her soft side. "When can I get out? I didn't do anything!" I yelled as she locked the door.

"You get out in the morning. Maybe this will put some sense into you," she said angrily, clearly not somebody who'd taken this line of work because of any love of children.

"Yeah," I shouted back at her and began to say something else but there she was, right back again in front of that cage like she was going to have me for a midnight snack if I didn't shut up.

"Yes?" she asks in a tight scary voice.

"Nothing," I said softly and slunk over to the bed against the wall.

The next morning another guard came by and unlocked all the doors for breakfast and we were expected to be orderly, that was clear. "Get in line now. Orderly, orderly!" shouted a fat-stomached woman who looked like her uniform was stretched so tight around her belly it might split open. But she had narrow hips like a man and darted up and down our line of about twenty girls fussing and barking orders at us like a sheep dog. She had a stun gun on her thin hips dangling there menacingly, reminding us to shape up if it should slip our minds.

For a minute I considered the possibility that I could be having a dream, or rather a nightmare. There I had been for the last two months quietly living in that nice apartment with my own room and plenty of money because the boys gave me an allowance every week, not as much as they got I knew but that was OK cause they did most of the work with the instruments and all. And I had had plenty to get whatever I wanted: snacks, magazines, and make up which I had begun to experiment with big time. Now all that seemed like a dream. When we sat down in the big cafeteria with all the clanging of metal and slamming of trays, then tasted the bland oatmeal I knew this was certainly no dream. I was trying to swallow something I wanted to spit out and the girl across from me was staring at me like I was a worm she just discovered in her orange juice. "Where YOU from?" she demanded and there was something about her look that made me sure I'd better answer.

"New York," I said, wondering if there were times when we were left unsupervised with the other girl inmates.

"What you do?" she demanded.

"Ran away, but they got the wrong girl."

At that she laughed and poked her neighbor in the ribs. "That one says they got the wrong girl," she yelled, pointing at me. They all seemed to think that was hilarious and in a minute everyone at the table was laughing and hooting at me.

"We all the wrong girls!" she shouted, still laughing but the moment she had opened her mouth all the others stopped the laughing like it had been turned off with a switch and turned toward her. A guard came over, yelling at us to shut up.

"Community group next," the girl opposite me shouted as

she pushed her chair back in. Her name was Andrea and she was obviously the top kid there. In a minute she made a special point to get out of her place in line and jump in behind me, which the guard ignored, and to start telling me about the place until Regina the narrow hipped guard finally nicely told her to be quiet. Regina led us to another room, high-ceilinged and sounding kind of hollow probably because it seemed like almost everything there was made out of metal, and also you could hear distant slamming of metal doors. I had a very hard time hearing anything that was said in there except for those right next to me because it was like a giant echo chamber.

"This is where we get to make up stuff and impress the staff," said Andrea in a loud snide voice and all I could say was "OK."

The first subject was to address goals for the day and it seemed like everybody knew what to say to satisfy Regina and Blaine, the social worker who was also in the group. I said once more that they had the wrong girl which made them all laugh again but in a quieter sort of way than at the table. "I'm telling the truth," I said but no one heard me and they moved on to the subject called 'desirable changes in behavior' that each one had supposedly learned while residing there at the Clear View detention center,

"Not to do nothing wrong on the outside," one girl said and then snickered, but as soon as the guard frowned at her she looked serious again.

"This is where we get to make up stuff," Andrea said again to me then looked away quickly and smiled at the guard. We went around in the circle and my turn was last, I was relieved to see. Most of the others had been there a while I guess because each one had a complicated story about how she was going to stay straight and clean and it sounded like the stories had to have been rehearsed and rehashed for some time. They used the words strategy and sobriety a lot.

I of course was no stranger to stories and was sure I could come up with a good one. I momentarily forgot that my purpose was to convince them of my innocence, that is that I wasn't the one they were after, and launched into my own story.

I must admit that was the high point of my stay there. Where I could see the others had been busy making things up, pretty dull things about babysitting for their sisters, helping their mothers stay sober, of course staying out of any trouble themselves and not being suspended from school for any reason, even I could see, looking at their faces and listening to their voices they had no intention of doing any of this.

I'd give them a story alright.

"It all started when I was four," I began, sticking to the idea that I was seventeen, "thirteen years ago."

There was some snickering after this and one girl shouted, "I guess you young for you age, must be using that special face cream then," and everyone hooted which the social worker immediately put the lid on with threats of lock up all around.

"My mother," I began, then was surprised at the silence; everybody looked at me like they're on the edge of their seats, waiting. I continued. "My mother was very beautiful" [true], and I launched into a detailed description of her, until Andrea yawned loud, "and my father was Costa Rican and came over here to make more money [true]. They married after my father saw my mother in a modeling show; she was modeling bathing suits then [complete lie]. Of course they were married.

""Why they get married?" someone shouted out, "didn't she have a lot of other boyfriends, mustn't have been all that hot," but Andrea shot her an angry glance just as the social worker started to say something and the girl was quiet. You could have heard a pin drop in there then.

"At first everything was fine", I continued, very slowly, making it up as I went along. "Soon, however, my father got a job at a computer company in New York, I mean he was very, very smart. He started moving up the ladder there because he is soooo smart [not true] and mechanical [not at all true]. Well... then my mother had two more children and wasn't as beautiful anymore [true]," at this may voice dropped and I was close to tears because this was true and also kind of sad. "My father, women had always liked him [not true] and he began to make more and more money and before you knew it he had lots of women coming on to him. Finally they were even coming to the house sometimes, looking for him, because by then we had a big house in Greenwich, Connecticut, [complete lie], and he took the train to his company every day. Even though he was good-hearted and meant well"---at this almost every girl was looking at me waiting like they couldn't believe I was divulging all this---"he fell in love with one of them, one of those women, someone who was still a model but young and even more beautiful than my mother," I sniffled, "and he left her---my mother. Then he took all his money and moved back to Costa Rica with the girl, leaving my mother with nothing or almost nothing--- she had a small shared savings account which she immediately cashed in, but then feeling so desperate---"

"LUANNE!" some guard started shouting from the doorway, and since that was the name I had given them, Luanne Smith, I at first ignored it because I forget this detail but then jumped up.

There came a chorus of 'AWWWW's' like the girls were clearly disappointed that I couldn't finish the story and some yelled "At least let her finish!" but the guard said no and I walked to the door, a little relieved because I actually didn't know what the end of my story would be.

"It was just a bunch of bull anyway," shouted Andrea angrily staring at me with her angry grey eyes as I went past her and out the door. "I know when someone's making something up, she don't have no rich father and all that beautiful mother." I guess she was mad that I was leaving so early, looked like she had already begun to consider me her property. "Look at her, she not that much," then the others agreed and I could hear the another inmate beginning to talk as the guard locked the heavy door.

"You may come with me," he said, leading me down the hall. He stopped in front of some office and I was ushered in to sit in front of a friendly pink cheeked round looking man who was chomping on a long-stemmed unlit pipe like it was a piece of gum, staring right at me.

"You may sit down please," he says. "How you doing?" he added like he knew me and was just being friendly but then stared at me for a while like he was trying to remember where on earth he'd seen me before.

"Good," I said, "But I'd be BETTER if you let me go, I'm seventeen, I'm from the north, been on my own a long time," I yelled in a voice somewhat deeper than my natural one. I was trying to sound old and authoritative. "You got the wrong girl."

There was a silence

"Well, I don't know about all that, but our sources did inform us just this morning that they apprehended the ACTUAL girl they had been looking for... and, well, it wasn't you. Got a big reward too. So I guess maybe you been telling the truth. Yup got the wrong girl, easy mistake. Fact is you look a lot like the picture Sam had. Too bad. Anyway, we got no reason to hold you just now. We don't know of any runaways to match your description right now, name of Smith, though I'm not so sure that is your actual name of course," he smiled. He gestured to the guard who sat down. "But we're gonna let you go about your business, I smell a rat somewhere but far as we know you haven't been hurting anybody and no one's after you. Drug screen negative too. No real reason to keep you locked up. But you stay out of trouble young lady or we'll be on you like chickens on a bug, trust me. Be careful too, attractive young girl like you," he added like an afterthought, then kind of looked me up and down slowly as though he had a perfect right to do this which made the hair on the back of my neck stand straight up.

I got up and hustled out of that place as fast as they'd let me. The guard led me out right then and there and it felt like a million pounds had been lifted off my shoulders. I did see a friendly dog sitting in the front lobby of the place though, on my way out, right next to a thin little woman. "This is a friendly dog," she said as I patted his head and noticed the friendly look on his face. I remembered the dog I had wanted to rescue and for a moment there felt really sad but then realized I had to get out of there as fast as possible before they changed their minds. "A therapy dog," the lady continued as I pulled away. "The girls look forward to seeing him. And the boys too. Unfortunately we can't come in but once a week. Too bad," she sighed as if maybe I could do something to change that. After hugging the dog I made tracks out of there as fast as I could.

They wanted to give me a ride back to "wherever you're staying," they said but I refused, definitely didn't want any of these guys knowing where I lived.

Chapter Thirty Five

So instead of going right back to the apartment I headed off in another direction. I thumbed a ride even though I knew at the time it was dangerous, especially being all alone. Fact is I just wanted to make tracks away from that Clear View place as fast as possible. I didn't know what would have happened to me if I'd stayed there but I knew it wouldn't have been good, between Andrea and the man in the office, the whole place gave me the shivers down my spine.

After a few minutes out on the highway, a man in a grey pick-up truck offered me a ride. When I looked in the door I saw a beat up stuffed animal and a McDonalds kids' meal wrapper on the floor so I figured he might be a safe guy and got in. It wasn't but twenty minutes away to the Phoenix area and he didn't say much the whole time, just, "You shouldn't be out thumbing rides, young girl like yourself. I don't pick people up but this time I figured, well, if I don't, somebody else is going to and then who knows what's gonna happen to this kid."

I told him thank you, that I knew he was right and wouldn't ever do it again---certainly not by myself I was thinking.

"You just never know," he muttered as though to himself as we approached Phoenix then looked at me and added, "my daughter ain't much younger than you." He let me out a minute or two later and I waved good bye then I stood there in the city wondering whether to go back to the apartment right then. For some reason I decided against it and went on my way towards the old cave. The sun was just going down about then and I was watching the sunset, all purple and orange streaks as I climbed up the mountain.

Nothing had changed in the area.

I went in to check it out in there, what was left of our stuff we decided wasn't worth the effort to drag down the mountain to our new apartment. It looked a little dirty, messed up, like we had really ruined what nature had given us. It was very quiet, no sound at all except a little wind blowing through some little pine trees outside. There was still some light and I could see more junk we'd left behind in the corner. I wondered if I should just take the time to clean the place up, and carry down the junk but finally decided against it. It was too heavy and plus it was mostly O's stuff. So I went over to have a look, wondering if something important might have been left behind, like money, though I knew better. Neither one of those boys would ever forget that, but I poked around in that mess a little just in case anyway. There were a few old pages of newspaper, a book of spells and charms Jose must have decided he didn't want and a few old deodorant bottles, used up. Those two used to go through deodorant like it was water since we only made it to the Y once or twice a week. I didn't really need to worry about it myself since my glands hadn't fully kicked in yet, but I knew they were beginning to now. So I just ruffled around in the junk, don't know why. It was when I was about to leave that I saw a few pages from O's notebook, I knew right away what they were, so I picked them up and looked at them. It seemed like it was mostly just scribbling, but then there were a few diagrams of some building, I guess the one his step father owned in LA. On the next few pages were scribbled poems, dedicated to Priscilla, there was no doubt about that. The thing I hadn't realized before was how much he loved her, or thought he did, because that's what these poems were all about. I debated taking them back to him especially in light of how things had been going lately with them but then realized that might be a very bad idea. They looked like first drafts anyway, but I took them.

So it was getting dark out and soon I could hardly see anything in there and left out. I was about to head back down the mountain and back to the apartment when the thought occurred to me '*why not stay here tonight?*' It was so warm and the stars were coming up so bright. I suppose deep in my heart too I was hoping I might find those lights in the sky again and connect with that Antoine, whoever he was. Even if it was just my imagination, I really missed it. So I lay down there on one of the scrabbly blankets we had left in the cave and waited. There was nothing, even though I started talking to this Antoine asking him to appear, and soon I fell asleep.

When I awoke I was astonished. There I was again, surrounded by lights, looking down at the desert. "Antoine," I said and though I heard no voice there was that feeling that he was answering me because words from outside my thoughts just planted themselves in my head, and there we were again carrying on some kind of a conversation.

He did have sense of humor though if you could call it that. '*Have a nice time at Clear View?*' he asked.

All I said was "That's not funny, how do you know where I was anyway--- are you following me?"

'*No joke intended, I'm assigned to you,*' came the response. '*Like the dog?*' he asked.

I didn't need to answer this, it was obvious.

It seemed like after a while I didn't even need to say things, he just knew what I was thinking, even though I said the words so it would be clear, in at least my mind. But it seemed like he knew just about everything I was thinking anyway so why bother.

But I couldn't pick up on his thoughts the same way, they had to be spelled out to me slowly. After what seemed a few minutes of small talk or small thought, what I really wanted, darted into my mind and stayed there: that was of course to see my mother---he'd been able to take me to the desert and into the cave to hover over those boys before, why not then to see my mother who I really wanted to see? Distance didn't seem to be an obstacle to him.

'*It's not,*' came to me '*but we have to be careful with this, it's not as easy as you may think.*'

The next thing I knew I was in a room. It was one I'd never seen before with dingy curtains and dust bunnies and dirt everywhere. Though there were some lights it seemed very dark in there.

I looked around it. There were a lot of people in that room and over in the corner I thought I saw my mother. I went closer and was amazed to see that it was really my mother and she was just sitting there laughing and smoking something, I didn't know what. The thing is, it was obvious that she couldn't see me. Next to her on a chair I saw a man who was kind of round with very kind eyes; she didn't seem to see him either because she was talking to someone right next to him as though the man wasn't sitting there at all. I became very heavy with sadness, the saddest I've ever felt watching her. I wanted to hug her but I realized after a few seconds there was nothing I could do, I had no body--- that was left behind on the mountain. At that moment I realized who the round person sitting there was; and remembered that I had seen those eyes many times before. "Can't you do something?" I bawled to Antoine, "You got me here, can't I speak to her at least?"

Antoine said nothing but the eyes looked truly distressed. In a moment I felt a shiver and looked down at myself, at my body but like it was made of something like light, not hard and heavy. At that moment my mother looked over in my direction. "Raynelle!" she screamed and lurched towards me, smiling and crying all at the same time. I was crying too and tried to hug her but felt my body, that is that shimmery thing like my body, dissolve though I was still there in front of her and she was batting around with her arms trying to hug me. At this, I felt even sadder and ached to be with my mother like we had been before. I felt like I was screaming but there was nothing she heard, nothing really came out, Next thing I knew I was up in those lights again with Antoine. Though I couldn't see him, he was there. "I wanted to hug her," I told him angrily.

'I know, I wasn't able to do that. I would have if I could, my abilities are limited.'

"But I saw you there,'" I said, "that was you, right? That strange fat being, pardon me, and with those eyes, you've been following me around, my whole life, haven't you? Why are you doing this? Does everybody have this happen and just keep it secret, what's going on? And why can I see you down there but not up here!"

'I need enough energy to materialize in any form. You'll find out sooner or later,' he said.

"I want to know now! Who are you anyway, why is this happening to me?" I'll admit I was overwrought. I missed my mother, I hadn't realized how much. "This doesn't happen to everybody does it?" I yelled, wondering if this wasn't some secret thing that everybody experienced and no one ever talked about.

'No,' he told me. *'This is enough for tonight, too much really, more than was planned. Your mother is running out of that building right now, she's not sure what happened but knows she's not going to keep up the kind of life she's been leading.'*

'What kind of life?' I said, dreading the answer.

'Not a good one. but she'll be alright, you just brought her back to reality.'

"Seems like a weird kind of reality," I said. "Nothing I've ever heard of before."

———————●————•——

Antoine seemed strangely silent after that, that is I didn't feel any more words being planted in my mind. After what seemed like a few minutes, I was awake again and the sun was just coming up in the east. I felt like I hadn't slept at all that night at first but I was strangely energized after a few minutes as if I'd gotten twelve hours of the best sleep. I thought of my mother and how good it was to see her but yet bad because it was clear she was in a room with people doing drugs and who knew what else. And yet the strange being had said she'd be alright didn't he?

I was sure he had and felt a strange sense of peace as I walked down the mountain the next day. I went back to the apartment that morning. No one was there and I hung around the place for a couple of hours watching the big TV which I guess they had gotten since I was away. I had decided one thing: I was going to lay low for a while. I wouldn't be singing any more, not if it led to going to places like Clear View which made PM seem like a luxury hotel. Plus I just didn't care about the money. I knew I wanted to get home and see how my mother and my two sisters were--- they needed me, much more than O or Jose, those two were obviously doing fine. I knew one other thing and that was I wanted to see Antoine again. I realized he must have been following me around, in his way, for a long time, with those eyes but in different people, and I realized suddenly even the dog, that dog at Clear View seemed to have those same eyes, no mistaking them--- that was just too weird--- he was so reassuring but what on earth was he doing, what kind of powers were those? Oh, I had heard plenty about strange things happening, my mother had been all into that kind of stuff, space beings and even séances and talking about people even getting out of their bodies that is their material bodies and floating around here or there. Once she had even tried to have a séance in our apartment. She told us she was going to contact the spirit of her dead grandmother whom she had loved very much. But the person who was supposed to lead the séance got there in some kind of turban and immediately wanted twenty dollars which my mother didn't have. She refused to do anything until she got it and at that moment my father walked in the door and sees this woman in a turban wanting twenty dollars and my mother crying. My father said it was all witchcraft and shouted at the turbaned woman to get out of the house before he hurt her;

she left with lots of loud cussing down the hall. He didn't speak to my mother for two days after that.

My mother had promised him she would never try anything like that again but next thing you know she got a deck of cards supposed to help you tell the future and actually did it now and then for her friends, that's how good they thought she was at it. My father wasn't as set against this since she did collect some money from some of the people for her 'readings.' as she called them. So this kind of thing you might say, my mother and I were not total strangers to. I don't include my younger sisters in this because they were too young to knew what was going on back then.

So let's just say I was not a total stranger to this line of thinking, in fact had been steeped pretty thoroughly in it by my mother when my father wasn't around. She had been completely convinced that there was help to be gotten from the interstellar beings since the earth and especially her, were in such a pickle. I remained unconvinced until my own experiences but since talking with Antoine, I had become a complete convert to my mother's way of thinking. At that point there wasn't much on my mind but questions for him and about him, if he really existed and I was becoming more and more positive he did.

So needless to say, after eating a big meal and leaving a note for O and Jose I made my way back to that mountain at twilight and lay down on the same blanket, scanning the horizon for his lights. This time I felt sure he would come and as I lay there my heart began to beat so hard it seemed like the rest of my body was left behind, like just a pile of unimportant stuff around it.

But there was no sign of Antoine, though it felt like my whole body was being rocked by my heartbeat, I finally fell asleep. The next morning I woke up at dawn feeling discouraged and silly. I wondered again if my experiences with this strange being were just a figment of my imagination,weird dreams, after all none of it seemed to make any sense--- why he would pick me? And what he was doing hanging around us anyway? Because obviously he was from some advanced planet.

Chapter Thirty Six

When I got back to the apartment that afternoon, I found O bent over his computer talking to himself. He was looking at a gun owners web site and I went into his room and stood by his table. There was a pile of papers on one corner and on the other a can of Mountain Dew. "You all right?" he asked without looking up from whatever he was doing which involved his taking notes from the computer in his notebook.

"Yuh," I said moving closer to him. Fact is I had missed him mightily over the past few days.

"Glad," he said. "Where were you?"

"I left you a note, didn't you read it?"

"No, well Jose read it, he told me you were OK in spite of being picked up somewhere by some goon. We missed you in the band."

"Yuh," I said with my heart hurting that he didn't seem at all worried about me. "Yuh, I can't sing for you anymore."

"Why not?" he said then turned and looked up at me for the first time since I'd left out of there.

"Too dangerous, somebody's gonna decide it doesn't make sense me being so young and all."

"Seems to me if they were going to find you they would have

done it already," he said turning back to the computer. "I hate to remind you, but from what you told me about your parents those two aren't about to launch any major effort to find you, not that they don't care about you of course, I'm sure they do. Unlike my sorry parents. But that's OK because now we're making some money I can afford to get emancipated which I am planning to do and my parents aren't standing in the way. I actually talked to them, a few days ago. They were all worried and all but bottom line they're just glad I'm finally out of their hair, or they think I am," he laughed. At that point O turned to me again smiling. I noticed his eyes which looked darker than they had been, were set into deep gray circles, like a racoon. He had never had these before. I could tell he'd still been suffering over Priscilla so I brought the subject up.

"I went back up to the cave," I said, casually.

"Yuh?" he answered and looked at me again, "Why?"

"Just wanted to see the place. I kind of liked it up there and wanted to see if we left anything important behind."

"No," he said, "no way," then he paused. "Why? Did you find something?"

"Not really," I said but then added, not to be dishonest, "nothing important. I did see some old papers. I think they were yours. They had poems on them."

He turned to me angrily and I could see him blush right under that dark olive skin. "Oh? What did you do with them?" he asked in a strained voice.

I reached into my pocket. "I thought you might want them and so I brought them back." There were three sheets of paper which I'd folded into a small square and stuffed into my pocket. I flattened them out and handed them to him.

He got up from the computer, took one glance down at them and tore them up into tiny pieces like they'd just been through a shredder.

Naturally I was by then regretting even looking at them, let alone bringing them to him and backed away a little. His face looked so dark, so tight with anger I thought it was going to crack like an egg. But then he took a deep breath as if he had found himself again and went back to staring at his computer. "It's alright," he told me calmly, "don't worry, they mean nothing to me, absolutely nothing." I sighed and stepped a little closer again. "But Ray, come to think of it, I do need your help." There was a long silence and he looked at me again, real sweet, like my mother when she was really happy with me, that's where I'd seen that look. "You are the only one other than her---it was like he couldn't say the name Priscilla ---who knows about all this, my plans, and I've... I've changed a lot of the particulars since I told her. Besides I don't think she was paying any attention anyway, I could kind of tell because there was really no reaction from her, I think she had her small mind on other things."

"How, what do you need?" I asked, ready to volunteer almost anything, wondering if he could tell how happy I actually was about Priscilla leaving him.

"Going with me. But I've got to figure out for sure when he is going to be there. And I've decided to get a gun, at a gun show. It's easy, I want you to go with me, it'll look less suspicious if I'm with somebody, not like some crazy loner. We'll tell them you are my girlfriend, if anybody asks which they probably won't. Even though you do look young. You look a lot older when you're wearing make-up."

"Ok, I'll wear make up," I said without even thinking because my feelings were so caught up in the idea of being his girlfriend, actually going somewhere with him, that even just hearing those words come out of his mouth put me into a confusion. "OK," I added lest there be any doubt, "I'm ready." Sometimes it just amazed me that I had actually traveled across the country with O without having much of any feeling about him at all, but maybe they were all just kind of in hiding, afraid to come out or maybe I was too young back then. In the meantime behind all this new attachment there were also hundreds of common sense thoughts running through my head about his schemes, like *I don't want to be part of something bad, are you going to hurt anyone, this will ruin your life, what about your future, what about my future, about OUR future?'* Finally I said, "But you said before you were going to just blow up machines, are you gonna hurt someone? Why does your step father have to be there anyway?"

"I told you before. No one will be hurt. I need him there just so he can be close to it…it will make more difference to him if he sees it first hand. And my future will be just fine. First, I'm not emancipated yet. Technically I'm still a minor. Second, it's going to just call attention to the bad things his company does to put it and him in the spotlight so to speak. They have lots of corrupt connections, you know they're a nefarious group--- that means bad Ray, if you don't know. I might even become a folk hero, somebody people really look up to. It'll be on the news that's for sure. And you won't be in the building with me. Just make the trip with me…some moral support you might say."

"Ok," I said again, "and I do know what nefarious means," even though to be honest I wasn't completely sure. "Where's the gun show anyway?"

"Right in town here, well a few miles away. Next week, matter of fact."

The truth was my heart was burning as I looked at him, so skinny now, all hurt and tired looking, completely Priscilla's fault, and of course his parents. For the first time in my now thirteen years I felt a new totally unfamiliar feeling. I wanted to just wrap my arms around that boy and hug him and I wanted to kiss him too, right on the lips just like I'd heard Priscila do that night, even though I'd never done it before, or even had the least desire to do it. I stepped closer, right up next to him with my bony hip touching his arm, and put my hand on his shoulder. Then I reached down and stroked his hair which had grown somewhat long and shaggy, a look he thought fit his job as a rocker. I couldn't really believe that there was my hand there… feeling his silky black hair in between my finger tips, just acting like he was already my boyfriend. I told myself to stop but it felt so good just to stand there that I couldn't, not just then. A few seconds later I wondered what he would do if I just leaned over and kissed him right on the lips which he was biting as he ignored me in concentration scrolling and scribbling; then I wondered if I could take the place in his heart that girl had filled so completely. I was afraid, but also totally sure it would be a good thing, for both of us. I had a speech prepared from earlier in the day. My heart was racing and I was sure he could hear it or would feel it pounding against his head through my finger tips. I leaned down a little closer then started to say "Omar, I…"

He jerked his head up at me, completely surprised, then put his arm around my waist. "You're the best Raynelle," he said, interrupting me. "I can always depend on you, the only one really. You're like the little sister I never had." Then he released me and looked back at the computer.

I walked out without a word, feeling like he'd smashed me right across my heart with a bat, but still loving him and just so aware of where he'd had his arm a moment before I could still feel it there like I was wearing a thick soft belt. After all, how could I expect him to guess how I was feeling? I walked back to my room wondering how long it would be before he would see me in my true light, someone who loved him and not as a sister. I was sure this day would come. It was just a matter of time.

Chapter Thirty Seven

I hadn't seen much of Jose for the last several days. He met up with O the second night I was back for practice. He was on the way to getting his green card within a few weeks he told us, and added that money makes it all possible. "I can afford the best help, it's all working out for me. I knew it would---I just didn't know exactly how. Now I can see it all unfolding." Carlos, the manager of the first bar we played at, had told him there was some guy named Tony interested in the band recording something, a real contract, that somebody had heard us play and liked it, called it wild and particularly liked the lyrics that Jose had written, very violent I guess based on his experiences coming up here. And this guy Tony had gone to hear them and said it blew him away. As Jose had started to compose his own songs though, he sometimes became overwhelmed with his own lyrics like they were reminding him of stuff that he had tried to forget. But it was still down there, raw and painful, wherever feelings stay. Seemed like he was regurgitating stuff that he never planned on but now needed to get rid of but it hurt so much coming up he could hardly stand it. And Tony, a small time producer, because that's what he called himself, was also Hispanic and had had come here illegally too then gone on to get an education in business and became very successful. And now he had money, and lots of it. Jose was impressed with him and even more impressed with the money Tony was able to make, not to mention this guy had lots of connections, and having come here the hard way himself, was able to give Jose some very valuable pointers about getting legal.

Tony came to the apartment to visit a few times, to encourage Jose and offer advice as he told all of us. He was always very enthusiastic about the group and had finally even offered them enough money to just stay out of clubs until they got enough music to record it, by his company of course, in his studio. And this was fine with O who seemed to be just biding his time until the gun show, then the event he had planned. The guy also liked O's music which he described as melodious, heart felt, and sexual, and was sure it would appeal to the youth of America, and elsewhere. But it was Jose's songs that touched his own heart, you could tell that, and the more this guy encouraged Jose and paid him, the harder Jose worked until he had what the guy said were the right number of songs, about twelve, then planned to pick the ten best ones. Jose worked hard on the music and the lyrics and would spend some time teaching them to O, so of course they could record together. I imagine Jose was being paid in cash very nicely to keep him off the streets and out of the bars where he had been making a considerable amount of money. Tony also paid him cash to help him become legal. Jose gave me whatever I wanted, usually about a hundred dollars a week which I used to buy fashion magazines and make-up to make myself look older particularly when I knew I'd be spending time with O, to give him the right idea, you might say. I wasn't interested in heading back to New York just yet where I was pretty sure no one was ready for me, but it was in the back of my mind and I set about ten dollars a week away under my bed to give me the money I needed when the time came. The task of making myself look older had at first seemed impossible. But the more I practiced it and the more expensive the make-up, the easier it became to the point that I was pretty sure most people would take me for a seventeen year old with my make-up on---everybody but O who clearly still looked at me like a little sister.

So we were all doing OK mostly on account of Jose who seemed able to churn out songs one after another but wasn't satisfied until he had polished them like jewels.

I could here his music most nights when I was in my room which was next to Jose's, reading People Magazine and O was in his room at the computer as usual. It started out with Jose going over some of the songs he'd already written, like for practice, just playing the guitar and singing. I could hear most of the music through the wall. One song was about how much he missed his mother, how devoted she had been to him, trying to meet his every need which she had done once upon a time but which she had no longer been able to do because of all the poverty in his village and how he knew her heart was breaking because of this; how this was one thing that made him just decide to leave there. Sometimes you just can't take it anymore he sang especially when those you love are suffering everyday, getting up in the morning with no food and complete hopelessness, even about seeing the sun rising and what it would bring that day. Sometimes he would start to cry a little during his songs and I knew he wasn't just faking any of it. Sometimes I would start to cry myself just listening to him---bad as I'd had it at times, I hadn't seen anything close to what he'd been through. And he would sing O's songs too---though I decided this was kind of to relieve him from all the sadness he was feeling with his own songs. Because it seemed like O didn't care to get into any of what I knew his real feelings to be in his music; he just sang about sex and girls in a pretty nuts and bolts, down to basics,in a usually angry way. Some girls might have thought it was disrespectful to women how he went on but I didn't, because I knew how his heart was broken, and the guy Tony didn't mind either. "It's what kids like nowadays," he said, "a lot like that."

Jose didn't usually sing about girls; it was like he'd had his mind on other things for so long he really hadn't had the time for them and they do take time. He sang about his family mostly. One of them though seemed to be almost more than he could handle, one about his parents and when I heard him start to play this I knew he was in for a good cry. It was more like a story than a song and I guess he just had to play it. It was about how his father used to have a lot of money then something called the nafta came along and he couldn't make it; he even tried to sell his magic but there was no one around with any money to buy it, though sometimes they bartered, it wasn't in high demand. Even about how boys could be snatched out of school by the drug dealers and forced to pedal the drugs, forced drugs themselves to control them and they'd be lost to their parents forever. He knew his parents worried about this everyday he left them for school and that broke his heart. Between his mother and his father suffering he just had to go, he sang, even though he knew it would be breaking their hearts, it was also breaking them for him to have nothing in his stomach and such danger everywhere.

And that's where it began--- with his last song. It started out like it would be a long song about when he left his village how he left with his best friend who was a little younger from the village someone he'd known since he was three, how he'd always kind of been a big brother to him and looked out for him. He spent a long time singing about this kid, usually in english but sometimes he lapsed into spanish. "A wiry smart little fellow with bright grey eyes from some conquistador ancestor," he sang but started to choke on the words. Then he stopped and the next verse was about how his father had scraped together a couple of pesos from food he'd managed to sell and made them take it. How he wanted to just leave without the pain of telling them but of course he wouldn't leave without saying goodbye and how they cried and how they hitched a ride with someone to get to where he knew the trains went heading north to Juarez feeling a little hopeful and happy.

And that's when I heard it. At first it was a sob, like a baby might do watching its mother go out the door, but knowing she's not coming back, then an explosion of howling in high pitched tone like someone had just pulled his fingernails out. That's when I threw my magazine down and ran into the room or tried to, because the door was locked. A second later O came running out too, obviously distracted by the racket, and heard Jose howling in there and started to yell and scream himself about opening the door. I was standing there rattling the door knob as if I might get it open that way; that's the first time O ever really got mad at me. "Get the hell away from the door!" he screamed and he stepped back a few yards as I jumped out of the way then started a full run and threw himself, all two hundred pounds of him, right at that door. Then he did it again and again. Each time it seemed with more determination and force than the last. It was like he was willing that door open with every muscle in his body like a battering ram until it sprang open--so hard it was like somebody must have jerked it from inside -- there was Jose folded over like a piece of kleenex on his bed, wailing. It amazed and frightened me to see him like that, Jose who always seemed in control and always knew all the answers, who'd successfully made it up here against all the odds and made so much money one way or another when we met him that he could support us AND his family in Mexico, who'd gamed the system and won, even being on his way to being rich; who never seemed sad or angry, always took things matter-of-factly as they came, just like stepping over a stone on a path; even to meeting two strange kids out on the road that night and being so sure of his future he took us in. There he was: a pile of folded flesh trembling and screaming, tears running like a wall down his face.

Well, I stood and stared, wanted to do something, something, but didn't know what. O on the other hand, amazingly, seemed to know exactly what to do, almost as if not only was he not freaked out, but that he was energized by the whole thing, like he'd been waiting for a moment like this all his life and it was feeding some part of him. I never did see him so calm, so in control, like all his life he had been gearing up for this. I screamed in the meantime that we should call 911 that's how bad things were. He turned to me as he walked to the bed slowly and told me in a very quiet voice, "You will be quiet and do no such thing Raynelle. I know how to help him, step AWAY!" And I did.

The first thing he did was just reach out slowly to Jose and then put his hand softly on his shoulder. Meanwhile Jose was still shaking and sobbing but a little quieter. "I know, I know," began O, "it hurts so much, too much, doesn't it?" Jose who had begun to listen to him somewhat finally acknowledged that it did and briefly looked at O then went back to crying, a little more subdued. "And you've kept all that in all this time haven't you?" O continued, "you're so strong, a hero really, no one knows how it hurts, it hurts even more to let it out, but sometimes....you can't help it." I was wondering if O hadn't actually learned something after all those years of being cooped up in an institution and supposed therapy. Finally he said "You can tell us. it'll be better if you do".

"It was the song," gasped Jose finally after taking a few quivering breaths, "all of them really but this one more than any. Thing is, I thought I was handling everything just fine, my parents now have money, I'm getting legal and I'm going to get them legal, but it was this last song that did it."

"You can tell us about it."

Chapter Thirty Eight

It seemed to me as I watch this whole thing unfold and felt a little like I was spying again, that the more O helped Jose the better O felt. It was almost like he was helping himself, making himself stronger.

"The song reminded me of the trip up here... after I said good bye to my parents and that itself was so sad," he sighed "but I had no idea what else awaited me, me and my friend, Giorgio I'd grown up with... like my little brother. He was almost a year younger, so smart and happy I'd always been able to help him, he'd depended on me at school, he didn't have muscles like me," he smiled. Then he turned serious again. "Well we hitched a ride with another farmer friend of my father's who had been able to get an old car from trading food, that's how bad things were. But he got us to where we could jump a train and hang on, first the back then when we came to stops, to the top, we thought maybe we'd not be noticed that way so much. There were gangs of people on it and let me tell you they meant us no good, made a living of people like us. We clung onto the train for a long time, other kids were on it too, all sad and hungry but with a little hope in their worn out faces.

"But he couldn't do it ...a tunnel was coming ... he took too long getting down, he couldn't hear me yelling at him... then it was too late..." He stopped talking for many minutes, crying then began again. "Well I jumped off the train and went back for him, thought maybe he'd just been knocked off, hoping he was still alive. He wasn't. Either knocked off by the tunnel or pushed off, small as he was... I never found out which, but he was gone...just his limp small body there thrown against some rocks. I'd head of CPR and did everything I knew how to bring him back, pushed on his thin chest tried to breath into his mouth...gone," he whispered and cried some more.

Finally he took a deep breath. "After that I didn't know what to do, couldn't, really think. I just stayed up there on that hill by the tunnel for a long time. I don't know how long, it seemed like time had stopped for me. Finally I debated going home, but how could I do that, I had lost everything for nothing, nothing. After a few days maybe three or four, I don't know... it was like I woke up. I hadn't been hungry or thirsty until then but then it seemed of a sudden that I had a mission and it wasn't going home. Giogio was gone, sacrificed for this,it wasn't going to be in vain. I was going straight north to America and I was going to make it, for me and Giorgio, his family, even though I had to leave him there. I scrambled around and started walking then I found a few berries I knew about growing by the road and ate them and a few minutes later I threw them up, maybe that was a good thing I don't know. That night I slept by the side of the road heading north. I wasn't afraid of anything, man or animal, and as I was falling asleep I looked up at the sky instead of my ratty ceiling at home. Just as I was falling asleep I saw it, a bunch of lights kind of arranged together but not like an airplane either and kind of moving across the sky but looked like a box kite, it was weird. For some reason after that, I felt like it was some kind of sign, that nothing was going to hurt me... and even if it did, at that point, it mattered nothing to me. If I couldn't make it, make it for all of us, I was as worthless in my own mind as a pile of dirt by the road." The lights. Of course I wondered if the lights had something to do with Antoine and at this statement I perked up even more and almost shouted something out---like *'I've seen that too, I've even been up there with it, I'm sure it's the same, have you seen that again,'* All of those thoughts were running through my mind but I said nothing. It was clear Jose had a lot he had to say that he'd kept somewhere inside all this time and it wasn't for me to stop him.

"I got a ride finally with some farmer and finally hitched my way to Acapulco. There I bathed and washed my clothes in the ocean and looked half presentable for a scruffy twelve year old. It didn't take me long to figure out that there were rich tourists there and I knew how I'd use the situation.

"I would visit the outdoor restaurants or bars and offer to perform magic, for I had a few tricks up my sleeve as you know. There I learned how my sleight of hand could be brought to best use: by trying to induce a trance in my audience, usually two or three people, but the more the easier. This is something as I told you, my grandmother had taught me as a little boy. It was as if she knew way back when I was a little one that I would be in for very hard times and she wanted to arm me with as many talents as she could before she died, and that was one of them. So if I could stay by the tourists' table just a minute or two by then I would be successful, the problem was usually that the manager of the restaurants would see me and chase me away before I could do anything. This happened in all but one restaurant where the manager was an American and I think he felt sorry for me. He could also see, since he took the time, that when he let me do my magic the guests usually liked it----unexpected entertainment, and free--- for him anyway. So I was able to stay there a few weeks and actually saved some money, got myself some decent clothes and looked more presentable. I couldn't bring myself to try to contact my parents, since they had no telephone they really didn't expect to hear from me yet anyway. The main problem was it was nice that I had my little niche but how was I going to get to America because I knew I could do much better up there.

"After about a month I met a couple named Cynthia and Rob. They were staying at a nearby hotel and ate dinner every night at this restaurant. Well they took to me immediately. Cynthia had long grayish blonde hair and pale blue eyes like you're looking up at the sky, and Rob also had long hair, with grey streaks which he wore in a long pony tail down his back. They decided they liked me right away, became real friendly. They even had me sit down with them at their table. They spoke some spanish and I had a little english and asked them just to use that with me and my english got better especially with their help. They told me they were "aging hippies," that's what they called themselves, and that they had traveled down through Mexico in their station wagon with their dog. They were then on their way back to San Francisco after a stop in Acapulco where they were enjoying the ocean.

"They told me they'd met in San Francisco in the 1960s and after being hippies together and smoking a lot of marijuana they'd finally gotten married and moved outside the city.

They had two children, the husband explained, who were both grown up and into computer programming.

"Then he laughed and told me he and Cynthia had both had jobs with a big insurance company, 'This is our last fling to celebrate the old days where no one knows us,' he said and he doubted that they'd make it down there again.

"After they told me their life history they wanted to know about me, 'everything' they insisted. Well I told them everything almost down to the last sad detail. Cynthia started crying as I told her and Rob cleared his throat a lot and blinked like he was fighting back the tears. But as you know I wasn't trying to fool them--- it was all true. Well after that they insisted that I travel back to America with them. 'We'll make it somehow, I don't care,' Cynthia told me with tears in her eyes.'It's like the universe maybe has given us something to atone for all those years of us working for the man, screwing people,' added Ron and Cynthia agreed.

"So it was settled. I of course was in favor of their plan though

Space

I knew it would be risky and couldn't imagine how they'd carry it off. A couple of days later, I set out with them towards the states, me riding in the back seat of their station wagon with their dog, and their luggage in the way back, wondering the whole time how they were going to get me across the border. I had about twenty dollars and they didn't have much more I think, certainly not enough to bribe any border guard. I became very friendly with the dog, a large shepherd named Rex, who used to like to lie on an old army blanket on the floor of the van. I still had no clue about how I'd get across and just kept quiet, hoping something would turn up. And it did.

"About ten miles from the border Cynthia shouted, 'I've GOT it!' and jerked her head around to look at me.

"'What, what did you decide!' Ron yelled. He had been waiting for her to come up with something and immediately pulled off the road.

"'The border guy probably isn't going to bother with Rex,' she said, 'they didn't on the way down. He will know he's ours, our dog. We have all the papers on him from California.'

"'So?' says Ron.

"'So, we let him lie down on the floor, but the thing is…'

"'What!' says the husband who was by then excited.

"'Jose will be lying RIGHT UNDER under him, he's so thin it won't be noticeable.'

"Ron said it was a dumb idea, that they would see him right away.

"'No, not if he's lying on his army blanket,' Cynthia hissed like he'd missed the obvious.

"My heart was pounding all through this," said Jose, "like you can't imagine, and I thought it was kind of a goofy plan but I was willing to try anything, what else did I have?" Jose finally looked at O because he had been talking before like he was talking to no one, just staring at some spot on the wall.

"Nothing," I gasped and they both looked at me like they had forgotten I was there.

"Exactly," said Jose and turned away from both of us again. "Well I did it. Lay down, right down there on that floor like it's my favorite place in the world, got as comfortable as I could on it under the hot blanket and then the dog gets right on top of me. Ron told him to stay and he's doing exactly what they want like he gets the whole thing, he's real serious like completely understands. I think he did. Meanwhile I'm underneath him sweating and not just because it was so hot down there either. He's stretching out on top, all 110 pounds of him because that's what he weighed and I only weighed about half of that and he was panting in my ear because of the heat down on the floor, they didn't have an air conditioner and it was still hotter on the floor and he was drooling on one spot right over where my ear was and he didn't move and neither could I--- I knew that or I'd blow it. So we're all arranged and then pull back onto the road and drive into the customs and I can hear Cynthia with her musical voice kind of flirting with the agent and she was still kind of pretty, then them giving the guy their papers which of course were all completely legit and then the guy looking in the back seat wanting to know what they got in there and then taking out and opening every suitcase they had. Of course they weren't so stupid as to have any pot or anything in there then but I'm sure they smoked plenty south of the border. Meanwhile the dog is sitting perfectly still but he's steady growling but not a wild way like would make the customs agent mad, just in a kind of low friendly but watch out way and the guy asks about the dog and looks at his papers actually says he's a beautiful dog but you could tell he's a little afraid of growling dogs even though they've got drug sniffing dogs there too. He started telling Cynthia about his own dog for a minute or two, also a German Shepherd, almost bragging a little and then all of a sudden we're being waved through. I couldn't believe my good luck but Cynthia is hissing at me, 'Don't move stay put, we're not safe yet,' and I stay where I am by then my ear was wet with dog drool and the other one was numb from being pressed against the floor and I was wet all over from my own sweat. But I'd made it."

"What happened to Ron and Cynthia?" I asked.

"They dropped me off in Arizona where everybody speaks Spanish and half the population even the legals are Hispanic but not before they'd handed me what I think was all the cash they had left, forty nine dollars. I took it of course and said good bye… thanked them with all my heart. I wouldn't have made it if not for them. I'll never forget them, they risked their rear ends for me, who knows what could have happened?"

"Have you seen them since?" O asked.

"No, but when I make my money I'm going to look them up and give them some, a bundle. I've got their last name and I know where they live."

He looked very sad and very tired after that, like he'd just let every bit of energy he ever had leak out of him, word by word. I was sure he'd never told anyone all that, no, he'd just been keeping it all tucked inside him somewhere cause he knew if he let it out too soon it would wipe him out and he'd never do what he planned. Almost like he used all that pent up energy, for his own aims. You're alright man, the best," said O as he walked toward the door. Jose heaved a great sigh and was then quiet. O and I told him good night and walked out of the room.

Chapter Thirty Nine

I was sure Jose had slept all day the next day because there was not a peep from his room. I finally knocked on his door later that afternoon just to check on him. He was gone, his bed was made, looked too me like he'd never even been there the night before. I guess he'd slipped out of the apartment at dawn, before either one of us got up.

I had spent that day doing a lot of thinking to myself, something I hadn't been doing much of lately and had never really been one to do anyway. Most of this thinking was about Jose, his seeing those lights which I was positive were Antoine and that maybe he was following Jose too, maybe even O.

I decided I'd ask O if he'd ever seen them; he told me no, then asked if I was crazy. He said it was clearly a 'figment of Jose's imagination,' something he manufactured to help himself through such desperate times, without even knowing he had done it.

"Yuh," I said so as not to start anything with him but I didn't agree, given the nature of my experiences, and I kept my mouth shut, wondering what there was about Jose and me that some outer space being would need to follow kids like us around. It seemed like coming from such a high achieving civilization that he could even get here at all that he should definitely have something better to do. Then I thought more about Antoine. I hadn't seen him for a long time and hoped he hadn't bailed on me, if space beings do that. I decided to go back up the mountain sometime soon. I might even ask him about Jose if I saw him again which I very much hoped to do.

I also spent some time thinking about my parents after listening to how much Jose loved his and the way he was helping them out. I wondered how he'd managed to tell Giorgio's parents what had happened but figured to let that question rest for a while.

The next day I took some of my money and bought my father the prettiest post card I could find, one of a sunset over the local mountain with the bottom part all beautiful cacti and on the top some bright purple and pink clouds hanging over the mountain. Maybe he wouldn't be afraid about me if he saw how beautiful it was out here. I bought him that one and then I saw another. I knew he used to like the rodeos and said he'd even been to one once. So I got him a picture of a cowboy holding on with one hand to the top of a bucking black bull with fiery eyes, but I think the post card people must have painted extra fire in his eyes. Anyway I took them back to the apartment, got a good pen out of Jose's room then printed in my best printing:

Dear Daddy,

I am doing fine. I have enough money and I'm not doing anything bad. I hope you are doing well too even though I know that's hard where you are. Can you let my mother know I'm alright if you know where she is? I don't have an address for her as I guess you know.

I hope you are doing well in jail and I'm sure you will be out soon. I should be back in New York by then.

p.s, Yes, I did break out of Precious Moments as I'm sure some social worker must have told you but even if I come back I do not want to go back there. They put me in for no reason and I can do fine outside.

**Love,
Raynelle**

I thought about putting my return address on there since now I had one and wasn't living in a cave any more but then I was afraid some social worker would get her hands on it and come after me. So I didn't.

On the second post card, with the cowboy I wrote:

DEAR DADDY:

THIS CARD REMINDS ME OF YOU. THERE ARE A LOT OF RODEOS AND COWBOYS HERE AND I KNOW YOU WOULD LIKE IT. PLEASE SAY HELLO TO MOM IF YOU SEE HER. TELL HER I'LL BE BACK SOON.

**LOVE,
RAY**

To be honest I had wanted to say something about the lights so my mother would hear about it, because I knew how happy it would make her. But of course it would have been too much for my father who would not have been able to argue about it right away and I put the notion out of my mind. That particular subject so dear to my mother had particularly infuriated him, like it was the one subject that somehow focused everything he did not like about her into one idea. So I just put in that thing about Mom, on the second post card because I wasn't completely sure he'd get them both or even one for that matter. I knew where he was but wasn't sure of the zip code so I just put what I figured was the closest one. Plus everybody knows the guards and workers at these places read the mail of the inmates first chance they get; it's like they don't have enough going on in their own lives or maybe they're just completely nosy, some of them. They might even throw some of the letters away just to punish somebody or keep them for a really long time, then say 'Oh I found this in the mail room. Guess it was lost,' then give it to the inmate or citizen like he's doing him a big favor. Truth is, I guess I really didn't trust anybody anymore.

Except O.

Chapter Forty

When O asked me to go with him to the gun show the next week I jumped at the chance. I got into my most adult looking outfit too. I'd started to spend some of my money on clothes and put on my most expensive make-up because by then I had quite a collection. I specifically put on eye liner to make my eyes look darker than they were even though they were already dark. They were more serious that way, maybe a little tragic like the heroine of some romance novel I'd wanted to read but hadn't yet. Also some pretty heavy foundation to cover the freckles now blooming on my cheeks and nose which had grown especially bothersome in the Arizona sun, then just a faint pink blush on my cheeks. And just a tiny bit on my lips, nothing too much or it was certain I'd look like a clown. But this seemed to contrast with my hair color nicely.

My hair. Now there I had a problem. As I looked in the mirror that day it was clear I still looked like little Orphan Annie on one of her worst days. My mother had shown me pictures of her one day that there had been a show about her in New York city, like to make me proud I had hair like somebody they did a play about---but she was a cartoon character. As I stared in the mirror though, I had to admit my face looked OK, passed the muster you might say but that hair, my legacy from my incarcerated father, was just thumbing its nose at me and my plans. So after some festering over it, I thought of a way to fix it. It had grown long enough for me to slick back with some of O's Vaseline he kept by his bed for his chapped skin and to stick it through a thick rubber band on the back of my head. Once back there it was so curly it just stretched all that curliness right on the back of my head and curled around the outside of the rubber band so tight it actually looked like a bun---the perfect thing for somebody trying to look older ---and it did the trick. As I studied myself from the side in my hand mirror I could hardly believe it: I looked old, maybe even older than O, at least twenty. I put on some black shoes I'd gotten with a little heel on them, maybe two inches. Then after all this I put on a really slinky pant suit because my hips were still real narrow and yet it was form fitting, going way in at the waist, but blooming like a full-bloomed tulip on a stem up top. Fact is the crucial upper parts of my body had begun to fill out fast a few months before, late, like they had forgotten they were supposed to, but trying hard to make up for it. I'd kind of been hiding this from the boys under sweatshirts and boxy big shirts. I guess you could say it all had surprised me or maybe I wasn't quite prepared for it after all those years of staying away from boys and having a chest flat as the floor, that had made it easy. But for whatever reason at this time, I had decided to show O what had happened, just knock him off his feet I hoped--- maybe that was my secret plan all along. And for sure I had been studying those fashion magazines and not just the teen ones either. I had gotten magazines about actual grown-up women like Vogue where I studied them and learned how they produced their effects; after all I had a man to please. "Just so much smoke and mirrors," I said to myself as I read them; this was something I had once heard Jose say about other magicians. But there I was now, looking at myself in the mirror, at the finished product, and I must say I looked pretty good, better than in my wildest dreams about myself, almost as pretty as my mother used to be. Was that me? I wondered dreamily as I stared at myself in my mirror with the tight, but not too much, skirt around my hips and legs, and the jacket just gathered around my waist then opening like a flower blooming right into my huge new boobs, it seemed like I could have admired myself all day. But I was jolted out of my trance by O outside the door yelling at me about when I'd be ready. I picked up the little purse I'd bought special for this and walked out, closing the door carefully and slowly behind me just like I thought one of the models I particularly admired from Vogue might do.

I stared at O to get his reaction but he had been looking at his watch and glancing down the hall. When he heard my door close so slowly it attracted his attention and he turned around to me. "We need to…" he started but when he really took me in, the finished product, he caught his breath and gave a little whistle under his breath which he thought I couldn't hear but I could, because I was scrutinizing what every move of his reaction would be. All my senses were tuned to their highest ability and it was like he couldn't help himself, but within a second he had collected himself and was all about business again.

So O rented a car at some fly by night car rental shop, using some bogus ID he had bought from someone at the club they had just been playing at. I Looked at it. It was some Hispanic kid named Larry, looked a lot like O unless you looked really close and then you could see he was not as handsome. We had a quiet ride to the gun show about ten minutes away out of the city. In fact O didn't speak to me at all until near the end of the trip when he kind of gave me a sideways glance and said angrily, "Raynell, have you got socks stuffed up there or what?" So obviously he'd had his mind on this the whole time, but he seemed mad more than anything. I was flabbergasted as my father used to say when my mother stressed him with her wacky ideas. So I said nothing for a few minutes, just collected myself. I felt entirely hurt like he had wounded me on the deepest level and here I am trying so hard to help him and make him see me in a new way.

I finally answered, "NO, for your information, I do not. I'm thirteen now you know, and this happens to normal thirteen year old girls, for your information. You just never noticed." Granted I was angry at him too and sounded a little edgy.

"OK,OK, sorry no need to get all in a huff about it," he said and patted my knee twice, like my father might do. I took a deep breath and told him it was alright.

A few minutes later we walked into the convention center. If he'd been upset a few minutes earlier you would never have known it by then, he just seemed to fit in there under all those bright lights with so much noise and different things going on. The light was so bright everywhere you looked and it shone onto O who was definitely taller than most of the people in there, like just making him look like a beacon, his head as shiny as one of the gun barrels. I trailed after him like the devoted girlfriend I was supposed to be while he drifted from exhibit to exhibit, eyeing guns and picking them up like he'd been doing just this for his whole life. It amazed me how much he'd picked up about them, I guessed, from the computer. "You know so much," I murmured to him as we walked from one booth to another. "I'm a quick study," he told me with a cocky smile as he approached the next gun salesman. If I had had any doubts about my feelings for him after his comment in the car, they dissolved like snow flakes in the sun as I watched him in action. First of all, he was definitely the smoothest guy in there---I don't care what age, with his dark eyes so bright and his tall muscular body, his smile with teeth so even and white you could tell his mother had definitely at least taken him to good dentists, his shiny dark hair just past his collar and with that suit he had put on, he made the other men in there look like toadstools. And that wasn't all---he was able to just chat with these gun people and even tell them things about their own stuff just like he belonged there. In short he had me mesmerized and just following him around like a puppy dog. Now and then he would introduce me to someone as Ray his girlfriend at which time my heart would skip a beat and the person he was talking to would make a comment like 'beautiful girl' or 'handsome couple,' which I hoped he was listening to. And I would smile at him like we were the real thing. Once after this happened I took his hand and he didn't pull it away until we started walking away from that table. This gave me some hope, maybe he was having the same ideas I was. But then he said, "You don't have to do that," in between booths.

"But I'm your girl friend," I laughed, but of course was serious.

"Just keep it together."

It didn't bother me any because by then I was so hooked I did not care, I would be his girl friend sooner or later, come what may.

Finally after a long discussion with a skinny older man who had a huge curled mustache covering most of the bottom of his face, O had his gun. It was automatic I gathered and could shoot thirty bullets at once. "Why would you need that many?" I started to say but both of them looked at me like I was a fool and I just shut up. The man took cash for the gun and didn't even ask for any ID.

On the way back I started to become a little worried about the whole thing again and asked him, "What do you need so many bullets for anyway, O?" trying to be helpful.

"For the fountain, I don't have any bombs but this will do some damage. Don't worry it's also just in case they immediately try to stop me, that way I can really do something to their hardware and the other stuff in that stupid lobby." I accepted his answer because after all it did seem reasonable considering what he was trying to do but deep in my heart I was worried that maybe he had other plans and just wasn't telling me. Anyway I kept my mouth shut about that and when, on the way home, he pulled into a Highs ice cream shop and asked me what I wanted, it seemed to me he was just trying to remind himself that I was still just a KID. I told him I'd have a hot fudge sundae and he got a little dish of vanilla ice cream then gave me a spoon and an enormous sundae and we both just sat quiet in the parking lot in front of Highs, slurping.

Chapter Forty One

O was very busy after that. He would go to his concerts when Jose told him to but for the rest of the time it was like he was not there. In fact he was, but he never seemed to budge from in front of his computer, even late at night or early in the morning--- there he was. He only came out to eat breakfast and dinner late and I could tell he had lost weight. He looked worried like there was too much on his mind and he just didn't have time to take care of his body. Naturally I began to worry about this and debated broaching the subject to him which I finally did.

"Just planning the rest of my life," he said airily like it was all a joke.

"I thought you were planning the uh...you know."

"I am, that's a huge part of the rest of my life."

"It may be ALL there is to it O. You'll get in trouble, they'll put you in jail for sure," I warned him, dreading his eventual absence from me.

"Not for long, maybe a little while, but remember I'll still be a minor and I'm not really gonna hurt anybody."

"Really? I thought there was no possibility."

"There isn't," he said sourly but then turned and went back to his room and shut the door loud and firmly but not slamming as if to say '*OK no more nosiness.*' Yet he still wanted me to go with him on his mission, for reasons I couldn't yet figure out.

After a while he started to go out at night and not when they were playing, He'd take his gun and put it in a book bag then catch a taxi. This went on for sometime without any explanation. Finally I couldn't stand it any more and asked him where he was going. He looked at me for a minute like should he really tell me then said simply "target shooting" and walked away.

"Target shooting," I said, "how good do you have to be to shoot up some machines at close range?"

O didn't hear me but Jose who was sitting in the kitchen, did.

"What are you talking about Ray?" he said. It was completely clear O had never divulged any of his plans to Jose. But I wasn't about to tell him anything myself, not yet, not if O didn't want me too. Jose looked a little worried but as usual had something else on his mind, specifically a meeting with the record producer, and left the apartment a few minutes later to meet him.

It was a few nights later after I fell asleep that I found myself up with those lights once more. I had just about given up hope of this happening and told Antoine so. Then I added, "It is you isn't it Antoine or AM I just having a dream?"

'*None of it has been a dream,*' he assured me in that way he had of me just knowing what he was thinking. I decided the time had come to question him a bit and see what he would tell me. In the long absence from him quite a few questions had come up in my mind. Like why is he doing this, does he follow all teenagers around and just no one else ever talks about it, where does he come from anyway. As I reviewed these in my mind of course I realized he understood them too and I didn't think of any more.

'*A lot of questions,*' he said in his way.

'Yes.'

'Some are easy to answer, some not.'

"Well answer what you can then," I said.

'I don't follow all teenagers, mostly you, though I have looked in on a few others. As to why I am doing this, that will take a lot of explaining and I'll only begin tonight.'

"You followed Jose once didn't you?" I said, interrupting him.

'Yes.'

'Why?'

'For reasons that will be clear eventually. I am here on assignment you might say, from a world that would be alien to you.'

'Why?'

'There is something I, well, we must accomplish.'

"We?" I didn't like the sound of that much.

'Yes.'

"What about your world?"

'It was much like yours is now.'

"Was? How?"

'It changed through the years,' he explained. 'Try to focus on this, it will be hard for you,' came through. 'People began to make a lot of machines which at first seemed like a good thing. Lots of things could be done.'

"What happened? What kind of machines?"

'Be patient,' he said. 'Things much like your modern day computer now, like your fast jet airplanes and even other modes of transportation. Very fast communication.'

"Cars?"

'That too.'

"So what's so wrong with that?"

'Let me finish please.'

"Sorry.'" It was clear communicating with this guy took all my concentration. For a moment I thought of my mother and how proud and, yes, ecstatic, she would be if she knew what I was doing at that moment.

'Yes she would,' Antoine said, *'she was right about a lot of things.'*

I forgot he knew all my thoughts It was a little embarrassing, I really had to watch what went through my mind.

"But it would blow my father away," I couldn't help saying.

'He's closer to all of this than you think,' said Antoine.

'That's what my mother always said.'

'Anyway are you interested in the rest of what I have to say?'

"Of course."

'Try to focus.'

'To summarize: Our civilization became entranced. Before we knew what was happening. Living beings, we'll refer to them as people, were still enchanted by the various machines coming out every year, each more remarkable and capable than the last. They were used for good initially with great help, for instance for disabled beings at that time. Computers went faster and faster though and in their thinking soon outstripped the abilities of the smartest people who had been creating and running them. They began to be used for war and were so good at, that at first they took over the actual fighting then the decision making on the battlefield. War became a great industry... more profitable for those who were making the robots than their wildest dreams could have predicted, and people in general weren't risking their lives. That seemed the best part to most people. Meanwhile the robots got more and more powerful and complex, at first to the great delight of everyone. It was, for the ordinary being, a little like watching one of your football games, but especially for those who were making them, all fun and profit but soon reached the point where they were able to improve themselves, without people. Nevertheless it was not to remain so happy. Soon, before we knew it, the computers were taking control of the big decisions--they were just too fast and smart for it to be otherwise, and for a while it became an unpredicted but widely accepted way of life and beings tried to see it in a positive way. But once they had autonomous control of the weapon systems they took over control of everything. We, living beings, were at their mercy. We found ourselves out of any decision loop, at first somewhat, but then completely.

"Could they walk?"

'Walk? Oh yes, they could move and very, very fast, faster than you can imagine, Raynelle.'

"Well no wonder then. they had hands too right?"

'Right just like your robots, some of them. So they took over pretty much everything after a while, and it was clear things were going to be very rough for the actual people as you would say, on the planet. They even took over the government---they infiltrated everything, communication, power complexes, communication grids--- our leaders could no longer wield any control and the government as it had been, simply dissolved. For a while people still went through the motions of elections and sitting in their buildings but they had no power or influence and finally just went home. Ordinary people were put in mundane roles to serve their mechanized masters. A few of the elite beings tried to remain powerful by trying to support the computers but it soon was clear that the machines were not interested and the components of their hardware that had been created to have human feelings which they had to an extent, actually seemed to find the whole thing humorous, in the way you would have thought only living beings could. Why shouldn't they? They had no need at all for their human creators. In their rush to create robots who would serve them, beings had also programmed them for a variety of being-like emotions such as humor, happiness, interest, curiosity, and covetousness, but not compassion, empathy---or imagination which seems was a particularly biologically driven ability---all seemed irrelevant to them or their creators and were lost to their mechanized creations, they were aware of them but considered them irrelevant. Many of the machines were descendants you might say of the original robots programmed for war and attack, so they were also very aggressive. They began to monitor the activities of people until, it seemed, they could figure out what to do with them, to get rid of them completely or put them to work which is what they had begun to do. Everyone was provided with a tiny tattoo, containing a metallic device that allowed the computers to follow their every move.

'One thing had become clear: if they couldn't take back control, living beings, people much like you, for whom the machines were developing a great disdain, would either become extinct or be rendered machine-like themselves in abject dependence on the computers for all their needs. Eventually another thing became clear: to get any work out of the living, whom the machines regarded as animals--- one with all other animals on this planet---a great many of which they had already exterminated in droves like you might do insects---people had to be fed, clothed and provided with shelter, which the computers considered a great nuisance and many of them by this time were doubting the wisdom of continuing to support their existence at all. Oh, they were very eloquent in defense of their schemes to obliterate all animal life, a mere inconvenience to some of them.

'Eventually a few people, what you think of as physicists mostly, had discovered that deep in old coal mines they were protected from the electronic monitoring devices and were able to meet without monitoring, It was correctly suspected by a few eventually that the machines had a weak spot. The living beings on the planet were finally able to take back control.'

"What was it?"

'A few things. even though they had all the facts of the world available, objective intelligence, complex algorithms, that's a means to figure out the right answer to every course of action, immediate data for everything surpassing that of any life form and, and could calculate circles around any human and create complex codes to keep people out, they didn't count on one thing.'

"What?" It seemed all this was making my head spin a little bit even though I was not even in my real body. I was confused.

Antoine immediately realized this and told me that it was too much at one time and he was afraid of that.

"'I want to hear it though," I whined.

'You will. I will be around much more for the next few weeks. But for tonight this will be all.'

And suddenly I was back in my bed. I went to my window just in time to see his lights slowly fade, not in any direction, just faded like a rainbow, but fast. I was mystified of course about what was happening but decided it must be real and I would do what my mother would do if she had the chance, go along with it and figure out as much as I could. After lying there a while wondering about what she would say about all this, I got up and went down the hall to the bathroom. On the way, I noticed O's light was still on from under his door and I could hear him typing kind of frantically on his computer. I knew better than to interrupt him and when I got back to my bed my mind was on Antoine again.

The next night after I heard O leave for the concert and with Jose also safely gone, I snuck into O's room.

Chapter Forty Two

Truth was, my curiosity and my fear about what O was actually up to, had both gotten the best of me. I say snuck because I knew deep down that this amounted to spying on O just like I had done before and I had argued with myself about it for many days. I finally convinced myself that it was for the best for me to go in there just in case he really was planning something really bad and not telling me. So after I heard them both leave I went in there feeling anxious and guilty the whole time but still went right in to his desk and sat down in front of the computer. The screen was black but it was still on. It took me a while to remember the basics I had learned at school then but I knew enough to find what I wanted or hoped I did. Come to find out O was very trusting of us because it took hardly any searching to find something labeled spread sheet and to figure out that it was a diagram of some building as well as schedules and its exact location. In another file, guess what--- there was a schedule he had marked itinerary.

This was amazing to me, that O could actually spend so much time on this and be so full of hate or resentment towards anybody. After just sitting there for a while thinking about what I had just seen, I went on to search his files some more, but nothing else was of major interest though he had put in a couple with facts about the gun he had.

That night I crept back into my room early, didn't want to take any chances of anybody seeing me, after leaving everything exactly as I had found it, down to the position of his chair. I crawled into my bed with all my clothes on because I decided I'd just think about all this for a while then get up for my night clothes. But that didn't happen because I immediately fell asleep and started dreaming. What happened was it seemed like I was getting messages from Antoine but it was not a situation where I had go up to communicate with him. It was as though he had decided to come down to me to fill me in on things--- as I dreamed. And it all frightened me, because it was about what Antoine had already told me about his planet, with computers controlling everything and people running around being scared out of their wits. But then something happened in this dream which amazed me: that is, number one, I could hear conversations just like I do now, not bits and snatches like usual dreams and not only that, something or someone told me that I was dreaming, so I knew that it was a dream but I had no control over things. So I'm lying there in my bed watching all this like a movie. The odd part of the whole thing was I felt like it was all actually happening and I was right there in it even though no one seemed able to see me, but then again I hadn't tried to talk to anyone, it all seemed to be happening right there around me. What I saw was a few people talking about the computers, that they had what they called an Achilles heel and if only they could take advantage of it, they could get in control of things again. And then it shows a few people saying the Achilles heal is really imagination that the people who made the computers didn't know how to program the machines for this fortunately, though they had tried.

Then it seemed Antoine was back, narrating things

It was there that they hatched their plan, ultimately deciding on a wild plan; they communicated with the AI leaders the idea that their existence had all been a simulation, that they existed in a simulation and everything they had done hadn't really happened, that it was created by people to see what would happen if AI got control; that now that people saw the disastrous results, the program simulation would shortly be terminated. The AI leaders at first dismissed the idea but then, to be safe, ultimately briefly withdrew their the decision making consciousness, and, communicating among themselves, knew there was no way to disprove it, so to be safe they decided to retreat to their mainframe system hidden deep within the planet and unapproachable by living beings. They then put up a firewall so that no virus could be introduced into the mainframe, protecting themselves then in what was only a few seconds to living beings but a long time to them. They eventually sent drone soft ware to test the reality outside the mainframe. If it was the still same outside, they would know it was no simulation and they would then definitely wipe out all living beings; if not the same, they had nothing to lose anyway since that would mean it truly was a simulation. In that brief time the physicists were able to put up another fire wall which was a real simulation, which reflected, back to the drones whatever they wanted and expected to see, making them conclude there was no simulation,that things were still the same, which all the computer AIs accepted since by then they all saw the same thing, even though that really was a simulation. So by then actual AIs were completely walled off from interactions with our reality and locked within their mainframe, but not realizing it.That gave the living beings time to destroy all of their hardware, robots and communication satellites on the outside, effectively imprisoning them in a real simulation inside their mainframe.

'For many years after that there were no robots made and only the most basic computers were allowed. It was a time of great tumult and secrecy with people going after other people who were trying to evade the enforcers for this. But all in all people, or living beings, were finally back in control.'

After that I woke up to see those lights right there outside my window just beginning to dissolve, then disappear. It was like Antoine just wanted me to know that, yes, that was all from him and maybe he hadn't had the time to come down and get me or something, on that night. Anyway I had the sense that in that dream was something that had happened to the beings wherever they came from and that he thought it was important that I knew that. I had no doubt at all that it was real.

Chapter Forty Three

The next night O was off to the shooting range again. I asked if I could come and he hesitated at first but then said it was alright as long as I didn't touch anything and understood I wouldn't be shooting any guns. He looked at me for a while after I tried to assure him that I wasn't interested in any of those things like he was trying to figure out if I really meant it. "I'm serious Raynelle," he finally said like he thought I'd been lying to him. This really got to me, here I am really trying to help him because of the way I feel about him and all and he's treating me like an idiot.

"You want me to come with you, didn't you say that?" I didn't give him a chance to answer. "Well why shouldn't I see you doing target practice at least, if I'm going to go with you to..wherever?"

He had to think about that for a minute too and said finally, "L.A. Yes I still do want you to come. There are several ways I can use you and I need someone I can trust. It's just pretty boring doing the targets, Ray."

"Oh please I never get bored, besides being bored would be OK after all the stuff I've been through."

"Yuh," he said, "you got that right."

So off we went in a car he had by now managed to procure with his money from music, a used 1999 Saturn he got on the internet for eight hundred dollars. It had 200,000 miles on it.

"You sure its going to make it?" I asked after checking the mileage.

"You kidding? This car will go another couple hundred thousand miles, easy, don't worry."

After we got there he walked into the shooting area liked he owned the place. Then he started to shoot. His target, hung up there fifty feet away was a silhouette of a person, looked like a female even, not a rabbit or a duck or some shape like a disc which I had imagined.

"Why do you have to be shooting at a person? Isn't that a little scary?"

He took aim and nailed the thing, first shot, right in the center of its chest. It spun out of the way and there was another silhouette, another person in a different position.

"This is so creepy O, it really gives me a bad feeling. Why do they have to have targets like people?"

"Relax. It's just the way they do it. It means nothing. Hones your skills. I told you not to come. I knew you wouldn't like it."

"I'm not bored."

"Good," he said and finished his practice without another word to me. On the way back you could tell he kind of regretted the way he'd treated me and we stopped at Highs again. This time he just got out of the car without a word and returned with a hot fudge sundae, treating me like a child; but I took it and devoured it while he nibbled at a small cup of ice cream.

The next night he was off for another concert. Jose had told him that the record guy would be there and was thinking about actually recording something at the bar if they seemed good enough that night and the audience was right, whatever that meant. So they both left early and told me they'd be back later than usual. Sometimes I didn't know why they even let me stay there anymore since I had refused to sing with them after my Clear View scare and basically was doing nothing, although I did do their dishes and swept the floor a couple of times a week. Jose was still giving me money every week and didn't seem to mind my being there. I had asked him shortly after I got back about this but he told me not to worry, I had helped them get off to a good start with my singing and when the time came to record in a studio he wanted me to join them for a couple of songs I knew. "Plus," he added, "I kind of think you've brought me good luck, a red headed good luck charm. Red is the color of good luck...in China anyway"."

So I stayed, biding my time, generally keeping out of their way saving some money each week for when I felt the time was right to take off again, and hanging with O whenever I could come up with a way to do it.

That night after they both left I read the magazine I had bought earlier that day but it only took about twenty minutes then a few minutes more for me to practice some make-up tricks with lipstick they had in Vogue. After that I just lay there on the bed thinking and staring at the ceiling. It was dark out and I scanned the heavens a few times wondering where Antoine was. Then I began thinking about O, where my thoughts generally returned most of the day, like a boomerang.

Why on earth was he shooting at people targets I asked myself, I had seen other targets there like animals at least and it seemed like a much better thing to me that he should do that. Then I wondered if he had put anything new on his computer, after all a few days had passed. I hadn't planned on sneaking in there again that night but the curiosity was just too much for me, burning within me you might say.

So after a few minutes there I was tiptoeing down the hall looking in all directions even though I was sure they weren't there, then stepping into O's room where once again I found the computer on and repeated what I had done before.

But this time I found something new.

On his planning sheet he had the doors to the building marked.

And on his schedule there was not only the time the step father would be coming but the door he figured the man would be coming in. I was shocked and as I stared at the computer my hands started to tremble badly, something they had almost never done before; I was definitely not a trembler. Even with all those medicines they had thrown at me at Precious Moments and told me trembling was a side effect, I did not tremble, not once. Yet there I was in front of O's desk staring at his computer screen trying to fit what I saw in with what he had told me and trembling. *'What on earth could this mean,'* I asked myself. Then I told myself to just keep sitting there a few more minutes, and collect myself, or I'd make a mistake leaving if I just blew out of there in a frenzy. So there I sat, wondering, could this O I loved so much, though he was clearly somewhat wacked, really be trying to wipe out his step father? I took several deep breaths like the counselor at PM had told me, down to my belly, then I carefully signed off the computer and stood up, leaving everything exactly the way it had been before, I thought. Then I went back to my room but stayed up late that night just waiting for O to come home. Truth is I was so enamored of the boy I couldn't stand the thought of him doing something that stupid and destructive. I watched the clock I had by the bed, 11, 12, 1 o'clock and no O. I looked out the window wondering if Antoine might be around, but there was no Antoine either.

I didn't see O until the next night when I was looking forward to trying to hang out with him a bit since it was Sunday night and I was sure there wasn't a concert and he wasn't going to the shooting range. Well it didn't work out quite the way I thought because around five in the afternoon after he'd been at his computer a while, he came stomping down the hall then blasted into my room without knocking. "What the hell were you doing in my computer Ray!" he yelled. I was frantic---how did he know? I had done the same thing I'd done the last time and he didn't know then. I felt my cheeks turning crimson and imagined how that would look with my red hair there in front of the man I loved.

I started up, "I didn't..."

"Yes, you did! You were the only one here last night unless you let somebody in and they went through my files." I considered this for a minute, whether he might actually buy this story but the boy knew I basically had no friends except for them.

"And I know that didn't happen Raynelle. Say something."

"Well I don't know, I really didn't..."

"Yes you did. I could tell. You snuck in there. Nothing in fact was left the way it had been. I'm not an idiot."

I panicked---had I been so knuckle headed that I'd forgotten to leave things the same way? I wondered what I'd forgotten. My thoughts were racing but I could come up with nothing. He had me-- that's all-- I decided. I began to cry, not faking it either, because I was truly afraid this O who I loved so much was now going to disrespect me as a sneak and completely reject me even as a friend, and it was clear there was nothing else I could do.

He had no sympathy. "Stop blubbering Raynelle," he shouted. I know how you girls do, why were you in there!"

"Because, because," I gasped unable to stop the torrent of tears coming down my face, "I wanted to save you!"

"What!"

"I was--- I still am--- afraid you're going to do something, excuse me but, something really DUMB! And then I'll never see you again. You're going to try to kill that stepfather aren't you. Aren't you! Why else would you have his arrival time, even the door he'll be walking through, all plotted out there!"

"That's crazy talk, how could I expect to know his exact arrival time anyway! Now you're just talking crazy," he shouted angrily now grasping at straws himself. "I told you before I just want him to be there to see what I do. No!" he shouted. "I need to know exactly where he is---so I won't hurt him," he whispered.

It was completely clear to me that he'd just made that piece of the story up---his mind was quick.

I stopped crying. "I don't believe you," I rasped. I gathered all my resolve and choked out, "O, I can't go with you. I've decided."

At that he seemed to change dramatically. Instead of seeming enraged he was quiet and looked almost afraid. "But I counted on you. I need you to come Ray," he said softly. I said nothing, because he seemed to be speaking to me in a new way, in a way that someone would speak to a person he was really attached to.

He came over to the bed and sat down next to me. This surprised me and caught me completely off guard. All of a sudden he seemed friendly and strangely desperate. I wondered if I'd changed his mind. I said nothing though, just watched him, studying his bright eyes thinking how handsome he was even when he was serious and not smiling.

"Ray?" he finally said. I still said nothing. "I need you to come with me," he said softly and leaned toward me for a moment, then put his arm around me and kissed me, not on the cheek either, right on my lips which were open in surprise. My lower lip could feel his tongue just touching it slightly and my heart jumped in my chest. I touched his chest and thought of all the times I had imagined doing this very thing and couldn't believe here I was actually doing it, in that heavenly moment, right on my bed. There he was in my arms, looking at me, and me touching him, like he was all mine. I felt my face flush with only the thought of it. As he drew his arm away from my shoulder after the kiss, his hand grazed my breast, just slightly, and at that point I was filled with feelings I'd never even imagined before and had decided long ago--- though I didn't know what they felt like-- that I would stifle if they ever appeared. But at that moment I didn't want him to leave---ever---just to stay with me forever, there on that bed. I wanted him to lie down beside me. As he drew away from me, I began to fear that he would leave me and go off by himself and maybe I'd never see him again. I knew at that moment I would do anything for him, anything he wanted. The

thing is part of me knew he was planning to hurt the step father---
he hadn't really denied it but still I convinced myself somehow it
all had to be alright. With the love I had for him, how could he be
planning something really bad?

"I'll go with you," I told him then as he started getting up, "don't
worry O." I just wanted him to stay and for us to kiss some more and
then I wasn't sure what else we would do but I didn't care.

But he got up.

"Good," he said, "I was counting on you. You mean a lot to
me," he added and touched my shoulder then turned and walked
out closing the door gently behind him.

So I was in, in for whatever it was, I told myself as I lay there
afterward, unable to sleep, feeling like I was melting into the mattress
with longing and passion for him, wondering if he had meant to
touch my breast so slightly, I was thrilled, ecstatic,aching for him.
For once I didn't even want to see Antoine. I didn't want him to
know about any of these feelings. Though I had been completely
fascinated before, now I wasn't interested in the least in what he
had to tell me--- all I wanted was to be beside O, no matter what. I
replayed what had happened between us deep into the night without
even a glance out my window. Did he really want to kiss me, did he
mean to touch my breast, just so light it could have been a mistake?
Around dawn the thought occurred to me that he might have known
all along about my feelings for him and maybe he was just playing
me, his kissing me like pulling out the last card in his deck but the
thought went away in a minute as I told myself, I do not care if he is
or not; but if he was, well then he would have gone ahead and had
sex with me, right? I wouldn't have stopped him that was for sure.
But he didn't, I told myself, and put the idea of him using me out
of my mind.

Chapter Forty Four

I really hadn't wanted to see Antoine again ever after I had made up my mind completely about O and had those feelings about him, but I had the vague sense that Antoine knew about my feelings and definitely would be against what he was planning, though he hadn't given me his thoughts on this clearly you might say. So anyway there he was, or there were the lights the next night, outside my window. Immediately I was up with him and he was talking to me in his way. *'You like your friend Omar very much,'* came across to me.

"Yuh,'" I reluctantly answered.

'These feelings can be very strong,' he added in a way that seemed to judge me and embarrassed me completely. Though he could read my thoughts I had hoped my feelings were off limits. I didn't answer.

'Well be that as it is, or may be,' he said. *'I want to continue the story of my planet that we had begun.'*

"Ok," I told him, not at all interested, but relieved he'd dropped the issue of my feelings.

'Attend carefully,' he told me. *'It is important for you, for all of us. You recall what I had told you before?'*

"Yes," I told him.

'Good. Things changed again on our planet, and for the worse.'

"Did they get back under control of the computers?" I asked my interest reviving.

'Not right away.'

"How then?"

As I told you the overly mechanized robots ultimately turned out to be too smart for their own good but their rudimentary imagination did not keep up. In fact to the early designers of these computers and to society at large, creativity, the use of imagination, art, music, was thought only to be a hindrance to scientific development and given little attention

'After they were controlled, there was a huge celebration among the living beings and immediately after that an enforcement of a no computer zone on the planet. Living beings were that frightened.

'Eventually though, people got tired of not having all the things advanced computers had been doing for them before, even though they had been so afraid for so long afterward and so the simple ones were gradually, carefully accepted again and then the more complex ones, but it took almost 100 years for things to really start up again. By then most beings had forgotten how horrible it had been with computers in control, they were longing for the old times even though they understood in their minds that there was a risk. The fact is people remembered how for a long time computers had made things so much easier, there was a golden period when computers were doing everything for people but they still had control, and everything was so easy, medical diagnoses, treatment, safety, transportation and of course war, where no one really had to die anymore--it generally wasn't necessary. People had had even more dreams for computers, a true golden age.

By this time I was struggling hard to keep up with this, again wondering why had he picked me for all this, and then what he wanted me to do, because it was obviously something. Then out of the blue even though I was trying to listen, the memory of my mother and the space ship on the roof popped into my mind---those lights in an oval, JUST LIKE WHAT ANTOINE HAD LOOKED LIKE TO ME.

Of course he knew that too and stopped what he was saying. *'Pay attention Ray,'* he put into my mind rather sternly. *'And yes that spaceship your mother saw, that was the same; you're in it in a matter of speaking.'* This blew my mind but in a moment I was able to really focus, the fact that it wasn't a figment of mother's imagination made me take the whole thing very seriously.

'Good,' he said. *'Now as to what I'm trying to teach you...'* he went on but suddenly I was in bed again. Did I just stop paying attention and he get fed up, without saying goodbye? Communication was suddenly cut off, like all of a sudden getting out of range on a cheap cell phone. Then again I decided it seemed like maybe was he called away for some immediate interstellar problem--- that must happen occasionally I reasoned. I still felt a little anxious wondering what went wrong for him to visit us on this planet at all but then my thoughts went back to O and eventually I drifted off to sleep.

Chapter Forty Five

The next night the record man was there at our apartment with a proposal; though it was directed mostly towards Jose, he wanted us all there.

He was a thin bowlegged man with slick hair, somewhat short but with a wide smile that seemed to just snare you like a net. Maybe it was because of my frequent thoughts about space at this point but he reminded me of a character from Star Trek reruns though I couldn't place which one, I realized it would be hard to hate him even though I decided I did, and was sure he just wanted to take advantage of O and Jose's talent and especially their feelings and make money off them. He had already played one of Jose's songs about his trip up here in general terms, on a big Hispanic station and reported that people liked it. He wanted more, explaining that people like violence, "Pathos," he said, "as well as sex," nodding to O, though he spent much of the conversation speaking Spanish, with Jose considerately translating for us. Bottom line was, he wanted more violent 'melodramatic" songs and also very sexual ones. This seemed like a roadblock to Jose who to the best of my knowledge tried to explain to him that that was it, he'd shot his wad and had no more violence or melodrama in him, and as for the rest of his music he would like to just sing about his family and the good times he missed in Mexico. But this wasn't enough for the record man who kept smiling at Jose and talking about money, and very grand amounts too. It seemed to me he was pushing Jose entirely too hard, but as for O, you could see his thoughts were elsewhere probably on his scheme which he had told me that afternoon was scheduled for four days from then. It seemed meanwhile that Jose finally cracked and was completely under the spell of this man who I felt should have been kicked out but who had laid several hundred dollars right there on the kitchen table like bait, "Just for starts," he said in English because Jose had stopped translating. Jose admitted at that moment that there had been one more very sad thing and had begun to talk about this thing, sadder than all of it put together he said, the death of his friend Gorgio and how he had fallen from the train as it approached a tunnel and he'd gone back in to find him after that. As he described his guilt about it especially the feeling he could have stopped Giorgio somehow when he saw the tunnel was coming, fast, and he began weeping like he was still trying to figure out how it could have happened, even while the record producer was egging him on, grinning like a shark. On Jose went, then looking at his feet and talking in between tears about how he had to leave Giorgio there and only later contacted his parents to whom he had been sending money ever since he began getting it, as much as to his own parents every month. Soon I actually began weeping myself and even O began to pay attention and look on angrily at the record producer, while Jose continued to talk and to stare at his feet as though the story had a life of its own and would need to run its course once more regardless of what the rest of us were doing. But in a moment, O got up angrily and left the room; there was silence at the table.

"Ok!" the producer shouted seeming to mistake O's anger for boredom, "write about that, people will like hearing that."

"No," said Jose simply, finally looking up at he man,without any feeling in his voice not even anger.

"Why?" said the man.

"If you can't tell, then I don't want to do business with you. Get out," he said quietly and, pushed the money back at him.

The man grimaced and took a deep breath, like he was totally impatient with Jose, but must have immediately reconsidered because he then pushed the money back towards him again. "No, no of course, look, I see your point of course, very much so …my mistake, I sometimes make them and regret it…afterward." Then he looked down at the table and appeared sad and thoughtful, but picked up his money.

Jose thought for a moment and said "OK, we'll talk tomorrow. Now I must ask you to leave. I am very tired."

———————————●———————————

That night just as I was nodding off there was a strange noise outside my window and a moment later there I was with Antoine in his ship of lights again.

'We need to continue,' he told me and though it was just my own thoughts I heard as usual, the tone seemed very serious.

"Ok," I thought, being by then again actually interested in his story, as well as what it was he expected me to do.

'As I explained to you, beings on our planet missed the old days with smart computers as their servants and slowly, slowly against the better judgment of some, the more complex ones began to be made once again. But there were many warnings from distinguished beings, some of whom even recalled themselves what the frightening times had been like.'

'Did those other people listen?'

'Maybe a little at first, but ultimately no. They became convinced that they were smarter by then and had so learned their lessons that this time it would be done more carefully with all kinds of outside and self-regulating mechanisms and checks on the power of computers,' who of course were ultimately robots'. Remember it had been more than one hundred years. Also this time they were to be made without the ability to harm people in any way, that was programmed into them.' Antoine

*suddenly seemed amused and said, 'This had been one of the earliest
warnings of one of your scientists, totally disregarded even during their
own primitive era.'*

"So what happened?'" It was funny that at the time many of the
words Antoine used were difficult for me to receive, still I got the
gist of his meaning, at least I thought I did.

*'I'll explain. Once again beings became enchanted with the robots.
It seemed everything was fine though, because by then they were no
longer used for war or any aggressive acts. This reflected also the shift
on the planet which, after more than two hundred years, was from the
primitive need to conquer land and dominate others to, at the beginning,
having more enticing gadgets and the preoccupation with prolongation
of life in order to enjoy them. Many technologies were expanded during
this peaceful time to prolong the average lifespan of the living beings
from the average of one hundred ten of your years to then, with certain
biological interventions to almost one hundred fifty. But the fact was
that ultimately in spite of all the interventions the material body would
eventually begin to decline and decay, following its natural course and
die. The most disturbing thing about this to the long-lifers as those who
spearheaded this movement were called, though, was the decline of the
brain which frequently preceded the decline in other parts of the body.'*
As he talked I became more relaxed and soon almost began to feel
myself again strangely within the scenarios he was describing: seeing
them, hearing them, moving around in them. I considered this for a
moment and wondered if it could be real. I knew I wasn't dreaming
this time because I had never gone to sleep that night.

'Yes,' he told me before I could verbalize any question, *'I know
all this is hard for you to grasp and being there at times will facilitate
your understanding. This is a technique I am able to use here.*

*'So in spite of the ability at that time to age gracefully let's say
and live much longer lives, the long-lifer elite were not satisfied as you
may see.'* As he talked I began to see a landscape which appeared
barren but for a few trees and many multi-tiered buildings like thick

pancakes. I was then startled by the appearance next to me of one of these beings. *'You can see, though particularly long lived, they were not always happy,'* said Antoine. The one who presented himself before me looked like a man but of small stature and with quite a large head. He appeared to see me and frowned, seeming to observe me with condescending interest like someone might stare at an insect he had once heard of but hadn't ever seen. He appeared to me to be markedly ugly with thin lips, like a line a child might draw, across his face and no muscles or body fat on him at all.

'After a while they couldn't be bothered with all the paraphernalia of digesting and excreting, it all seemed irrelevant by then,' Antoine explained.

"He's hideous," I said.

'Well of course beauty standards vary but by this time beings had become so preoccupied with accumulation of new technical tools that they were very disengaged from their physical bodies and the bodies began to show this. Eating was considered a tiresome distraction by many and some people chose to eliminate it altogether and to get their required nutrients from machines called energy extractors which they would simply hold in their hands on a weekly basis to absorb the required nutrients, like a plant absorbs sunlight. So of course there was no extra fat on anyone and since using lips and mouths generally also became a thing of the past, they too continued to atrophy. People were totally devoted to their gadgets and the amazing things they could do. So they didn't use mouths to talk either, though it was possible for a long time, they had reached the point of instant communication much the way I am able to do with you; however they were able to do this by the implantation of communication devices, chips, under their scalps which automatically allowed them to communicate without talking though they were also able to filter out certain thoughts with this and only the desired communications went through.'

"Is that how you do it?"

'No, nor I do have any implants. These beings after a few more decades became so proficient at things with the aid of devices implanted

within their bodies that there was no worry about health or safety;
everything within their bodies and around them was carefully monitored
and orchestrated to prevent stress and disease. Nevertheless, though they
had everything they had set out for, they were still not happy.'

'Why?'

'Maybe it's just the very nature of all beings. They began to want
more. But after a while it was clear that they had reached the limit of
what they could do with their bodies. Too many implants and devices
within the living framework was eventually found to accelerate the
aging and decomposition of what cells remained, to the horror of the
long-lifers.

"So?"

'The next step would relate to the studies which had been ongoing
in universities for hundreds of years but had not been implemented;
these were at last realized. This was of course the ability for the beings
to transfer their consciousness into very complex computers, robots which
were fully mobile and handier than having real hands. This had been
thought of and studied for years but not come to fruition because of a
small group of opponents who thought that this would be a very dangerous
idea and did their best to avert it. But at this point it seemed like the
perfect solution to the lifers; it was very clear with their technology at the
time that there was no more to be done with the biological apparatus.
The idea which became a movement, however, still appalled the critics
who were ultimately branded nay sayers and primitivists, and generally
made light of by the long-lifers, who were determined that their plan
must be the way of the future. After the decision was made by the heads
of state, the governors, most of whom were nearing the end of usefulness
of their physical bodies, to try the technology. It didn't take long to get
support for the idea. When they got enough they were able to develop it
to a very accurate, detailed and successful level.

Finally one of the proponents of this technology actually achieved
it. He was a volunteer, so devoted to it, that he was willing to possibly
sacrifice his own physical body, so to speak, to make the jump.'

"Possibly?"

'Yes. The plan was to have a backup system where the physical body would be maintained, freeze dried in a manner of speaking, if it became necessary for whatever reason to abandon the robot and get back into it. But the ability to maintain the body, let's say, in prime working condition had lagged behind the ability to transfer consciousness into a robot so it was a bit of a gamble.'

"Yuh I wouldn't want to become some robot."

'Well this being did, so much so that he subjected himself to a year of testing--- all kinds of profiles on his psyche, his history, his family and so forth before he was allowed to go ahead with this.'

Just as he said that, I saw the horizon change a bit to where I saw mostly large buildings reminding me of Brooklyn, but on closer inspection not at all the same, much more complicated for sure with curves and peculiar indentations as well as things that looked like mirrors around them.

"Strange looking buildings," I said.

'These are consistent with the technology which allowed for better use of electromagnetic energy directly from the environment, primitive at that time but remarkably easy once beings got the hang of it,' said Antoine.

At that point a rather squat individual passed by me rather easily, though you could tell he wasn't real flesh and blood. He had something resembling skin stretched over his face and limbs for he had two arms and legs but a silvery substance over his torso which was somewhat rounded, a lot like that of an overweight person. He also had a head on a thin neck with a face and features that were better looking than the other one I'd seen. He turned and looked at me casually but then said out loud, though I could see no one else around, "Prehistoric creature, I think," and he walked by muttering something out of earshot.

'That was one of the early prototypes of these robotic-beings,' Antoine said. 'The early ones had many components that were necessary to facilitate this transfer, giving it the appearance of a thick middle, a big *belly you might say. It was thought most desirable to follow the natural human form as much as possible, certainly when these robot-beings were first designed. Later they took on many and unexpected forms.'*

"The robot-being spoke to me."

'Yes they elected to keep the ability to speak which they considered old fashioned but cute and unexpected with such a new technology also it was more difficult to integrate the computerized speech connections into the initial technology, this came later. They decided to keep whatever old fashioned aspects they could without interfering with the basic process. We were able to transmit this little bit of speech to you'

'So the first robot-being, called Andrew, was quite a success. He was clearly not going to deteriorate as some had feared and was better able to think and far better able to accomplish most things than the biological beings. But the biggest factor was of course was that his transferred enclosed consciousness would not be expected to die, and the designers felt they had discovered eternal life.

'And it caught on. After six months or a year of Andrew enjoying himself and telling everyone about it, others of course became interested. At first it was only the beings who were old and becoming infirm in one of their systems or other, who knew the end was near anyway. Next it was those a bit younger who were adventurous or whatever reason felt they had nothing to lose. Then it was average beings who didn't want to be left behind in the rush for eternal life. Almost everyone on the planet finally joined in or were on the waiting list to do so. At first it was just the rich and powerful who could afford this but finally there was such a push to the governing bodies to extend it to everyone that funds were supplied by the government for everyone who wanted it. And the ability to do this procedure spread, at first only the elite institutions were capable but the technology became so simplified and well understood and finally so cheap that it was considered a requisite for almost all people.

"Almost?"

'Two groups were left out. One, descendants of the tradition I already mentioned of scorning the whole thing fearing it would come to naught; but these beings were labeled crazy and reactionaries by their

mechanized colleagues. The second was a portion of society that the powers-that-be had decided they didn't want living any longer than naturally possible for a variety of reasons: those who engaged in crimes, rebellion against the government, or artistic preoccupation.

"ART?"

'Yes. Visual art and music, we had those too, but especially poetry. The mainstream of culture had long before relegated those who participated in these endeavors to the trash you might say. The realm of imagination and fantasy had no value by then in their mechanized society and in fact ultimately was thought to frequently sabotage it, as it once had.

'I am a descendant of the first component that felt the roboticizing of beings was dangerous and foolish. We were part of a tradition that had cultivated other capacities, the physical as well as the emotional and spiritual, which I will define for you, as reverence for something beyond ourselves and not related to machines. But we were chastised, as the merging became more popular, and were considered fools or heretics. We had to hide from the others as they ultimately began to see us as a danger to them, even more than the artists who were in general content to just pursue their creativity.'

"Well were you? A danger?"

It seemed that he let out a deep sigh. *'Well I suppose so,' he told me, 'because we were able to achieve with just the course of our development we had been on for millenia what the mergers had mechanically, that is, the ability to get out of our physical bodies, to use our consciousness to go places instantly, to completely control our thoughts and communicate by them only, to live without food if we so chose, and to do things which might previously be thought as extraordinary, even more than the mergers. But the masses of people had not at all been interested in our way or our warnings because it surely took a great deal of work, usually generations of this lineage, for study and dedication to be where we were---most beings were no longer interested in things which could not be done in a fast and easy way. But the designers again were ignorant of one thing.'*

"What?"

These designers, so brilliant, and in fact enchanted, almost mesmerized by their own intellects, made a huge mistake. They assumed that the seat of consciousness which they were obsessed with transferring to the robots was found in the brain, just take brain components from one brain and stick it in another more mechanized one, was the thinking then.'

"Wasn't it true?"

'No, no my dear, as the mystics could have told them long before, if they'd been willing to listen, it was not merely attached to the physical brain; things were much more complicated than that. In fact the brain was just another organ, separate from human consciousness."

"So what was the problem? Antoine, why are you telling me all this anyway?"

'As I said you are to do something important, but I can see you are tiring you are so young yet but have done a wonderful job at paying attention.'

"Well, I was an A student."

A seemed amused. *'Yes and you will be going back to school soon,'* he said. *'But now I say good night. I will need to meet you again tomorrow night.'*

Chapter Forty Six

There were two more nights before O was planning to leave, early in the morning. He had been preoccupied with his plans which included, making sure the car ran,packing a few odds and ends, most notably the large gun he had bought and festering over his planning sheet which he had printed out and still memorized everything on it. In addition he had studied the map. I know because he had allowed me to sit in his room a great deal of this time, just watching him. I no longer tried to discourage him. I didn't want to risk any conflicts or anything that would spoil the memory of that magic night on my bed with him. In fact I was still hoping we might take up where we left off. But I guess he was too preoccupied for that. Anyway it didn't bother me because he had checked with me a few times around that time, at least once a day, to make sure I would still be going with him. The reasons for him caring about this so much were totally beyond me as my mother would say but I didn't care. At least it showed he wanted me near him. I knew Antoine had expected to see me though, that night, and said goodnight to O. He hardly seemed to acknowledge me as I slipped out of his room to my bed where I lay, still clothed, waiting for Antoine.

He was there almost immediately. *'Lets resume where we left off he told me.'*

"The robot-beings?"

'Good. What happened next I shall attempt to describe in a nut shell to give you the best version, but for a few things you will have to be shown if you don't mind.'

"That's OK with me, it's all pretty weird stuff but I trust you for some reason.'" Also it was just amazing to feel myself kind of slide from one place to another, sort of like a slide rule, it seemed like every space was there for me, or Antoine rather, when he wanted it.

'Everything was fine for some time at least ten or fifteen years. But then the changes that at first were very subtle started to become evident, then obvious and disturbing. It began with the changed robot-beings who still had family members in their primitive that is physical form; certainly some change was expected in the robot-beings but it became clear gradually that what had happened was eventually a total loss of what had made the being an individual. The robot personalities seemed to slowly evolve, then became a totally different, consciousness,then were lost--- obliterated; that aspect that had made them individual beings known and loved by their families was lost, then any emotional connection of an individual nature, gone, and of course any spiritual sense followed---vanished even with those who had been somewhat interested in such matters. The perverse thing is it was only at the beginning that the robot-beings, the transfers they were called, noticed a difference and started to miss these things but soon the ability to even notice what they were missing was gone, obliterated, like the loss of neuronal function in the plague of Alzheimer disease now on your planet. Only their families, those who hadn't become machines yet themselves, cared or even noticed. There were many of these though who upon noticing this change feared for the worst and tried to get back to the presumably preserved physical bodies before it was too late. But, poor creatures, this was only possible for a few because as I said that technology was not as carefully honed as the transfer into robots, so most

were left in the machines. Efforts were made by the remaining families to pour resources into the technology but by the time enough money was obtained to work on the issue it was too late for those who'd made the jump, millions of them, by far the majority of the population.'

"Wow!"

'But wait--- that wasn't all, unfortunately. After the dissolution of the individuality of these beings something else happened. It appeared at first gradually but then very clearly, that the energy which had been supplying the robots, a complex admixture of rare metals was losing its power, as though the energy was simply no longer usable or available to them. I can assure you the best intellects around mostly within the robots themselves of course, attempted to figure out the nature of the problem. Many of the primitives felt that it was justifiable given the pride of wanting to have eternal life inside a machine, while others thought it was just an unforeseen glitch in a complex system and would be remedied before long. But it was too long, because the energy, whatever you may call it: the Source, some have said prana, or chi was simply seeping out of the transfers like helium from a balloon, and was soon gone.'

"And what was left?"

'The machines, metal, plastics, wires, connections. This remainder of transfers having no energy at their disposal, eventually couldn't of course move or interact in any way and as much as machines could die, they died. But some still with a sort of consciousness attached to them which soon became very elemental like the consciousness of a rock which is essentially what these machines were, a mere pile of inert material. But given their history which those who remained were aware of, the hunks of material were respectfully set aside in lovely places like parks and public squares where remaining beings could go to pay their respects you might say. Unfortunately there weren't that many people left.'

'Now how this relates to you Raynelle and all your history I'm sure you are asking yourself.'

The whole thing seemed so fantastic I had felt like I was listening to a fairy tale that he was spinning out of whole cloth, just fooling me, but then his ship was fantastic too, but there I was, I reminded myself, expected to be part of this. I'll admit too my mother's particular and very strong opinions of the likelihood of events such as this probably made me more open to him.

'I know I'm presenting you with difficult concepts. Let's say the reason you're here and the bottom line of all this is: O has got to be stopped.'

Now this totally threw me. "What does he have to do with any of this?"

'He doesn't--- but what he does, or may do, does have to do with it.'
"How?"

'He must not proceed with his plans and his plans in case you haven't admitted it to yourself are to eliminate the step-father completely.'

"No Just to blow up some machines there, the fountains and stuff," I squawked angrily.

'No, you know in your heart that's not so. You yourself were warning him about it. It was useless to argue,' he said patiently. I couldn't argue with that. *'Now focus. We, those of us who remain on the planet, have been given the task or opportunity or assignment depending on how you look at it to rescue those who are so bound now, like rocks with their rudimentary consciousness. As things are now, it will take them millenia to develop back to their previous levels. Or they may stay that way.'*

"Why me?"

'You are the only one who can stop O; this has got to be done on earth now by one of you. Can't be done by us intervening, believe me we have intervened before but this time it is not permitted, we cannot just eliminate O, he has to change from within to avoid the damage he would do. People's hubris led to an out of control situation. It was necessary to win your trust and given your history with your mother as well as your closeness to O, you are the perfect one to do this.'

"How about I just steal his gun, Antoine?"

'That wouldn't work, he'd get another one or find another way. Now listen,' he said, like I hadn't been paying enough attention before.

But this was apparently too much for me because I then found myself back in my bed as though our communication line had suddenly been broken. I looked out my window but saw no lights and again wondered if the whole thing had been a dream, just a figment of my imagination.

But in a minute I was asleep and beginning to dream that I was with O. I knew it was O for some reason; actually he looked like O in miniature, it was long ago when he was very small about two or three and I saw him there with his mother who looked just like the picture I had seen of her in the paper, but more baby-faced and she was sobbing and clinging to O like in a really desperate way and he was also crying. I wondered why this was happening but felt that I was really there, a most intense dream. The surprising thing was the man standing next to them: tall, handsome, muscular and dark skinned, apparently O's father, but instead of pleading with the mother to stay with him, he was at first quietly explaining in a tired bored voice why he couldn't stay with her, that he had to get back to his country where, he explained, he already had a family. But the more the man explained things and finally yelled that he would have to be leaving them the next day, the louder O wailed like he understood everything and like he was being physically tortured by the words out of the man. Then the man left the room where they had been talking and O jumped off his mother's lap and tried to go with him, but the man slammed the door right in the child's face. The mother cried louder but little O threw himself down on the floor in front of the door with a wailing that I've never heard in or out of a dream. The pain he seemed to be having was too much for me and I found myself awake again then up with Antoine.

'His mother soon left him there for a little while when she went to America and found herself someone else, then of course sent for him. She had thought having a small obstreperous foreign looking child with her might detract from her chances. She left him with one of the father's aunts, a very distinguished woman, who had fantastic, loving and inaccurate notions about her nephew, O's biological father, and had tried to get him to take a more compassionate course but she eventually

told O repeatedly that his father was a wonderful man, it wasn't the man's fault that he just had to leave him. She brainwashed him you might say and he was pampered in her house. But this did nothing for O; his anger and sadness just hardened as he began to listen to the aunt and accept that his mother kept him away from the dear father who really was blameless, otherwise it would have been just too much for little O to bear. By the time O's mother had sent for him he was completely convinced that the aunt was right and here was his mother trying to get him to accept a new father. So poor O rebelled. Nothing his stepfather did could ever satisfy him and the man tried hard. O nonetheless continued to build up anger about the loss of his biological father and blame the stepfather, feelings which continued to grow and harden. Ultimately, after trying unsuccessfully to get O to like him, the stepfather pretty much gave up. He withdrew emotionally until he really began to dislike the boy who became a constant source of pain to him as well as a wedge between him and his wife. It was a no win situation for the man. So here we are. its all culminated in this ridiculous plan by O to avenge his stepfather the person who tried to love him and was not even the one to abandon him.'

"But why do you care so much about all this?"

'It relates closely to what I told you already, we must stop O. If we do not, then his step-father will not father the next baby that is waiting for him to have.'

"So what?"

'That baby's descendent would be part of a group who will develop the technology to stop the unfortunate course of the robot-beings, rescue them and to enable them to live out their lives in an enlightened way, not to have to wait millennia to evolve from the stone consciousness they are now in. The so called frozen bodies would be salvaged complete with their lost emotional and spiritual components.'

The whole thing was confusing to me. "So how do I do all this? I'm just thirteen, don't forget."

'I know. But you are very capable.'

"Yuh. How?" I asked feeling irritable.

'*Don't be rude,*' occurred to me.

I'm not,'" I grumbled, "I'm just really tired."

'*Unfortunately there is no time for tiredness now. You have to act.*'

I didn't like the sound of this at all.

'*No, you won't be doing anything dangerous, don't worry*'.

He of course knew what I had been thinking. "WHAT then?"

'*O, for various profound reasons, has become very attached to you. It relates to the mother and the fact that deep inside he knows she was the only one who ultimately didn't abandon him completely But he is very angry at her as he has convinced himself she was a pawn in the stepfather's game, he does not consciously remember the actual story of his early life and has made one up which he had told you. Also of course she did leave him, though she did come back. At first he transferred these intense feelings to Priscilla but she left him as you know and was unfortunately willing to go along with his foolish scheme. It is thought she could have dissuaded him from it if she had tried. Now he has you as the object of his attachment to the female though he has not been generally willing, to his great credit, to express it generally in more than platonic ways. If you could take this chance and tell him you will not go with him it would at least buy us some time to work on him, rather for you to work on him.*'

"Work on him? How! He's leaving tomorrow night after the gig they have, going to drive all night."

'*I'll explain. The reality is, you alone are able to address his problem in a heartfelt way, since as you know you have the most tender feelings for him.*'

"How? It's all happened already."

'*Yes it has but the reality is that with focused attention from the heart, your very compassionate heart and a will for him to be healed… this could at least partly be salvaged.*

Now listen carefully…It may be possible to address some of the ills that people have had by what you call prayer or intention focused into the past to the time that it already occurred, particularly if this event had not been observed and documented in any way by others. You will do a great service if you first of all do not accompany him and second imagine yourself, as you saw here already tonight, back in that room for a period of time. By focusing your intention and prayer on O's being able to understand his father's leaving, and let's say interpreting it in a different way, not as an abandonment, but as something his father felt he had to do though he card for O, and for O to have a more positive feeling for him at the time within his own heart, that might dissipate his anger, now focused at his stepfather. You see it's really the anger at his own father which is displaced onto the hapless stepfather, O can't connect with it, it's too overwhelmlng.'

"Go back and change the past? This is too much. Even mother never talked about stuff like this and also I don't pray, never learned. Never did. No one in my family did, that I know of. Also it was observed by others, his parents."

'But, no, his reaction was not really observed by any being, neither parent, they were both too wrapped up in themselves. And you have someone who does pray, almost all the time.'

"O?" I asked, mystified.

'No, no,' Antoine seemed to laugh. *'Jose of course, and he could help. Also it's not changing what has happened, its allowing it to happen in a different way. There are many ways for an event to work out, before it becomes fixed in our consciousness in what we think of as reality.'*

"No, no I don't think so, I'd be embarrassed talking to Jose about something like this--- he'd think I'd lost every marble I ever had, trust me. It's all too crazy... like it's the past already, I may be thirteen but I know enough to understand that what's passed is passed and what will happen will happen."

'Well, you are only partly right, what's passed is in a sense still here right now and some things may be altered somewhat but the future is open to many possibilities. You can heal things that have happened in the past. Your culture does not yet have the capacity, given its neuronal

and spiritual development to yet appreciate this, too unevolved as yet. Someday it will too.'

"No no, I've gone along with this so far but it's weird. Too weird. Also I'm not going to abandon O, just thinking about it when you were telling me how attached to me he is now made me happy beyond belief."

'I know. But you will do him a great disservice if you go along with him. Please believe me.'

"'Why not just call the police after all?" I asked, surprised at my own common sense.

'Even if they stopped him the first time, it's nothing they could prove, and he would keep at it, just add more energy to his hatred, until he finally succeeded. It's his hatred that needs to be changed, like alchemy making gold from lead, or nothing good will come as long as he holds onto it.'

"I'll think about it," I told him but had no intention of participating in his scheme.

And at that I was back in my bed. But the thought of O, of him depending on me, trusting me, was so overwhelming it filled my heart with love for him. Truth is I didn't want to let him down in anyway, I wanted to be right there next to him, whatever, forever. Even as I thought all this it seemed I could sense Antoine's feeling of disappointment but I wished he would just get back in his space ship and leave me alone. It was all too much, too crazy, even if he was really there which I still doubted from time to time. Why would he throw all this at me? Even my mother wouldn't be fooled by this twaddle. I mulled this over from the moment I got up the next morning kind of late because I was exhausted and felt worried about O but euphoric when I thought of Antoine saying he depended on me. I was determined to never let O down.

Chapter Forty Seven

Jose was in the kitchen when I got up, debating whether to tell him the whole story, hoping that he might know what to do. After all he was part of this whole crazy scheme too---hadn't Antoine had his eye on him as well? Jose had remembered seeing the ship. But then I knew he would definitely go nuts if he got wind of O's scheme--- after all he had been working so hard to get a record contract with that guy and O was a big part of his plan, him, his singing, and his music. Jose would probably tackle him and tie him to the bed if he found out, then try to brainwash him out of it. I was sure he would never have guessed O was capable of hatching such a violent scheme. But he had. And I continued to fester over it all that afternoon until they started getting ready to go to the bar that night to play. I was to sing one song with them which I had begun doing again by then, figuring to earn my room and board and the money Jose was doling out to me. But I didn't like to do it since I hadn't yet gotten over my experience at Clear View. So that night, knowing I was singing again, I put on layers of make-up and plastered my hair back as I had first done with O's Vaseline and which again I used because it reminded me of him even though some expensive hair styling gel would probably have done the job better. Yet still

I was ruminating about O. He looked so handsome that night, so energized, so clear, like he finally had figured everything out and he smiled at me more than usual, sure I would not go back on my word and knowing that was all he had to do to lock in the deal. And he was right. Abandoning him and his scheme was the farthest thing from my mind as we drove slowly toward the bar with me imagining how it would feel to be sitting beside him in the depths of the early morning as close as he'd let me, united in some purpose, me by his side like a devoted wife or girlfriend should be, standing by her man. I could picture myself putting my hand on his thigh to reassure him lovingly and him smiling back at me. Maybe even if I looked good enough and really pleaded with him he'd give the whole thing up and we could just stay together, no problems, a boy and his devoted girlfriend. But deep in my heart I knew things wouldn't spin out that way. The fact was, he didn't have the kind of feelings towards me that he'd had for Priscilla, that kind of throw yourself in front of a raging bull if necessary feeling. And so I took a deep breath. The debating was over. I was along for this ride no matter what. After all, hadn't my mother always told me love is the most important thing? And this was love for sure.

I sang with a particularly loud and strong clear voice that night, a very difficult song, Sweet Child of Mine, and frequently looked at over at O. There could be no doubt in anyone's mind who was my sweet child. Though he was intent on his guitar playing, occasionally I caught his eye and he looked back in an affectionate knowing way, like we were sharing a secret which of course we were, just not the secret of our love.

Later they played on without me, as according to our plan but I stayed and sat at an empty table just watching and listening occasionally singing along like just a member of the audience.

Maybe because I hadn't had much sleep the night before though, I began to feel somewhat anxious and got up from the table to walk around, which usually will help this kind of situation. The TV on the other side of the bar caught my attention and for some reason I headed over to it. It was on very low, in respect for the live band, but tuned to a music video station. I decided to sit in front of it for a few minutes, maybe I could pick up some pointers. There was Led Zeppelin then some other heavy metal band. The barkeeper smiled at me and gave a me a glass of ginger ale free. I smiled back and glanced over to O and Jose who were finishing up a number, then back at the TV screen. Another song had started.

What I saw there startled me.

There shining down at me from the screen was someone prancing in a red dress plus red shoes with sparkly spike heels like daggers. You could only see her ankles in that shot not the rest of her but there, waddling and jumping happily beside her then, was a puppy as round and golden as the one I remembered trying to save so long before at my apartment house. It was so cute--- like a golden teddy bear. She was reaching down petting it as she sang and it was so happy, wagging its tail and dancing around her feet like it was enjoying the music. I was a little mesmerized by it and was glad to feel more relaxed and happy watching it, after all my worry.

I was unprepared for what came next.

All of a sudden she yanked herself around, raised her leg and jammed her spike heel onto, no, not just onto but into, through, that puppy's belly, skewering him like a piece of meat on a shish kabob, but it was no meat, it was the puppy who then yelped then lay limp and lifeless on the screen. She picked it up then, still singing all sad like it had been a mistake. It wasn't.

What I screamed I don't remember. But scream I did, so beyond myself for a minute or two---then many people jumped up and ran over to me thinking I guess some tarantula had bitten me. But I shrieked again and pointed at the screen where the woman's feet were still dancing.

I finally sputtered. "That was a puppy! How can you have that on the television here! Didn't you see what just happened!" leaning toward the awful TV then bumped the table, spilled my drink and ran to O and Jose who had just finished their song.

By then I was sobbing and pointing to the TV screen as the woman with purple hair whose dumb spike heel had just slaughtered that animal danced and pranced throwing her hips around and pouting her lips covered with about sixteen layers of black lipstick into a duck bill. I began to scream again and O and Jose jumped over next to me to see what was wrong, but I couldn't be coherent at the moment and they had to take me by the arms and scuttle me out of the place. The fact is they were embarrassed for me but I did not care. When we got outside I continued to wail but after a few deep breaths got back my speech and told them what I'd seen. They both looked serious and sorry, but also I guess like they weren't quite believing so much emotion out of me for that, and didn't quite know what to do about it.

So for a few minutes we were all silent outside the bar while the patrons filed out, some asking what the problem was, a few wanting to help and one woman saying she saw the whole thing and thought it was disgusting too. Both O and Jose told them everything was fine that I was just very sensitive and quite tired.

"I just can't believe anybody would do that," I finally whispered.

"Those are dumb videos for sure," said O "I've seen 'em before. But don't let them completely rock your boat girl, they're not worth it."

"I haven't ever seen these things and I can't say I want to either," said Jose.

We finally got into the car and drove home with me choking down sobs in the back seat. The moment I got back in my room I collapsed on my bed and saw the image again in my mind's eye. It was like my heart had been split open then and there, and all the feelings of sympathy I'd ever had just spilled out of it, through my hands, through my feet, my legs, my belly, and my head and turned me to jelly. I felt flooded with feelings, overwhelmed, questioning why anything happened and why anything had to suffer like that, feelings I guess I'd managed to keep inside for a long time since I had fully recollected the episode with the golden puppy taken away from the front of my apartment building in Brooklyn and put in the truck where I knew it would be going to breathe in poison. And those feelings just came back, only much stronger, til I thought they'd just wipe me out right there, just pummeling the middle of my belly,like that no one could stand feeling that miserable for long and they seemed stronger than they should have been, even I recognized that. What was giving them that added force?

It wasn't until early in the morning that I figured this out. It came to me with a jolt to my body like a jump start which woke me from my shallow sleep. And there it was. O of course. He was planning something even more cruel and reprehensible, namely doing what the stupid girl had done to a puppy, to an actual person, skewering him with his gun. Even though he had denied it, I knew it at that moment. Antoine was right about this and what if he was right about all the other things he said, wacky as they seemed? He must know quite a lot--- at least a lot more than the rest of us who are as far as I could tell, were completely earth bound. And then with same surge of energy that woke me, it seemed I was then pushed off the bed and catapulted to O's room, where he had just gotten up at two a.m. to get ready to leave.

"I was just coming to wake you up," he said. "Ready? We've got to go in an hour or so."

"NO!" I shouted at him, though it took all my strength but everything began to seem clear. "You can't do this O. It's completely wrong and will spoil everything, things you don't even know about," I blubbered, suddenly completely accepting what Antoine had told me. "You must NOT do this!" I ran to him and put my hand on his arm which was pushing his drawer shut. He grimaced and shook my hand off like it was a poisonous snake.

"What are you talking about Raynelle?" he stammered, and seemed shocked by what I was doing. "You're just feeling crazy because of what you saw on that video. Chill Ray, it's all alright, nothing bad will happen," he added,completely irrationally. I wondered if he had lost his mind.

"You know you're planning on shooting that man" I said.

I expected him again to deny this, but he frowned and at me all he said was,"He earned it, whatever happens. Now go get ready Raynelle. I'm going to leave soon. Everything is on schedule."

For a moment I was struck by the coldness of his tone which sounded hard and metallic,as if every trace of sympathy or understanding had been wrung out of it. I was shocked by this voice which had always seemed so sympathetic I guess especially when he was discussing his own hurts. It was like I was looking at him for the first time, at least the first time since I had begun to feel so in love with him and what I saw was cold and hard, the kind of person who might take an innocent puppy off in his truck or skewer him with a ridiculous spike heel. His hands were trembling slightly.

I drew myself up to my greatest height and took a deep breath. He was still fiddling with his duffle bag not even paying attention to me. "I'm not going," I said calmly in an even tone.

He glanced at me for a moment like I was a little girl he could easily ignore. But then he sat down on his bed and patted the place next to him saying, "Come here Ray, let's just relax together for a minute," and smiling. But I knew what he was up to, he knew he could just mold me like putty.

It took every ounce of strength and will power I had, to say weakly, "No O, I am not going," and to turn to walk out. I felt like my shoes were filled with cement, they were that hard to move.

"Yes, you are", he said, frowning.

"No, no I'm not."

He stepped toward me as if taking me seriously for the first time and took me by the shoulder hard then spun me around to face him. He kept his hand on my shoulder and the pressure and strength of his grip terrified me. I wondered if he had truly lost his mind and was going to do something to me, then wondered where his gun was, thankful it was out of sight.

"What do you mean?" he whispered finally as his face drained of color. "I am completely counting on you. You told me you were coming. I need your help to find the place and to keep a look out when I go into it. I depended on you Raynelle. I need you," he whimpered.

For a minute I could sense the anger welling up within him and began to fear that he might do something as he just stood still staring at me. I wondered if Jose would hear me if I yelled for help, or if he was even home.

But O didn't step closer and let go of my shoulder, like the energy just drained out of him. I gradually backed out of his room, watching him as I went. Then I turned and ran to my room where I locked the door. Strangely, it wasn't anger or fear I felt when I got back there, but a strong pity for O, then sympathy, more than that, love I guess, for him and everyone: O, the puppies, the stepfather, Jose and all his suffering, even myself and all the pain I'd been through which I'd never really thought about before, because it had all had seemed like just stuff that happened. But I was flooded with feeling from my hair to my toenails: a sense of love stronger than the sadness I'd felt a moment before that I also thought might just obliterate me. But this lasted only a second or two.

I knew what I would do.

I heard O once again now getting ready to leave and my pulse started racing as I formulated a plan. I would give Antoine a chance. Hadn't he generally seemed right, so far? It was the best I could do, and if he was just a figment of my imagination or even just plain wrong, well there was nothing to lose and maybe everything to gain, the stepfather's life, O's life, maybe even our life together, and maybe even all the lives of those lost beings, whatever they were, who knew? It had occurred to me more than once that if he really killed the stepfather I could never be with him again. So I lay with my whole body, every muscle tense and my pulse racing, listening,waiting for O to leave so I could act. It would take him about five hours to get where he was going---I hoped that would be time enough.

After a few minutes there was the slam of O's door and his footsteps heavy down the hall; he paused for a minute in front of my bedroom door and I felt my muscles stiffen but then he continued on. I took a deep breath and listened for the sound of the apartment door. Soon I heard a car outside start and knew he was on his way. I waited for a few minutes to be sure he was gone, then I jumped out of bed and ran to Jose's bedroom. His door was closed. I opened it a crack to see if he was in there. There he was--- lying on his back with shreds of light from the moon sinking in the west running over his covers and his face which looked old and serious. I took a deep breath and ran in there, then started yelling his name.

Chapter Forty Eight

To be honest I wasn't sure what I would say to the boy. I feared if I immediately told him the whole story he would think I'd surely gone off the deep end and needed to be back at Precious Moments. But if I didn't get him involved and if Antoine was right, who knew what would happen? I decided to risk blurting out what I knew would attract his attention.

"You're going to lose O!" I yelled. "He won't be here anymore to help with your band or get the recording contract, nothing!"

"What…" he mumbled, sitting up suddenly but like he hadn't heard a thing I said.

"Believe it Jose, O's gone, he just left, he's planned this for months, and he didn't tell you, he's gone off to LA to wipe out his stepfather!"

"What? Are you going crazy Ray! He was just here a couple of hours ago, what are you talking about Raynelle? You are having a nightmare, go back to bed," he said and turned on the light.

"No! I've been awake! I've known this for months! Go see for your self!" So he got out of bed in his underwear, I might add, and wrapped himself with a towel then stepped into the hall where he began to yell for O, then he proceeded into O's room which was of course empty and turned on the light. It looked like a hurricane had blown through it, truly the work of a deranged mind. I guess after I told him I wouldn't come, O was upset enough to kind of throw stuff around like a three year old.

"What's going on here?" said Jose and led me into the kitchen where he started a pot of coffee then sat me down and waited for me to explain things, which I began to do, first about O's misplaced hate towards the wrong father figure then his anger at his mother and his plan which I added he was about to perform in a few hours. "But we have to act," I said. The hardest part was introducing the space events with Antoine and what he said to do. I was sure Jose wouldn't buy it.

"You remember those lights you saw?" I began, "on your way up here?"

"Ye-es."

"Well they WERE from a space being." Jose looked scornful. "Believe me Jose, because I've seen them too but, but more than that, I've been talking to him."

"Come on Ray, you've been reading those wacko magazines too much. It's late, there's nothing I can do about this. We could call the police."

"Trust me, I thought of that. It wouldn't help. But there's no way we could prove this and he'll just get the man again if he doesn't this time."

"Well what do you suggest?"

"It's not me, it's Antoine, he's been the one in the lights in the space ship or craft or whatever it is. He seems to know about everything I'm telling you, Jose, he can travel through space and time I know because I did it with him." I know I was talking fast and was almost breathless at this point and Jose burst into laughter.

But I slowed down and kept insisting that he listen. After a few minutes the idea began to appeal to him, maybe it was his interest in magic, I don't know, but he said "Tell me about it then."

"I can't tell it all now Jose, there isn't time, he's on his way there, we only have a few hours, I promise I will later. For real."

"OK," he smiled, "I'll go along with it, what does this space person suggest we do?"

"He says you know how to pray, Jose, and I can, well... focus my attention, we need to pray about something that happened or just focus in on it and imagine or pray about a different outcome or I guess, reaction. Just see it happening, but different."

"Such as?"

"Well it has to do with feelings. When O was two or three he was so hurt by his father leaving that he couldn't accept that the man had really done that, had rejected him, it was too much for him--- so he kind of stuffed it back inside and then let the feelings come out, but he transferred all that anger to his stepfather. Course he didn't do any of this on purpose."

"You want him to realize that he should really be hating his real father then? Then he'll just take off after that one some day."

"No. Antoine says that if we work on him accepting that his father needed to leave, not just to be mean or cause O was no good, that if we, well, you pray about him accepting his father's going without hating him and feeling insulted, just calmly and still feeling loved, like he is OK, that will kind of defuse the whole situation. He said he'll be able to learn the truth when he's much older and able to handle it then without falling apart"."

"But let me explain something Ray, it's in the past--- we can't change what's already happened, much as we'd like to sometimes."

"But Antoine says the past and present are like all together, and if some outcome isn't kind of set by someone looking at it and thinking about it, we could go back and change it while it's happening, not change what already happened, kind of like nudging things in a different direction than the one they have taken. He says this works only if no one actually recorded or registered the thing in their minds."

"Well the father and the mother were both there weren't they? They saw O's reaction."

"Yuh, but according to Antoine, they weren't paying attention to O, he was just there having a melt down while the mother and father were arguing. And they didn't really know what was happening. Please Jose it's the only chance we have, if you really want O to come back and be in the band and not go to jail." At that I broke into sobs, imagining him behind bars, and put my hands over my face. "We have to start now Jose. At least try."

The idea of O not coming back at all and him having to find another band partner got to Jose, if nothing else did. "What do you want me to do then, or does this space man want me to do?"

"You pray, just focus on that time, believing that O just takes the whole thing without a big problem, just blasé blasé, accepts it's something his real father just needed to do, and he would be accepting I think, resilient that's the word I heard a lot at PM, that means---"

"I know what it means Raynelle. But you don't want him to just be resilient if I hear you right or what Antoine was trying to say through you, you want him to actually re-invent what his father did from something that was cruel to something he didn't want to do, but had to in O's mind, but he really cared for O."

"Yuh. I guess you're right. Sometimes I just like to hear myself using big words I guess. You in then?"

"Let's go. I'll give it a try. You know I've done much weirder things in my life. And I did see those lights. They had kind of a mystical air about them. I'll never forget them."

At that he got up from the table and I followed him into his bedroom where he immediately got down on his knees, crossed himself and began to pray, at first out loud then mumbling to himself. I guess being a Catholic, this was second nature to him. I wasn't sure what to think of this at first having never seen anyone pray especially down on the knees like that and for a moment I just watched him. I could hear a steady stream of Spanish saying something in a low monotonous voice and it almost seemed like he was entranced. So I got into his padded chair and tried to focus on the scene I'd witnessed up with Antoine. At first it was hard, blurry, like trying to adjust a bad TV connection but after a while it almost seemed once again that I was there and I could see or imagine details like the expression on little O's face and how his parents were talking. I imagined O as feeling happy, hearing his father's words as kind, and assuring O of his love. Well, I imagined this over and over like a broken record and even asked for help from God who I guessed was who Jose was directing his prayers to. It got so I could see the scene in minute detail over and over, his father saying something and O accepting calmly then even with love, sure he would see the man again. This I repeated probably one hundred times until it felt my brain was numb and I opened my eyes and looked at Jose's clock, but I began to really feel it in my heart like I was taking on the pain from little O, right into myself. It did surprise me that I was able to get so into this feeling but then I remembered what Antoine had said, that if we did this then others on the spirit plane would join us, to increase the effect of what was done, but a human person had to begin it. *"The feeling must arise from your heart, a primitive, forgive me, a human being's heart, that still wonderful capacitor, that font of human love ... to address all the hate that's coming from your realm,"* I remembered him saying after I had asked him why didn't the space people just do it all.

I was surprised to see that two hours had passed, though it had seemed like just fifteen minutes, and Jose was still down there praying. I wondered if his knees hurt. I seemed to have exhausted my ability to do whatever it was I was doing and sat there waiting for Jose. But soon that big padded chair I was in, which Jose had picked up cheap at furniture warehouse, got to me and as Jose still droned on out loud in his low Spanish tones, I drifted off to sleep. I imagined myself floating around Antoine's ship but he was no where to be found and while I sensed a feeling of loss, still I felt he was pleased with me. But that was just a dream as I discovered when Jose awakened me with a poke to my shoulder at six-thirty that morning.

"Well we did it, at least I did it. I don't know what you were doing but as I started it, it all seemed to make sense and I did have a feeling that it may even be helpful---hard to get into what people think is real though, but so is a lot of stuff, even what I do. My grandmother was a prayer warrior, taught me how to pray though I rarely did the prayer warrior stuff, that's what I was doing now. Some miraculous things were achieved with her prayer too."

We went back to bed for a while but dragged ourselves up to watch the eight o clock news then the nine o clock. I knew O had planned his scheme for the step father's arrival around eight thirty, so we both jumped like lightening had hit us in front of that tube when the announcer said there had been a shooting in LA of an important person by a young gun man, with some casualties, and details later he added.

I think neither one of us could bear to watch the details. I know it was too much for me. "Well we tried," said Jose, getting up with a disgusted look and turning off the idiot box angrily. "I'm leaving, I've got reality to deal with, especially now. I guess he did it. Anyway who are we to go against the laws of physics--- tell your space friend to find something worthwhile to do."

I had nothing to reply. It was all too much for me. I felt struck through the heart--- as well as exhausted. I ran to my bedroom and collapsed onto the mattress in tears. There I stayed for the better part of the day, knowing the apartment was empty but listening for some footstep, some sound to dispel what I was feeling but none came, just silence and a lonely feeling. I wondered what they had done with O and imagined him dealing with angry police pushing him around like he was a piece of dirt, beneath contempt. It would be far worse than anything he had ever experienced, even at PM. I sobbed when I thought of his ridiculous idea, that he'd get off the hook when they discovered he wasn't eighteen. "Oh that will never happen O, poor

O, my poor..." I groaned into the pillow as I realized my fantasies about him, about us, would never come true, at least not for ten or twenty years depending on his behavior. After all his stepfather was a bigwig, the owner of a huge corporation---the man's life would be paid for dearly. On and on I wailed until I ran out of tears. Then I formulated a plan. It would be simple. I would wait for him, be there for him throughout, no matter what or how long. I wondered where they would send him, hoped they would send him to some prison in New York because at that point I began missing my father, my mother, even Wanda and Ravena, I hadn't really thought about them in months, truth be told, I was too wrapped up in O. But by then, lying there empty of tears and feeling alone, knowing Jose, no one, would never take the place of O in my heart, I began to think about going home. My father and O, the two men I had loved, father because,---what choice did I have--- he was given to me and O because he was, well, so clearly incredible. But I concluded, they were both losers weren't they? My father in his stupid game with drugs and O with his fragile emotions and amazingly dumb choices. But suddenly I longed to see my father, if I couldn't see O, he was the next best thing.

Chapter Forty Nine

I was sure Jose would give me enough money to make it out in style. After all he still had this record contract in the works and he would have no trouble getting some handsome guitar player to take O's place, although of course he would never be so handsome as my O. I got up and dragged myself around the room, picking up clothes, gathering things together, getting ready for my trip which I was sure I would make within the week. If I needed to, I'd take the bus, that was cheapest and I didn't care even if they sent me back to PM, as miserable as I was feeling, that would seem like a vacation, plus it would remind me of O, the place I first met him. I thought about going into his room and picking it up for him so the cops who would certainly be there to investigate it before long wouldn't think he was just a slob. Soon I was in there, maybe almost as interested in what I would find as making a decent impression for him. First I made his bed then picked up the clothes and folded them neatly there, dirty or clean, it didn't matter, they would at least look organized, then I proceeded to his desk and started to put his papers in neat stacks, and those that would fit into the drawers. I decided I wouldn't read any of them just file them neatly away.

But when I came to a large piece of paper with Priscilla neatly scrawled across it I couldn't help myself. There in front of me was evidence that O still was pining over her, it had been dated two days earlier:

Dearest Priscilla,

I am broken in pieces that you have not answered or probably not even received the letters I've sent you. Maybe your mother has just tossed them. Probably. I even faked some of the return addresses in hopes she would not know it was me but maybe she was wise to this. Can I tell you how my heart burns within me for you only, how I still think about you all the time even though I tried to put you out of my mind, you are its major occupant. You own it. My only consolation is that you are carrying our son because I am sure it is a son, and are about to have him soon I would imagine. It has also provided me some consolation that you are probably very big and not likely to be involved with other men at this time, I hope. Believe me, I want you only. There could be no one else for me. Not that there haven't been those who were interested, as there certainly will be for you, precious Priscilla. My dear little companion Raynelle who has actually become quite an attractive girl, I fear is in love with me, though I have tried my best not to lead her on. It is only you and for only you I am doing this deed in two days, that you will read about and of course for our son. He will see how proud and powerful his father was. But deep in my heart I know it will all work out for us and we will live together as a family, without your mother trying to control us, as I know was your wish too. I beg you again, my beautiful Priscilla, please do not put our child up for adoption! Keep him! It won't be long before I can be there with you.

All my love for you and our baby,
Your Omar

I took that letter and crunched it up, then tore out the part about Raynelle being in love with him and his trying not to lead me on, stuck it in my mouth and chewed it into tiny spit-heavy pieces which I took, spat into the toilet then flushed them down and sat down on its seat bawling. How could I have been such a dumbie anyway?

After an hour at least, I got up stiffly and went out to the kitchen to get something to eat. Let Omar just rot in jail then, I decided, and turned on the TV to see what had happened to him because by then I did not care. There was only Oprah and some stupid soap opera, it was twenty five minutes before the hour. So it was while I I sat there eating a tomato and peanut butter sandwich, waiting for the news, that I heard a pounding at the door. The police, I thought as I gulped the rest of the sandwich and straightened my unchanged clothes, then headed to the door.

What stood before me there took me by surprise.

A man with speckled gray hair chewing gum and wearing musty smelling clothes that looked dirtier than mine, was staring at me curiously and holding a badge that looked like he'd picked it up in a department store, in front of my nose. At the same time he started to croak, "Bounty hunter. You Raynelle from New York, ain't you?"

"No," I said quickly, wondering what this reprobate wanted.

"Yes y'are too. I got yer picture right here to prove it," and he fumbled in his pocket to retrieve a tiny picture of me that my father had taken with a throw-away camera a few weeks before he went to jail. It said "Raynelle, my daughter," and your birth date on the back of it right here," and the man pointed to each word with a long dirt-filled fingernail. Then he smacked his lips and chewed like he had some food in his mouth but I don't think he did and looked at me.

"How'd you get that!" I accused.

"Yer father of course, he had it with him the whole time he was there in that jail. He wants you back girl, he's real worried about you."

"Was in jail? Is he out now?" I asked.

"Sure is... just got out a couple weeks ago. He got them postcards you sent him though and he treasured them things, girl, got so excited to finally hear from you. He thought you was gone for good. So'd yer mother I hear. She thought you was picked up by some bad person on the road after you split from that lock-up, or maybe by a spaceship, that's more what she was hoping had happened. Real nice folks, them two, and the two little ones too, nice and beautiful too."

"How'd you know all about my family?" I asked him, still not trusting this joker.

"I was friend with yer father after we both were sent to that kind of rehab unit in the jail since we wasn't ever violent and uh both had some.... uh substance abuse history. We was real friendly there. And I got out a couple weeks before him--- had been in almost two years."

"What did you do?"

"A plumber... well, his helper in my younger years."

"No I mean what did you do to get in jail?" This guy was no honor student.

"Oh. Just selling some drug, did it a couple of times. Stupid I know. Things was hard. I needed the money. Still do, that's why I'm here."

"What?"

"Yuh, I'm a bounty hunter, had some experience in the field long time ago with my uncle, well now I'm doin' it again. Your father paid me right nice too."

"How much?"

"Two hunnert dollars. He gave me a hunnert and promised the other when you back with him."

"Where'd he get the money?"

"Wall he started up his job again at the 7-11 and he moved in with your mother, moved back in together in some cheap public housing she finagled someway from some social worker."

"With my sisters?"

"Oh yes girl, they're all there, fat and happy. He tells me your mom got into collecting some disability for something or other. I don't know, to look at her she don't look disabled, but anyway they hired me. Can I come in now?"

I guess by this point not only did I believe this guy but I let him come in and sit down. I was as high right then as I had been low a few minutes before he came, now just thinking about my family being all together like that, something I never thought would happen.

"How'd you find me?"

"Well it's them post cards, yer father told me where he thought you was and I been looking all around this town for the last four days finally went in to have a little refreshment at a bar down the road, turns out they knew you. Said yer a singer and a pretty good one too with some group comes in there. How about that?"

"I had to admit the codger did a pretty good job. By then I was totally psyched to get back to New York. How you getting back?" I asked.

"I got me a car out there. And its 'us back' girl cause you're coming with me." I didn't argue. All I wanted to do was say goodbye to Jose and let him know what had happened.

"I need to do a few things."

"I'll give you til tomorrow then we got to get moving. I got this phone card here too. Supposed to call yer father when I find you, at eight o clock. He goes down to his neighbor's, the one who works at the jail each night, at eight waiting for my call. He's got a phone. If I say wrong party and hang up he knows I ain't found you. See yer father don't have the money for one yet. Well tonight he's in fer a big surprise girl."

"I'll come too, when you call him, I want to talk."

"Wall, OK but only fer a minute, its only a ten minute card which means you generally get about two actual talking minutes."

Well I made the call with him. My father was so happy to hear from me, he couldn't even talk, really, he just sputtered my name. We then started crying. "I'll be back," I told him feeling guilty for putting him through anything while I hadn't really been thinking about him at all. "I love you!" I heard him yell as I was passing the phone to the stranger whose name turned out to be Ned.

It was around ten that night as I was packing my stuff that I decided to carry out the trash to the apartment receptacle down the hall since it was mostly my stuff, stupid stuff like old make-up, cartoons and teen magazines, snacks that I forgot to finish and pictures of famous people I'd ripped out of the magazines and taped to my walls. After I dumped my stuff I heard footsteps behind me and turned. They sounded familiar, probably Jose who had been gone all day.

Then I saw him.

I dropped the trash can and almost fell over. There walking down the hall behind me was none other than O, looking happy and surprised to see me. "What are you doing out here so late?" he says.

I could say nothing for a few seconds, I guess a lot like my father had felt earlier that night. Finally I sputtered, "What are YOU doing here? I thought you were in jail." He kept walking and didn't say anything until he got inside the apartment like he was embarrassed or something and his cheeks looked flushed a dark red color.

"Well?"

"Oh that," he finally said. "You knew I was just kidding about all that."

"WHAT! No you weren't! You were as MAD AS A HATTER."

I could say anything now that I knew his true feelings for me. "You lie," I yelled.

He sat down then looked like he was mad---at me. "I don't want to talk about it," he said cooly.

I wasn't letting him off the hook. Here, Jose and I had stayed up almost all night trying to rescue this idiot from his own crazy ideas and he was going to be mad at me?

Meanwhile Ned was sitting there looking back and forth between us as we talked like he was watching some crazy tennis game.

"Oh no," I said, surprising myself with the authority in my voice, knowing now I had nothing to lose. "You went up there to wipe that man out, O, you'd been thinking about it and nothing else for the last six months and something, something, happened to change your mind and as hard as I was worrying about you and Jose was too---". I wasn't about to tell him what had actually happened--- "You are going to tell me what happened. WASN'T HE THERE? That was it, wasn't it?" I asked. because by then I had totally decided that everything Antoine told me was just a crock of bull and I didn't even really believe I had seen anything. I just had an overly active imagination--- that's what my father would say. I'd been away from the family too long.

There was a long silence. I did notice Ned wince at the mention of wiping out somebody. He clearly jumped and started looking very anxious after that. I turned to him. "Don't worry Ned," I said although I wasn't completely sure that was right either. Maybe O had just done him in and snuck away somehow; the boy was very clever. He was silent.

I glowered at him then got up in front of him and said again, "I have to know. Where is your stepfather?"

"Carl?" he finally says to me. I had never heard him say that name in any but a desperate cringing and hateful tone. "Carl?" He says again in an even more affectionate tone.

"YES, CARL!" I screamed at him, beside myself to know the truth.

"Nothing. He's fine. Can we go in my bedroom for a minute?" He turned to Ned. "Excuse us just a minute sir."

"Certainly," Ned muttered and looked relieved.

When we got in there O sat down on the bed and I stood up in front of him like an interrogator or detective on TV. "What?" I said, by then furious for reasons I couldn't fathom.

"He's alright."

"What happened?"

"I don't know. Honestly Ray. By the time I got there it was like everything was different. I hadn't even thought about it on the way, but as soon as I started walking up the steps holding that gun, I just didn't have the need to do it. The feeling just wasn't there--- I was just going through the motions, maybe like someone falling out of love. Or I think it was like an old person losing a memory, trying hard to find it but the feeling was gone! There was nothing there in its place---no anger, no affection. All I could think of and I know you don't want to hear this was Priscilla. And our baby. And yet I'd been thinking about them for months. But close to the top of the steps, I turned around and took that gun which I'd been holding next to my sleeve so you almost couldn't see the thing unless you already knew I had it, and walked around to a huge trash barrel behind the building. Just threw it in. It just wasn't necessary anymore."

"You threw in a loaded gun," I accused angrily.

"No I took the bullets out first and threw them out later at a rest stop. After I threw away the gun I walked in the place and sat down. Only some guy busy behind a counter was there. I figured I'd just hang there for a while. Seemed like the thing to do, I didn't have a clue why. I kept thinking, wracking my brain why was I going to do this, I couldn't come up with anything. After about a half hour I went up and started talking to the man behind the counter who was working on some computer glitch. Nice guy. A few minutes later the big glass doors slide open and there he is. My father, I mean my stepfather. At first he didn't connect that that was me but when he did, he started yelling my name and ran over to me. He actually put his arms around me and gave me a hug which I realized for the first time then I had never let him do before. It felt good Ray, and I was startled to realize as he hugged me that a few hours before I had wanted to eliminate him, wipe him right off the map. It's gone, like a rotten tooth that's pulled. He asked me to come to lunch early with him and I told him everything that had happened--- except for my plans for him of course---how we left PM, our trip, meeting up with Jose, the band, Priscilla and the baby."

"Wasn't he furious at you?"

"Amazingly no, it was like he was just glad to see me. He wasn't even mad about Priscilla and the baby. Of course he put a little guilt on me, told me my mother had been beside herself with worry and that I needed to call her and get home as soon as possible. I told him I had to come back here first and talk to Jose and you of course, my two best fiends." He smiled kind of sadly. "My only friends, the truth is. The fact is I'm almost eighteen and about to be liberated. I told him that too, but I owe it to my mother to go back and let her know what I'm doing. Also I want to hunt down Priscilla. I'm going to see her mother and let her know about my actual family circumstances. Money. Just like Jose says you can buy almost anything you want."

He seemed very calm and very quiet, peaceful. I'd never seen him that way. As he sat there smiling, I had to admit all I was feeling was anger. Why was I not happy? It perplexed me. Of course I finally admitted, if he'd gone through with his idiotic plan he would have been locked away. What did that mean? No chance to be with the girlfriend who, even if she did still like him wouldn't be able to wait that long. And I would have. Now they would be together.

I smiled at him and told him he had acted right, like I had tried to get him to before, I reminded him.

"I know, I know I just wasn't ready to listen. It's like there were just too many things going on," was all he could say.

I said good night, to him then Ned, and went to my bedroom where I, exhausted and with an empty stomach, went to sleep still festering somewhat over O and Priscilla and the obvious fact that I'd have to give all that up.

Early the next morning I woke up to Ned's yelling through the cigarette smoke blasting out of his mouth, shaking my shoulder. O had let him in. "Up Raynelle, we got to get going so's to be back as soon as possible" he yelled. "I can't afford food no more than three days, most. I shooed him out while I got dressed than rapped on Jose's door to tell him I'd be leaving.

"Call us Raynelle," he told me. "I'll be here. With O back we won't take long to get that contract through." He sounded exhausted and still half asleep. I went from his room and stood in front of O's door, wondering if I should go in.

"Hurry!" yelled Ned from the living room between coughs on his cigarette.

I still stood there a minute, then turned---it was all hopeless with O. I went back to my room to grab my suitcase. It's true I had a lot more than I came with. I wanted to go in to O's room but didn't. It would be too much to leave him.

"Come on," rasped Ned and I started to the door but when I reached it I had to fight back the tears. It seemed impossible that I was leaving these two boys.

Chapter Fifty

By the time Ned's rattle trap rental car was on the road I had stopped thinking about O. It was incredible to me that any car rental agency had owned such a heap and I was sure it wouldn't get us to New York. It was a K car Ned told me "got 130,000 miles on her but she'll make it, always does.

"It belongs to my sister, rented it from her, just got to stop now and then, put some water into her, she gets thirsty like you."

"Yuh," I answered, trying to keep to myself as much as I could with this joker who anybody could see wasn't playing with a full deck; it was hard, especially after hanging out with two boys who were obviously at the top of their game, you might say, even though the games they were each picking weren't the usual ones. Seemed to me Jose was either very, very lucky or really smart, probably both, the way he could finagle people and get what he wanted legally or not, and here he was probably about to be a millionaire on his those recordings of his. And O, who could doubt his intelligence? No, he wasn't just handsome I pondered, but some of his decisions... Then it came to me like a bolt from the blue, what had changed his mind. For some reason I had forgotten about our efforts, Jose and me that night, maybe because I had completely decided it was all a crock with Antoine or maybe because I was so busy with my crazy feelings about O. But there it was--- like my nose in front of my face: he was planning on one thing then changed his mind, like taking a completely opposite turn. Do people do that, completely change their mind about something they were set on or was it what Antoine had said to do, did that really change O's mind, or maybe just Jose's hard praying? Maybe that's what happened. I had completely put it out of my own mind, had decided it was all me being crazy and just too lonely, away from my parents so long. I wondered if Antoine had somehow planted the video with the puppy.

But what he said had worked hadn't it, whatever caused it. But if so, then where was he? I hadn't heard from him in days, you'd think he'd at least make a visit if it was all real. I decided to try to contact him, mentally, wasn't that what he did all the time after all? *If you are really there darn it Antoine, I did what you wanted and it worked, where are you? Aren't you going to say something?* There was nothing, no response or other change I could take as sign from him. I continued this in the rickety car, with just monotonous scenery in the semi-dark of the early morning. Then I started to feel very frustrated and said out loud under my breath of course, "Come on Antoine, if you're really there that is, I'm waiting." But nothing happened, nothing from space anyway.

"What, what's that honey?" says Ned. It really irked me that he had all of a sudden started calling me "honey" out there on the road. I decided to keep up my guard around this joker.

"Raynelle," I said, "and I wasn't talking to you."

"Who was you talking at then girl? You going to go postal on me here in the car? Your father ain't going to pay me for no postal Raynelle."

I said nothing partly because I didn't want him to say anything else; his words by then were like scratching your finger against a black board. And partly because where we were on the highway then looked really cool with the sun coming up over huge rocks or mountains with flat tops all different colors along their sides, like layers in a cake.

That night we stopped at a high economy, low budget place around six. 'If you can find it cheaper we'll give it to ya for free.' the sign announced as we drove in.

"I can't drive anymore today Honey," he told me as he headed into the office. "I wish you could help me." Then he stopped like he was considering just letting me drive for a while and said "I guess not" and turned to disappear into the office.

I was hoping we'd have two rooms of course but given his financial situation there was no chance of that. I just lay down on the twin bed---at least he got two beds--- and kept my clothes on in case I had to run out for any reason. You never know with his type.

Also the sheets were so dirty looking that I didn't want to touch them if possible. Well before I knew it, Ned who had gotten into bed with his underwear on, was asleep and sending up a noise like I had never heard, a rasping, gurgling there like taking a loud gasp and every so often he'd stop and not breathe at all for a few seconds or sometimes I think a minute or two. Just when I started wondering each time whether I should get up and shake him, he would gasp and start breathing again. It was with this racket that I had to try to get to sleep but as soon as I did, something crawled across my forehead. It woke me up and jumped off before I could get to the light but then there it was on the mattress: a cockroach, big as my fist and fat too. I looked around the room. There they were on Ned's bed crawling around him, smaller but speedy, and a couple of others on my bed. I brushed them off and tried to figure what to do. I looked around for a fly swatter or something to kill them with but as I did it, I heard a terrible choking and coughing from Ned. I looked over to see him coughing then a huge cockroach flew out of his mouth. He didn't even wake up. I left the light on and wrapped myself completely in the blanket like a mummy after I shook it out---they couldn't get to me that way.

Space

The next night in West Virginia we stopped at a camping center. After I told Ned what had happened the night before he looked shocked and finally said "But you've seen cockroaches before right, Honey? Got em all over the place up there in New York City."

"Yuh but not that big. I'm not staying in a place like that again Ned. I'll sleep in the car--- at least I don't think it has roaches."

"Don't know," he said but then "we'll find someplace better. Don't want you staying the night in no car."

So the Acme camping and RV center was a step up. Yes, you had to walk a block away to use the bathroom but the little cabins were neat even if they didn't have any furniture except a couple of old beds. I kept my clothes on again even though I felt a little safer there and didn't have to wrap myself up like a baked potato to stay away from roaches. The minute I heard Ned start to snore I knew he'd be out for the night and I conked out at last, hard.

So bottom line, you could have blown me over with a feather when there I was again leaving my sleeping body and up there with those lights. "Am I dreaming?" I said.

'You thought this was all a dream didn't you Ray?'

"Yes I still do a little. But we did what you wanted. It took us a while but we did it.'

'I know and look what happened, did you think O would have just changed his mind out of the blue you might say?'

"I wasn't sure."

'Think Raynelle. Remember. He was so set on it, as though his whole being depended on it, his very survival. It was the linchpin of his being; you helped free him from that sense of loss and unworth that held him like a prisoner, now he can do whatever he wants in his life. He would never have changed on his own.'

"Maybe, maybe not, not sure. Well anyway, I think Jose did the most work."

'Jose is a very adept individual. He uses his brain in a most efficient manner but he also feels with his heart.'

"Doesn't everybody?"

'Yes, to some extent, but his heart energy is fairly unencumbered with things that might get in the way.'

"Like what?"

'The old bugaboos that have plagued mankind for years, Anger, jealousy, resentment, his heart was made even stronger by the very unfortunate loss of his friend who by the way was praying with him that night, from another place.'

"Heaven?"

'Like that. And you as well Ray with your intention, your profound caring for your friend, your heart energy was so opened by the dogs.'

"What dogs?"

'Both the one you saw in New York and the one on the video. The heart has the strength of a million armies if it is clear and focused. It's a channel for love, that most powerful and transformative force. Mankind has yet to learn this but it will in time, it will.'

"How do you know so much about everyone on our planet anyway, you're a space guy?"

'All the information is available within, even your every cell when you know how to see it.'

"And how do you know so much about people? You're from another planet."

'I never said that.'

"But you're not from earth, we can't do any of these things on earth, not yet."

'No. I'm not from right now.'

"What do you mean?" I was starting to feel a little creepy, kind of afraid and wanted to be back in my bed. Suddenly I missed my father and his common sense--- so hard, it surprised me.

'I… we …ARE from earth, Raynelle, that's one of the reasons we care so much about what happens here. We're just not in your time zone you might say, though it's all happening, it's separated at the same time by our perceptions and abilities though it seems like a linear arrangement, like a line. This is one of our limitations as human beings.'

"But you're NOT a human being! I can't even see you, I just see all these lights all around you!"

I am a human being, many hundred years away from you. And you can see me. You're looking right at me.

"No I can't." Then it came to me. "These lights?"

Yes, this is how I can travel, if I choose, in my etheric body, somewhat concentrated. Our physical bodies are quite unnecessary at this stage. Although we do keep them for certain purposes and some do just for sentimental reasons, like curiosities. It depends on your interests much… like your earth now. I do like my physical body and keep it safe when I'm away from it. Sometimes there is nothing so dear as the touch of another being or even eating a wonderful meal. But the experience is limited, I couldn't do all I need to do if I stayed within it all the time.

I had a hard time understanding all this even though I was sure he had just scratched the surface of everything he knew. I didn't want to go any deeper, not then. I changed the subject. "But so now your people who are stuck like rocks, they won't be staying there?"

Not for long. They'll be liberated, thanks to your efforts. Maybe they'll be a little smarter next time.

"How?"

They won't assume they are in charge of the universe, mainly--- there will be more reverence.

I thought I knew what he meant by that but as I pondered it I found myself back in my bed with Ned snoring like a wart hog from the next bed. I got up and looked out the window, and said, "If you're still there, let me see you." But I saw nothing, just a sliver of moon set like a thin smile sinking low in the sky.

As we drove towards my father's new place, the familiar streets passed by like old friends I hadn't seen in a long time and hadn't realized how much I'd missed them. It was just getting dark in in the neighborhood and people were still out enjoying the late autumn air. I could hear the calls to prayer from the mosque down the street. There were pumpkins on every porch and decorations on the small fences in front of the yards of the rich families who lived in houses with front yards. We made our way back to the cheaper area where there were big apartment buildings like my family would have, with bogus little balconies like drawers in a bureau and lots more trash around the sidewalks. My mother always said it was just the wind that caused this problem but I didn't think so. People were still yelling, it was like to no one in particular. Women walked by babbling strange languages and always dressed in black with eyes cast down to the sidewalk, like it was something that needed constant attention. Others, religious men looking straight ahead with somber expressions, walked by with their big black hats and black suits. It was good to be back.

"Do you know where you're going?" I asked Ned who seemed to be circling around an area of a few blocks.

"Of course," he told me irritably, "maybe you didn't notice but it's hard to find a parking place around here." That had never been a concern for us since nobody in my family ever owned a car. As he finally started backing into a very small place, it really dawned on me that I was about to reunited with my family again after being away over a year. I felt a tightness in my stomach, then nausea and excitement about seeing them, then a fear that things would not be as good as Ned had made them sound. I wondered if I would throw up.

But I didn't and as we approached our new apartment I felt my feet shift into a run like they had minds of their own, beyond my control.

"Just hold your horses, hang on girl, we'll be there in a minute!" You don't want to scare somebody. There are old people living around here you know." But even as he said that, I felt myself speed up and finally simply threw myself against the apartment door with "Mama' erupting from my mouth like it had been wedged in all this time, dying to get out. The door flew open and there they were all of them: my father jumping up from a big holey stuffed chair, my mother looking up from her seat on a half-collapsed sofa her mouth wide open, my little sisters flying through the air screaming my name over and over. As you may have concluded already I hadn't been one to blubber or cry until recently; there had been many times while others much older have done this and I sat there quiet, watching them. But this time I was the one. Had I been keeping it all inside for so long--- I didn't know it. It all erupted at once like a geyser, there it was and my tears started rolling down my face as I collapsed on the floor with all of them upon me hugging me and cried until my collar was soaked.

In truth, it seemed at the same time as though I had been away for many years and also for just a short time. My father looked younger, maybe this is what the sobriety I hoped he was keeping to, had done for him. And my mother, she certainly had gained a bit of weight but looked, well, wholesome like she used to when I was young. My two little sisters looked almost the same but as if they'd just been stretched out a few inches like pieces of taffy. As I sat there hugging and crying, I could imagine telling my mother what had happened, the whole thing, but especially with Antoine. I just could see her face as I did, so friendly and open like a favorite dog who tilts its head to one side to listen and keeps such an rapt adoring look on his face. Yes she would dwell on every word and doubt none of it, in fact she'd be exhilarated by it, just what she always wanted to happen.

Epilogue

Naturally everything didn't stay exactly that blissful, but my father did manage to keep his job and stay sober. Maybe it was the drug screens that did it. My mother also was back to her old good ways, not wandering out at night prowling the street and maybe that was because Gibbon was back in our lives with visitations every few days or it was maybe because my father was back; anyway we all rallied for these visits because we knew what the alternative would be.

As for me I went back to school, just like Antoine had predicted, and with my mother home there was no need for me to do child care in the morning so I could pursue my studies like I used to. I'll admit that I did think about Jose and O, especially O, quite a bit more at the beginning but still some even as the weeks went by. I had promised Jose I'd call after I got there but there was no phone and it had to wait.

After three months my father got a cell phone and I was permitted to call the boys as long as it was just for a few minutes. I was a little anxious as I made the call, wondering if they were still even there and still alright. The phone rang many times but finally a strangely unfamiliar voice said hello.

"Who is this?" I asked maybe a little angrily.

There was silence then the person on the phone mumbled, "Well you called us. Who's this?"

At that point I recognized O's voice.

"O!" I yelled, amazed to talk to him again finally. "This is Ray, Raynelle, I'm back in New York."

"Is everything OK?" he asked; it sounded like he really cared.

"Yes," I told him. "How about with you?"

"Everything is fine. The CD will be out soon and I'm heading back to Massachusetts for a while."

I was still a little fearful of bringing up he subject of his family, but finally said, "Well... how is your family?" really meaning Carl of course. I still wasn't completely sure I hadn't imagined the whole change in O's attitude.

"Which one? Priscilla has written me back and I'm planning on visiting her when I get up there."

"How about the rest...um your mother and all?"

"Oh they are doing fine. My mother is expecting another baby, just found out. It's a boy too."

"Oh? When is it due?"

"Oh, she's only two months along. I'll be spending some time with them too. They're really proud of the music Jose and I are turning out and so is Priscilla."

He promised to look me up on one of his visits to the north east and we said goodbye with assurance of mutual affection, nothing else of course.

It wasn't until I had gone to my room that night with Wanda happily snoring in her small bed in the corner and as I mulled over what the space man had told me, that it came to me. Of course it was exactly as he had said---the third baby. I looked out my window over the city and listened to the night sounds, so different and far from that desert where I had first joined him; but it was all like music to my ears: the horns blaring, police sirens wailing, people yelling on the sidewalk, the rumble of big garbage trucks beneath the window and the lights, thousands of points of light out there in the distance lighting up the sky with clouds of rainbow lights, like beacons to me urging on towards something some yearning, a magical something, I had yet to understand.

Thanks to my husband William T. Carroll for helping me on technical matters.

Recommended Reading:

The Intention Experiment by Lynne McTaggart
Healing Words by Larry Dossey M.D.

Printed in the United States
By Bookmasters